The Hunting Dog

by Louis Powell

Ford, Falcon & McNeil Publishers

. . . . . .

The characters and events in this book are fictitious. Any similarity to real persons, living or dead, is coincidental and not intended by the author.

ISBN:978-0-9827252-8-3

Second Edition Dec 2014

You can contact the author at:

LouisPowellTHD@gmail.com

What People are saying

"Just finished chapter 17... I am hooked good! I've been reading two books at the same time; gonna have to put the other aside for now. I loved Tim's conversation with Jacob Dabe! Bravos to your refreshing mind! Many quotable quotes there! *"There's not a dime's difference between slavery in the 1800's and the way some companies treat employees today."* & *"There's no leader free enough to lead."* Tim may have unwittingly struck a deal with the devil." **Charles Lefory - Computer programmer, Dallas Texas**

◆

"Mr. Powell uses his local knowledge, business experience, and skill with dialogue to create a fast-paced narrative that will carry you down main street and the into the board rooms to provide both a treat and meditation on cultural consequences." **Gary Sedlacek, author**

◆

"Powell weaves a story of greed and power as . . . Tim Lichten finds himself entwined in a world . . . difficult to distinguish between the respectable and the dishonorable. . . A good read, with imaginative twists and turns." **Linda Peters, author**

◆

It has greed, humor, and even murder. The suspense builds chapter to chapter. I simply couldn't stop, until I finished. **Ed Robinette, author**

◆

Reminiscent of Faulkner. But just a flavoring. I would say a diamond. The ending was eye-popping. **Don Betzen**

◆

Wait until you meet Mord: CPA/contractor/friend of the "family"/fixer. You will never see concrete pads under small stores the same way again. **Cal Hayes, author**

◆

". . . a fascinating read with interesting side characters that help make this book hard to put down. I recommend this book for anyone who likes a mystery." – **Monique Holeyfield, author**

◆

Very well Written book. Excellent character development and dialog. Cannot wait to see where the next book will take Tim. I enjoyed the book from beginning to end. **Francine Fuqua, author**

The Hunting Dog is a brilliant oreo of big
family business with prominent exposure of
greed, corruption, and murder. . . It is a
perfect, intelligent balance of good verses
evil where the good prevails, even through the
array of fallen bodies. An honest rewarding
contentment. **Scarlet Richards,author**

◆

Louis Powell has a fresh and gripping novel that subtly
balances avarice, mystery and pathos. . . It an odyssey from
the shallow life Lichen finds himself in Georgia and a return
to the virtues of his youth. These ethical conflicts are artfully
handled by Powell in *The Hunting Dog* with strongly
defined characters, two murders, and the mysterious role of
a trans gender, and local color of scenes in suburban Georgia
and the French Quarter of New Orleans. **Julian Goodrich**

◆

"This first rate crime novel with a new twist is provocative in
style and presentation. It is utterly compelling. A must read"
R.K. Diwan, author

◆

"This is an excellent read. It's more than a murder mystery. I found
its study of how business is done within mall owners lives
compelling. Finally I enjoyed the characters and would like to see
more of these people. I highly recommend it." **Robert Metzger**

◆

. It is worth a read just to get us thinking about our way of life,
not to say finance, sales, making a living are wrong, but to point
out that the values inherent in all of this are perhaps becoming
skewed. Nice work Mr. Powell. **– Charles Dunlevy**

◆

Prepare to be shocked! Powell certainly knows how to
employ the power of the written word. This story gives the
old adage "Money is the Root of All Evil" a whole new
meaning.- **Eddie Price, author**

———

After reading **The Hunting Dog** please post your views on
Amazon, Goodreads or any other public review of books.

Dedicated to the memory of Dr. Tom Bibey, author
The Mandolin Case & Acquisition Syndrome

1

The Visitor

Joan refused to smile when she heard Cecil would be the new manager of Cypress Tree mall. She had not talked to his family for years. She thought it was insane that Malifer would hire him. On his first day she pitched the mail on his desk when he was in the restroom. At lunch time she left without telling anyone. She returned two hours later, only to leave at 2:30 muttering she couldn't take him anymore. She broke every speed limit to her home liquor cabinet.

Soon she had killed half a bottle of scotch, but still mumbled curses about the bastard.

The incessant doorbell woke her and pissed her off enough to make her stagger to open the front door revealing a hooded stout figure. "Well, I haven't seen you in years. What do you want?"

"Joan, you must go back."

"Never!"

"You know too much."

"Did he send you?"

"No, he doesn't know I'm here. He needs your help. You know the mall's history."

"Tell him to go to hell."

"Then stay for a month."

"Hell no! I should have quit when he was announced."

"But you've been there for years."

"Go to hell." Joan slammed the door but it was pushed back so hard it hit the side of her head. She fell and gashed her head on the marble floor. She tried to stand but a black plastic bag went over her head. She struggled, gasped for air then passed to infinity.

The intruder waited until she was dead. Then crumbled the bag and put it in a coat pocket and laid Joan's head in the fresh pool of blood.

The killer stood, looked around then stepped outside and closed the front door. With their head down they quickly walked to the car and slowly drove away.

2

The Interview

Tim's plane rolled to the gate. It was fifteen minutes late, so when the seatbelt light went off, everyone crushed into the aisle and waited for the door to open. They streamed out, around and up the escalator like one long line of ants in search of sky, light and food.

At the top, in the rays of the sun, stood a young man in a pin stripe suit. He held a business envelop with TIM LICHTEN in thick black letters. Tim made eye contact and nodded. "Gil Palm?"

They shook hands, "Tim Lichen, from Chicago."

"Tim, welcome to Atlanta."

"I like your maroon tie."

Gil felt the tie, "Do you have luggage?"

Tim held up his briefcase. "This is it. My flight leaves at 4:45."

"Great, that gives us time. I plan to give you a tour of the mall, like you will do with future prospects. That is if you accept the leasing position."

"I have never leased malls. I am a sales dog. What are you looking for in me?"

"If you can smell a deal. Jim Franks told Dad you might fit in. If it is not a good fit for both of us, neither will be happy."

"My wife wants me to take a good look."

"I understand she is from Fenton."

"You've done your homework. I don't remember putting that in my resume."

Gil smiled, "Jim told Dad."

Tim had seen Cypress Tree Mall many times when they visited her mother. It was the place Aimee would show off the kids to old classmates. This time the mall's large windowless cold brick buildings looked like some giant child had left blocks on a cracked sea of pavement. There were few cars.

Gil drove around the outer edge of the lot, "The Pizza Hut's vacant, but McDonald's is still open." He drove past a pylon sign. "Our hotel is new."

"I thought it was a Hilton."

"It was, then a Red Roof, but now it's a Shenir Hotel, named for the owner."

"Never heard of him."

"This is his first in Fenton, but he owns about twenty in the South."

The cracked asphalt reminded Tim of a huge spider's web. But the mall entrance had new bronze doors. Inside, Gil's leather shoes echoed on the cold floor.

"Wow, you guys have made some changes!"

"This year our cash went inside the mall. Next we'll do the parking."

"The hanging banners make things come alive. And you added twenty-foot trees!"

"They're plastic."

Tim reached for a green leaf.

Gil smiled, "With plastic we don't water, and they don't die."

"Like heaven on earth."

"We must wash them once a year."

"I guess everything collects dust."

"But that is Cecil's job. Yours is to find stores for the vacant spaces."

Tim started to count store fronts. "You have a lot of dark spaces."

"Think of them as inventory on the shelf."

"Dark stores scare people."

"Your job is to change that."

"How?"

"Paint dreams in the stories you weave about sales."

"Sell the sizzle, not the steak."

When they arrived at the main mall, store managers rushed to open their doors.

Across the hall, a bug-eyed man raised his store gate, then turned to watch Gil and Tim. When they passed the man squeaked, "Gil, did my attorney call you?"

Gil did not turn around, only waved his hand as he shot back, "No, Cyrus he hasn't."

"He will."

Gil walked faster. Tim rushed to catch him.

At center court, Gil waved at a thin man in the back of Falconi's Estate Jewelry. The small man with bushy eyebrows waved back as he put rings in his showcase.

In the middle of the mall was an open area with a high rotunda skylight. Below stood a large flowing iron fountain surrounded by a pool with goldfish. Three gray-haired men sat on benches.

Gil pointed to the greenery around the fountain, "Now those are live plants."

"Gil, why is it there are always three or four old men at center court?"

"They want to be where the action is. If they go away, we might as well lock the doors."

Down the mall a thin hunched over man waved his rolled-up newspaper at them. Gil waved back and the two went to greet him, "Archie, great to see you. I want you to meet Tim Lichten."

Archie took off his checkered 'Bear Bryant' fedora, "My name's Archibald Seher, but call me Archie."

"Tim may come to work for Malifer."

Archie, raises his rolled paper to give a mock blessing like some bishop. "Well, I'll pray for him."

They laughed.

"Archie, you make things sound hopeless," said Gil.

Archie tapped Tim's chest with his paper. "On the darkest night, always hope."

"That one star might shine?" Tim asked.

Archie whacked the rolled-up paper in his hand. "Just a twinkle, that's all we need. Tim, give us one small spark to follow."

There was an awkward silence. Then Archie shook their hands, and turned to the fountain. He popped his paper in his other hand every few steps to announce his arrival.

Gil and Tim continued toward the hotel.

"Archie couldn't massage numbers the way we needed, so we retired him. One of our bankers suggested Cecil."

"The world moves on," said Tim.

"We thought Archie's assistant, Joan would cover the gap. But she fell at home and died."

"When was that?"

"Months ago. We didn't know she was a drunk. Cecil never ran a mall so Dad moved me here to help."

"And what do you do?"

"I focus on our southern properties. So I am out of town a lot. We need someone local. That's why we are talking."

"Change is constant."

At the end of the hall they stood at the hotel's entrance. On the left was a rock waterfall with overgrown vines. Tim sneezed. "I'm allergic to mold."

"The man who built the mall couldn't get Macy's, so he talked a friend into putting in a hotel."

"I've never seen a hotel in a mall."

"It was a mistake."

Gil leaned in, "Tim, don't let clients stay here."

"Why doesn't Malifer buy it?"

"We have a full plate."

They crossed the hotel lobby. A paperback "We The Living" lay on a Naugahyde covered couch. Then exited into the mall's parking lot. Cold wind nipped at their ears.

Gil turned to an outside door on the left. "Let's go to the Mall office. Cecil's off, but you can see your office." He pulled his coat up around his neck. "You brought Chicago's air with you."

Gil unlocked door and turned on the lights. He walked past a large reception desk with a small goldfish bowl to an open area with private offices along the walls.

"Tim, this one will be yours." He turned on the lights and watched Tim's face. "Pete will hang your pictures."

Gil was giving him the pitch he gave potential tenants. It wasn't like any interview Tim had seen before.

Tim's hand felt the cinnamon cherry desk. "Damn, this desk is larger than my cubicle in Chicago."

"We like to impress," Gil said. "It helps clients pay more rent."

Tim sat in the dark chair, swiveled side to side and nodded, "I can see this." He looked at the empty bookshelves, the two chairs for visitors. Then out the glass wall into the central area. "The glass makes this office feel larger. Makes up for no outside windows."

Gil pointed to a larger corner office, "My office is over there. Then Cecil's and Louie's."

"Who are they?"

"Louie leases the office tower. Cecil is the mall manager. Bobbie is his sister and his secretary. That was her desk with the goldfish." Gil moved closer, "Don't tell Cecil secrets."

"Why's that?"

"He uses everything."

Back in the car, Gil fell into a robotic pitch. "We are going downtown." He curved around a pothole in the lot and said nothing until he was on a main road. "This is Chestnut Boulevard, but you won't see any Chestnut trees. Blight killed them, and the city planted cheaper pines."

When they arrived at Davis Street with its new brick sidewalks, Gil waved his hand, "The stores have new fronts, but little business."

"Sometimes a face-lift has toxic results."

Gil nodded agreement, "Fenton could make something of itself but its leaders are divided and asleep."

"They don't even smell the coffee."

Gil smiled, "They just complain."

Gil's car ended up at Star's, a fifty's diner across the highway from the mall.

"You're late Mr. Gils," said a waitress with a gold front tooth.

"Ruby, I've been showing Mr. Lichten the town."

Ruby eyed Tim and waited for more. When it did not come, "I'll bring you both coffee."

"This back booth is where we have daily breakfast meetings." He glanced around to see who else was there, then pulled out Tim's resumé and took a deep breath. "Instead of my going over this, you tell me your story." He put the paper back in his pocket.

"Nothing special. I was raised in a small Oklahoma town. Dad owned a jewelry store, but died. Mom had to sell the business."

"That's too bad."

"She sold houses to support us."

"So you know real estate."

"Not anything about malls."

"But you know selling."

Tim laughed, "Boy do I. She would listen to tapes her broker gave her on how to close a sale. She'd make me act as the buyer so she could practice. One was called: "100 Ways to Close a Sale.""

Gil's eyes flashed.

Tim continued, "I have sold everything on the road; chemicals to factories, store fixtures even washing machines to farmers. My present job supplies restaurants."

"You could help Louie!"

"With the office tower?"

"Dad says he needs training. Mr. Roy says he needs a kick of motivation. You might give him both."

Tim was at a loss what to say, then continued, "We hate Chicago. It's too big. Everyone wants in your pocket. Malifer's a good company. Aimee's from here so I came to look."

"Isn't Chicago cold?"

"Too damn cold."

Gil watched Tim's eyes, "So your wife is from Fenton?"

"And related to half the town."

"Children?"

"Two boys - one's six and the baby's two. The baby was in a major car accident with Aimee. We still owe the hospital."

"Did they come through OK?"

"They are now, but Aimee was on drugs for a long time. Aimee's mother came up to help. Now she wants us to move closer to Fenton."

"Malifer has great health benefits. Mr. Roy has made sure of that."

"Aimee's mom made me realize the importance of roots."

"Today's families are scattered."

"Scattered and shattered." Tim sipped his coffee. "Gil, I'm leery of Fenton."

"Why?"

"There's such a thing as too close to family." Tim looked out the window to the stalled traffic.

Gil said, "Chicago has too many cars."

"And a lot of other things I don't want."

"All life's a search. You trade one job for another to get something better."

"I guess," said Tim. "We have had enough of Chicago."

"For a second I thought you wanted to stay in the snow."

"No, it's between Fenton and Memphis." Gil's eyes widened as Tim continued, "I interview there next week."

"We won't control you like a rat. Do your best – that's all we ask." His voice rose in pitch and sounded like a little-league coach. "Teamwork - everybody's on the team." Gil waited for Tim's head to move in agreement. However, Tim stared motionless.

"Sometimes you can take the family. It's on the clock. There's always a mall to see." Then Gil's voice became smooth as Godiva chocolate. "Do you want to make a lot of money?"

Tim smiled, "I love the craft of a good salesman. You're one of the best."

"A pro goes unnoticed."

"But real pros see quality."

Tim then asked, "What's my potential?"

"What do you want?"

"To be heard. I want to make a difference. I want to add value."

"What would it take for you to join us?"

"Proof that I be respected."

"How much will you need?"

"Fenton might make Aimee happy, but Memphis might be better."

Gil's eyes looked away, "Life's polluted in many ways." He took a deep breath and turned to Tim, "With your background, your knowledge, your ability - Malifer's the better choice."

"Glad you think so." Tim's eyes smiled, "What do you know about Memphis?"

Gil's jaw tightened like he heard a car crash. "If you want a big city, why not live in Atlanta? It will give you all the traffic and crime. Aimee would be close to her mother." He took a breath. "Tim, in Fenton you'll live in a small town, but you can take clients to ball games in Atlanta."

"And a mother-in-law on my back."

Gil gritted his teeth. "You'll be a few hours from the beach. Your kids will love it."

Tim focused on Gil's eyes, "I've always felt real estate was a con."

"Why?"

"Someone takes good open farm land, builds on it, collects rent, and sends it out of town. It's like a circus. They take your money and leave town."

Gil sat up straight, "A developer creates value. Where Cypress Tree is, there was a closed factory with so much poison in the soil the feds listed it as a 'Brownfield.' It had a chain-link fence with big yellow warning signs."

"Who cleaned it?"

"Well — the developer scrapped off the topsoil then sealed the subsoil with plastic, and the feds allowed him to build Cypress Tree on top."

"Making silk . . ."

Gil slapped his hands, "That's what we do. Take failure and make something to make money."

"So what would I do?"

"Talk to locals. Give them a vision, a dream."

"But I'll be pitching something used."

"Everything's used. Value's not something you put in a safe. It's something you create from someone's failure."

Tim closed his eyes then nodded and Gil continued, "When you create value, it makes money. If you can't, dump it and let someone else do it."

"Gil, you make it sound so mechanical."

"Hell, everything is from burnt-out stars."

Tim sighed, "My problem remains —— Aimee's mother."

Gil's shoulders slumped.

Gil lifted his phone, "Excuse me. I forgot to call Dad . . . Dad, make sure Mr. Roy signs those bank papers today!" He glanced at Tim. "Yes, we've been talking all morning . . . much better than I thought . . . I'll call when I know more. Bye."

He quickly checked for emails. "My dad, Zack Palm, is number two. Roy Parino started the company after Oxford. Mr. Roy appears shy, but his glass eye can pierce in a way you don't want to feel."

"Silent control?"

"Yeah, but he bleeds profit like I want someday."

"To be rich?"

"It's the only security."

"You think you can buy happiness?"

Gil gave Tim a vague look, "After Oxford, Mr. Roy met a lot of the arts crowd. You into art?"

"No."

"Mr. Roy and his wife are. They go to the Basel Art Fair every year." Gil cracked a smile, "Mr. Roy eats prime aged steaks, drinks 18-year-old Macallan and enjoys expensive art. But . . . "

"But what?"

"Profit. He worships profit."

They sat for a long while as Tim sipped his coffee, looked at the tile floor, the red booths, and the Tabasco standing between the salt and pepper. "I guess all we want is a cozy life with things to enjoy."

"Mr. Roy has that. He collects Renoir, Monet and Henry Moore."

"Art, a rich man's stamp collection."

"Investment," Gil interrupted, "Everything is an investment to him."

"Like stocks?"

"You can't insure stocks, but you can a Degas. Famous art only goes up in value, and you can avoid the tax man."

Tim shook his head, "That's worlds above me." "Everything is for profit. Once he bought a two million-dollar Rembrandt. Then kept it a few years and sold it for 15 million.»

"I could live off the taxes he paid."

"No, you couldn't."

"I could try."

Gil rolled his hands. "There are ways . . . " His fingers jumped spasmodically in the air, "He knows how not to pay taxes on art."

"He's a Midas?"

"No, he's human, and my dad owes him a lot."

"Why?"

Gil turned away, "That's another story." When he turned back his eyes were watery.

Tim looked outside to the Interstate. "If I take this job, what's the secret?"

"What do you mean?"

"What's your advice?"

"Meet people,» Gil said.

"That's it?"

"Get to know merchants. Spread cheer. Make them feel good. Get them to trust you."

"I just talk to them?"

"It is more than that. Talk, listen, interact. In short be with them.

"So I become friends to convince them they can make money in Cypress Tree?"

"You talk Southern don't you?" Gil said.

"I married a girl from Fenton. I have to."

"Right you know: talk slow, play golf, buy them Chivas and steaks and cheesecake. Get to know them."

Tim laughed, "You don't, do you?"

"I don't what?"

Tim leaned over, "Gil, to talk Southern you join a deer camp, drink beer, eat BBQ. And for god's sake, no cheesecake. Maybe a fried pie but not cheesecake."

"You're right, but we need to win them back."

"I'll try."

That afternoon they had to rush to make the plane. At the airport, Tim asked, "When will you decide?»

"If we make an offer, will you accept?" Gil asked.

"How can I tell? We never talked salary."

"What will it take?"

Tim shrugged, "Proof you want me more than Memphis."

"Let me talk to Dad." Gil's eyes searched for a reaction from Tim. "If the pay's good, will you accept?"

"Malifer must be fair."

"I'll talk to Dad."

"First of next week I'll be in Memphis." Tim then turned to catch his plane.

"We'll be in touch." Gil shouted.

The Hunting Dog

3

Decision Time

When Tim walked outside the Chicago airport, snow flecked in the overhead lights. Then he saw Aimee's smile and walked toward their faded car.

"Where are the boys?"

"Pam's watching them. As soon as I put dinner on, you called. Nice to have a baby sitter next door."

He gave her a kiss, "Sorry I'm late. We had plane problems in Cincinnati."

"How did it go?

"I think I'll get an offer."

"Did you see mother?"

"Didn't have time. Gil Palm, the VP's son gave me the third degree."

"Daddy's home!"

Two boys ran to the door. Ray, who was now walking, grabbed Tim's leg and stood with both feet on Tim's right shoe.

Aimee escorted Pam to the door.

"Junior, where's Ray? I don't see him. I can't walk to look for him — my foot's too heavy."

Tim lugged his right leg with Ray on it. Slowly he lifted it, waited for Ray to hold on, then dropped his foot while Ray held tight and giggled.

Junior laughed but eased near his mother.

Tim spun towards the door. "I'm going outside." He felt Ray's squeeze, "I think my foot's asleep. Maybe the cold air will wake it up." When he jiggled the door knob, Ray hopped off and waddled as fast as he could to the couch.

Tim kissed Aimee again, "I met with Gil Palm. His dad is at the home office." Aimee's car wreck scar above her right eye was almost gone.

"Will he be your boss?"

"Most likely, if I get an offer."

"Is he the mall manager?"

"No, I'll be in leasing. Management is separate. Some man named Cecil Malcour is manager, but it seems Gil is sort of over both."

"How much will you make?"

"They haven't made an offer - yet."

"They flew you down there, and you don't know how much?"

"We are feeling each other out." He gave her a reassuring hug. "It should be good."

"Enough so we can live on Bluff View?" asked Aimee.

"First, let me hear the offer."

Tim picked up the kids' empty plates, "I see Junior had corn on the cob."

"He loves it, but that's all he wants."

"You can't have too much of a good thing."

"Men don't understand," Aimee said.

Aimee put an ice cube in her wine, "I wish you would have called Mom."

Tim moved his fork of spaghetti near his nose, closed his eyes and took a deep breath. Then he started to talk about all the questions he was asked about his background, why he wanted to leave Chicago but most importantly if he was an experienced salesman.

Aimee was more interested about when the move would be. If it was going to be before Christmas what would he and Mike do with the two Christmas carts that they ran for the last few years for extra income. Tim assured her he would not start until after the first of the year which gave them time to make plans. But first they must wait for the offer.

Tim reached for more spaghetti.

"Leave some room." Aimee opened the freezer. Like magic, both boys appeared pulling at their chairs.

Aimee smiled, "Boys know when Mom thinks ice-cream."

Tim shook his head, "Amazing."

"I want some," Junior said.

Tim lifted Ray into his high chair. "Ray too."

Aimee looked at Tim, "They think you married me for the ice-cream."

"Who told them?"

"I hope you get this job. We've been here two years. Every month, someone else quits, and you only work longer."

"Malifer sounds good."

"I hope so."

"Do you think we can live with Mom?"

"Until we find something."

"The boys will love it," Aimee said.

"Yeah, or we might all end up with shingles."

"Maybe we could rent something on Bluff View."

"Let's find something we can afford."

"I can dream. I used to climb our oak tree, now the boys can do the same. It'll be a big vacation."

"Playing in family dust," Tim said.

Aimee had that sparkle in her eye and a tilt of her head that cut through all his defenses. "We'll survive," she said.

The next morning, Jim Franks, the recruiter who got him the interview, called and told Tim that he was in the running but it would be a few weeks before big companies made a decision. Tim saw the stress on Gil's face when he told him he would be interviewing in Memphis and was quite sure they would get back quicker. He might have to fly for an interview in Kansas City with Gil's father and others, but they were not going to wait weeks.

Tim looked up Chet Quinn. They had been in college together in New Orleans, but always talked a couple of times a year. He had worked for the Kansas City Star before his move to Louisville's Courier Journal. He called him and asked what he knew about the Kansas City company Malifer. Chet had heard of them, even remember someone coming to talk to his Rotary Club and promised to call the business editor and see what he could find out.

An hour later Tim's phone rang.

"Tim, the business editor says Malifer is growing fast with private money. They have several malls and strip centers. The latest one they bought is in Fenton, Georgia. Last month, they bought a small jet. The president and his wife are major art collectors."

"That's Roy Parino," Tim said.

"Their number two, Issac Palm, is the man who came to Rotary. He goes by Zack, wears a red bow-tie and tells great stories. His father came to Kansas City with nothing, but they now have property on every block. Zack's a deacon in his church."

"Did you smell anything I should know about?"

"No, not at all. In fact, my man said to ask if they need an old hack to do their newsletter."

"Thanks, Chet."

"One more thing, if you hear of anything for me, let me know. You never know where the ax will fall."

On Monday, Tim told Aimee if Malifer called, she was to say he was in Memphis and take a number. He set his phone to take messages. No one called. By Thursday, Tim couldn't take it any longer, and called Jim Franks who laughed and told him they may be talking to a couple of others, but he was in the running.

Tim was now sure Gil knew there was no real interview in Memphis and wished he had not played games.

It was the following Wednesday, after supper, when his phone rang. It was Zack Palm, Gil's father.

Tim took two deep breaths. They chatted. Zack told a couple of jokes with the rhythm of a Jay Leno. Tim returned one about eating ice-cream in Chicago in winter to get warm.

Zack said Tim's job would be to hunt for local and regional stores for Cypress Tree. He had talked it over with Mr. Roy, who agreed that Tim was what they needed in Fenton.

Tim began to breathe easier.

Zack asked, "What kind of salary do you need?"

Tim froze. He knew rule number one in a negotiation was to get the other person to make the first offer. He was being tested!

Zack listened in silence.

Tim bit his lip.

Zack then asked about his former jobs. Tim saw this was a round-about way for Zack to judge what he should propose. Then he asked Tim's present salary.

Tim had rehearsed several times. He would say twenty-five percent above what he made. He paused, then spit out the lie.

Zack quickly offered 50% higher!

Tim's mouth became dry. He tried to talk. Lips moved, but nothing came. His tongue stuck to his teeth. He squeezed his cheeks to produce moisture but all he could say was "aahhh".

Zack broke the silence, "I understand your wife is from Fenton. Has she picked a house?"

Aimee passed Tim a glass of water.

Tim's tongue quivered against his upper lip. "We'll rent until we find something."

Zack cleared his throat, "Mr. Roy suggested -- that we could help you buy a house."

"What do you mean?"

"We'll loan you up to three times your salary to buy a house."

"I don't understand."

"There will be no interest, if you stay three years. If you stay with us three years and a day, we will excuse the whole loan."

Tim's mind bounced. What did the man say? Tim had never heard of this. He didn't want to sound stupid, "I don't know what to say. I'll have to read the paperwork."

"We have concerns in Fenton. We're convinced you have what we need. Are you willing to work like you never have?"

"Mr. Palm, to use a mid-west term: I will keep my back strong and my eye on the corn." Tim sipped more water.

"If you stay the loan will be paid in full."

"That's one hell of an offer," Tim said.

"Gil has a high opinion of you. People in Fenton respect your family, and we expect big things."

Tim gave a quiet, "Thank you."

Zack came up with another joke.

"When should I start?" Tim asked.

"The second Monday in January, but Gil will be out of town. Cecil, the manager will show you around."

"I'll be there at nine a.m. on the second Monday."

"Great to have you on board."

"My pleasure."

Tim hung up the phone stunned. Aimee waited for a report.

The time frame gave Tim eight weeks to give notice and move. He wondered who in Fenton had given him a good reference. The only people he knew were Aimee's relatives. If they were asked he would have heard.

4

The Announcement

Tim's Chicago cubicle was in an industrial park near the airport.

When he started, there were twenty salesmen who made daily visits to restaurants. When one salesman died, Tim took his territory and soon doubled his commissions. But the company computerized and more salesmen left. Face to face sales visits turned to phone calls, and commissions changed to straight salary which was docked if quotas were missed.

Recently his job morphed again. His time was now spent calling late payers. Some days he and his best friend, Mike would double up and together collect late payments. Since September 1st, they were down to only four salesmen in the bullpen. Each with headsets and focused on computer screens while they took orders and begged payments.

The sun had set. Tim stood to stretch and rub his neck. It was 6:53. Out his boss's window he watched a plane land at O'Hare. He was alone. He locked his desk, turned off his computer, and walked to the exit.

He heard steps behind him, so he turned to hold the door. "Mike, I didn't see you."

"I was in the file room. Looks like we're the last ones here."

"That's what we do," Tim said.

"Any word about your Georgia job?"

"I'll give my notice tomorrow and start right after the first of the year."

Mike gave him a thumb's up. "Soon I'll do the same. Beth's papa wants me to work for him."

They gave each other the "high five" hand slap.

"He gave me an offer I can't refuse."

"I guess that is what life is about. You jump ship, learn to swim to a new boat then jump again."

On their way to their cars, Mike told him Beth's father had an idea to make some money with government contracts and he wanted Tim involved. "We worked together on the Christmas Mall Carts. This would be our next step."

Tim hesitated, "Can I hold off paying my part on the carts until we are open?"

"No problem. When we bowl Saturday I want to talk to you about her papa's idea. He says it will pay more than any mall carts."

Tim held up his empty hand and waved off the invite, "I'm still paying the hospital. I don't have anything to invest. I mean nothing."

"You won't have to. He going to teach me how government contracts work." Mike made a 'zero' with his thumb and index finger, "with no cash up front."

Tim laughed, "Sounds like he took a 'get-rich quick' retreat in the Wisconsin Dells."

"No, he's smarter than that." Mike looked around as if someone was behind him, "Does $100,000 profit sound serious?" Mike held up his index finger, "With no investment!!"

Tim waved his hand, "I'm going to miss your crazy ideas in Georgia."

Mike shouted from his car, "We're still bowling Saturday aren't we?"

"Sure as hell!"

"I'll bring a bid list. There're billions of things."

5

The Move

"Let's go," Tim said as he raced the motor of their faded Toyota.

Aimee put the purple African violet on the floor of the car and glanced at the boys buckled in the back seat. "Here comes the apartment manager. I need to run through with her, so we get our deposit back." Aimee rushed through the snow.

Tim double checked the straps holding the rooftop carrier he at rented then adjusted the car's heater and waited.

"Have a good trip Mr. Lichten." The driver of their moving van waved, slammed his cab door and started his truck.

"Dad, they're leaving!" Junior said.

"We can't leave Mom," Tim said.

"They might get lost!"

"They're going to store our stuff until our new house is ready."

"What about my toys?"

"Mom packed them. Ray has Teddy."

"Teddy, Teddy, Teddy," cried Ray.

"Damn," Tim got out and opened Ray's door to dislodge the bear trapped under his car seat. He then gave Junior the worn copy of *'Where the Sidewalk Ends'*.

Aimee came out, glanced at the steel colored sky, and got in the car. "Can we drive around the complex one last time?"

A plane screeched overhead.

Clouds hung low as they passed dead factories and rolling barren mounds of land.

"Daddy, why did they cut all the trees?"

"That's an old garbage dump. Those pipes release methane gas."

"Mom, will it choke us?"

"That's why we're moving. To find fresh air," said Aimee.

"Can we get corn at Grandma's?"

"She grows it in her garden."

"Can we grow some?"

"Sure, and tomatoes and okra. She even has tall trees you can climb," said Aimee.

"Make sure the kudzu doesn't catch you," said Tim.

"What's kudzu?" Junior asked.

"The only thing bad in the South," smiled Tim.

Outside Indianapolis, the clouds started to thin. When they crossed the Ohio River into Kentucky, patches of clear sky appeared. By the time they reached Lexington it was a solid deep marine blue.

The boys watched horses run on the rolling green fields behind black wood fences.

Aimee cracked the window. "I'm glad we're moving; smell that air."

"Dad, can we fly a kite in Fenton?" Junior asked.

"Sure."

"And your dad will get a tent so you three can camp outside all night!"

"Wow! Are there bears?"

She looked at Tim. "Your father will protect you."

"And Grandma will teach Mom to make biscuits every morning," Tim said.

Aimee squeezed his leg. "Touché."

In Nashville, they ate in a mall food court where the snap of plastic trays fought for attention with the clash of chatter off the tile floor. Aimee wanted to shop, so Tim took the boys to play-land. Their heads bounced like they were at a county fair. Tim sat with three retired men who eyed mothers watching their kids.

Back on the road, the sun danced between tall pines. Tim began to dream how he'd pitch Cypress Tree Mall to store owners. He would first find out about their history, exchange a joke or two, schmooze them, and convince them they would make a profit in the mall. It would be like selling to restaurants, only his product would be space. He would pitch the mall's foot traffic with eyes looking to buy. It would be easy to get them to open in Cypress Tree.

They spent the night at the Chattanooga Choo-Choo Hotel, a converted train station. Before leaving the next morning they had a family photo taken in front of the antique train engine in the courtyard.

On the highway, a billboard announced a huge fireworks store. Another, larger one with exploding glitter colors, shouted the exit. Tim held his breath, but saw Junior focused on his book as the exit passed.

"There is a God." Tim smiled at Aimee.

"Quite, the world is distracted," whispered Aimee.

They made the turn south onto I-75 and crossed into Georgia. Aimee said, "I don't want to live up North again. I don't understand the people."

"Why?"

"They're different," Aimee said.

"Everyone is."

"They use English, but in an odd way. It's hard to explain. It's like another language," she paused, "and sometimes they're mean."

"We met some great people in Chicago."

"But some want to tell you how to live your life."

Tim rolled his eyes, "You don't have that in the South?"

"No, not at all."

Tim smirked.

Aimee looked at him, "Do you think so?"

"We all live in a fish bowl."

After reading an article about an estate on Lookout Mountain, she looked up and burst out in song, "I get my house on Bluff View!"

"I hope it doesn't take too long to remodel," Tim said.

"Meanwhile we get to live with Mother."

Tim nodded his head. "That should make your headaches go away."

"If not, I have some pills Beth gave me."

"I thought you quit those."

"I haven't needed one for days."

"Good. Throw the rest away."

"Do other companies give help to buy a house?"

He shrugged, "Beats me, but I'm not complaining."

"Me either."

"Sure made me a loyal employee fast. But it makes me wonder."

"Why?"

"Dad always said if someone flashes cash, grab your billfold."

"Maybe you're not used to being treated with respect."

"I only got dinged once big time."

"It's not right to take a hundred bucks out of your bonus for each time you are a minute late for work. It snows 75 inches a year there!" Aimee said.

"That's past. Malifer's our future."

"I hope so."

"Malifer treat employees like family."

"Some think different."

"What do you mean?"

"They use families. We live them."

"What in the world does that mean?" Tim asked.

She laid down the magazine. "I'm glad we're moving." Aimee was in one of those moods when it was best for Tim to keep quiet and listen. "I get a house with a new dishwasher and granite counters!" She read some more then said, "Mama says if a neighbor from the North doesn't like you, she'll knock on your door and shoot you. In the South, she'll bring you a pecan pie with a smile, before she stabs you in your back."

Tim smiled, "Southern hospitality at its best?"

"Mom calls it 'Nasty Nice'."

"Well, I have learned something," Tim said

She added, "Good southerners always respect manners."

"Before they kill?" Tim shook his head miffed.

"Eudora Welty makes me feel safe. Not only her, Faulkner, Tennessee Williams, Robert Penn Warren – all of them. I hope our children grow to know them."

"I agree but . . ." Tim knew it was about a tradition that went back two hundred years.

"But what?" she asked.

"We need to start a college fund."

When Charlie Daniels' song on the radio stopped, Tim said, "That man can flat burn up a fiddle."

"You will have your own battles to fight."

"Listening to him wears me out."

Aimee turned the dial until she heard the cadence of a preacher. When she heard the slap on a Bible she knew he raised it high for all to shout "Amen."

She became solemn, "You know it was about property?"

"What was?"

"The war."

"Oh."

"The Civil War."

The preacher chanted, "*His time is near. . . His time is here . . . He's on his way . . . He's here to stay . . . Lord Jesus . . . He's in the world today.*"

"His rhythm tells me I'm home," Aimee said.

"Listen close. He'll tell you where to send the money," Tim said.

"Don't be a cynic."

Tim pulled into a truck stop, "We need gas, how about a snack?"

"With your pay I'll be able to get my own car," she said as she went inside with the boys.

Tim stayed back to pump gas. A lone oak's dry leaves shivered in the north wind.

6

The First Day

Tim rolled over in bed, but Aimee wasn't there. Where was she? It was Monday. It was cold. His legs were tangled in the covers. There was a man's voice on a radio. A spoon clinked. Aimee mumbled something, and her mother answered. A newspaper ruffled.

Tim freed his feet and set them on the ice cold oak floor. "Damn!" He pulled them back under the covers. Now wide awake, he listened to two female voices.

"Sounds like your husband's awake."

Aimee called from the kitchen, "Good morning, Tim. It snowed last night. The most in thirty years."

Tim turned to the window but dropped his head back on the pillow. He smelled biscuits.

"When it snows in Fenton, no one goes to work," Aimee said.

Mrs. Maples added, "Nothing opens."

Tim lifted his head, "Oh yeah?"

Aimee came to the hall and looked into the bedroom while she straddled the floor furnace to let heat fill her nightgown. "Mom made biscuits."

"It's my first day. I've got to go to work." Tim lifted the blinds to see a thick white blanket all the way to the street. He could not tell where the curb began or see any car tracks.

"I'm glad we packed the kids' snow clothes."

Tim got dressed, then threw a blanket over his shoulders and shuffled to the kitchen. "Well maybe we got four inches."

Mrs. Maples sat wrapped in an old purple and green Fenton high school hooded parka over her floor-length night gown. "Radio said nine inches, twelve in Alpharetta."

"I must go in to work!"

Aimee looked out the back window, "Mama, this has to be a record."

"It's my first day!" Tim said.

"You going to walk?"

"There's not a snowplow in the county," said Mrs. Maples.

Tim walked to the table and riffled through the paper. "Mrs. Maples, where's today's sports section?"

"Paper hasn't come. We're reading 'Sundays'."

He put it back on the table.

Mrs. Maples hobbled to the oven to remove biscuits. "Aimee, what about Billy? Your brother's proud of his new four-wheeler. He'll love to show it off."

Aimee walked to the phone.

At 8:25, Billy's big wheel jeep was in the driveway. The horn sounded. Aimee looked out the door and Billy shouted, "Snow Bird Taxi!"

"Thanks for picking him up."

"Yeah, I appreciate it," Tim said as he stepped into the Jeep. "I was the first one down the road. It looks like ten inches." "Hope you don't mind."

"This is why I bought this baby. We might even see a foot before it stops."

Billy tapped the dashboard light that showed he had engaged the four-wheel drive. "Now this is what life is about!"

They arrived at the office door at 9:07. Tim was late, but there were no footprints. He hopped out and pulled on the office door, but it was locked.

Billy asked, "You want me to stay until you get in?"

"I'll be fine. I'll wait in the mall or the Hotel lobby until someone comes."

Tim walked to the mall entrance about forty feet to the right. It was unlocked. From there a set of footprints ran out to McDonald's in the parking lot. Steam rose off its roof. There were two cars in its lot, and its sidewalk was clear.

He thought about walking to it, but snow had started to fall again so he stomped his shoes and went into the empty mall. Quiet echoed down the dark cavern. He stood at the door and watched a car creep like a turtle to McDonald's. Three passengers went inside but left the car running.

A tall bundled figure with a red hunting cap came out of McDonald's side door, swung a coal shovel on his shoulder and trudged toward the mall door.

When he got to the entrance, the leathered man set the shovel down outside and stomped his boots. Tim opened the door, "Good morning."

"Morning sir! You must be the new leasing man. Mr. Cecil said you'd be coming."

"My name's Tim, Tim Lichten." He held out his hand to the old man who in turn offered his gloved hand. The handshake was limp like a dead fish.

"I'm Pete Gravel, but call me Pete. I'm the maintenance man. I'll let you in the office."

"Thanks."

"If we go down the mall a way, I can let you in the office back door." Pete pulled off his cap, "Boy, did we get snow last night - Woo-wee."

"You did a good job on McDonald's sidewalk."

"They give me breakfast."

Pete led down a small hallway between two stores. In the back, Pete stopped and opened a large door. "This is the belly of the beast." Tim looked at the large pipes and train size boiler loaded with gauges.

"That is my desk with the clipboards hanging. I have to log them."

"Looks like you are the captain of the beast."

Pete furrowed his brow. "I just record numbers. Mr. Cecil is boss. Mr. Gil will be your boss." Pete lowered his voice, "Mr. Gil's dad is Mr. Cecil's boss in Kansas City." He smiled and looked at Tim.

Tim said, "I hear you."

They returned to the hallway toward a black door at the end hall.

Pete unlocked the door and turned on the lights. A bronze plate with Tim's name was now on his office door.

"Your Christmas tree is still standing."

"Mr. Cecil needs to tell me to take it down."

"Gil said this space used to be a doctor's clinic."

"They went to prison." Pete said.

"For what?"

"Billing Medicare for dead people."

Tim chuckled, "Did the patients complain?"

"Well somebody did, because the doctors now take care of patients in jail. I took their offices out."

"You did?"

"Yes sir, after their stuff was sold, I hired some Mexicans to take out the walls, so we could build this office. The ceiling was loaded with asbestos, so I took it home."

"Asbestos? Isn't that bad news?"

"Not in my attic. My power bills went way down."

"Did you breathe it?"

"Not enough to hurt," Pete gave a look so Tim knew to drop the topic.

"Can we start the coffee?"

"Yes sir, make as much as you want." Pete tapped the thermostat. "If you need anything else, let me know."

Tim started the coffee, but when he asked where the cups were, Pete had vanished.

Tim turned on a small radio, sat in his leather chair and looked at the mail on his desk.

In a few weeks, Aimee would be in a home on Bluff View. Their hospital bills would be under control, and they could start saving for the boys' college. Life was good.

At ten-thirty, the phone rang. Tim answered and it was Cecil Malcour, the mall manager.

"Glad Pete let you in the office."

"Did Gil order this snow to test me?"

"You know he is out this week. How is the fort?"

"Fine but it's only Pete and I."

"In Fenton, when it snows no one goes to work."

"That's what my wife said, but I promised Zach Palm I would be here."

"I like your attitude. Bobbie put some mail on your desk. You might want to go through that."

"I have been reading the magazines and have coffee waiting. The office is warm and waiting for you."

"We'll see you in about thirty minutes."

7

History Lesson

Tim spent a week having breakfast with Cecil at Star's. Then they would go to the office and read the morning mail. Bobbie showed Tim the filing cabinet with letters sent to prospective tenants. She told him no one had made visits to local tenants in either Fenton or Atlanta.

On Tuesday Tim met Louie Vick, who took him through the office tower. At the list of tenants in the lobby Louie gave a history of each tenant. An accountant, two doctors, a dentist, a psychiatrist and several offices that were rarely open.

Wednesday Tim wondered into the boiler room and surprised Pete Gravel eating a sandwich.

Thursday Tim picked up a map and drove around Fenton. With a orange marker he circled various areas where small shops existed. He put an "X" where he found a bank branch. He figured bank managers would be good people to know. At least they would know who could to afford to go into business.

On Friday he started at one end of the mall and went store to store, introducing himself to each store manager. He asked what they thought would go well in the mall and who might be interested. The bookstore did not want another bookstore. The dress shops thought there were plenty. Shoe stores were not making their sales as is, etc. He started to get depressed.

The following Monday Gil Palm walked into the office, "Bobbie, I see your Christmas goldfish is still alive."

"Welcome back stranger. Cecil's in the mall supervising set-up of the antique show. Louie hasn't come in, but Tim's here."

Tim stepped out of his office when he heard Gil.

"Damn, Gil, you hire me then abandon me."

Gil's open shirt exposed a winter tan. "You been to Star's Cafe?"

"Every morning, but Cecil's in the mall today."

"Let's go. I need breakfast." Gil turned to Bobbie, "Tell Cecil and Louie we already left."

At Star's, Gil led to their regular back corner table.

"You all's early this morning," said the waitress.

"Morning, Ruby. We thought you'd give us an extra biscuit," Tim said.

She smiled. "Mr. Gil, did you tell Mr. Tim we call this the 'liars table' for a reason?"

Gil asked, "Has he shown up every day with Cecil?"

"Yes sir. You thinks he'll understand crazy Cecil?" She eyed Tim who turned red.

"Ruby, Bobbie will take care of Cecil. We need Tim to find out how," smiled Gil.

Ruby rolled her eyes as she poured coffee. "Why don't you bring Ms. Bobbie in? You sure talk enough about her."

"She knows too much," Gil said.

Ruby looked over her glasses, "Too much truth."

Tim nodded, "Ruby, you sound like my wife."

Ruby motioned the coffeepot to Gil's new Rolex. "I sees Santa was good to you."

"It tells time better." He showed it to her but quickly pulled his coat sleeve over its gold.

"What ya'll want this morning?"

When they ordered, Ruby went off passing the coffee in front of patrons on her way.

Gil asked, "Well Tim, what did you learn last week?"

"The importance of words."

"What do you mean?"

"It's like I'm in a foreign country."

"Words have their own baggage," Gil said.

"About the time I learn a real estate term, I find there is a southern version. Then there is Fenton's translation and finally a Malifer dialect."

"That's everywhere," Gil said.

"But it depends who I am talking to, what words mean. I want the truth."

Gil's eyes sparkled, "I told Dad you were smart enough to talk in different sales tongues."

"I was in sales, not real estate." Tim shook his head, "I always thought words were the meaning."

"Mr. Roy said your time with Cecil would give you time to learn how we use them." He sipped his coffee, "Besides Dad wanted to stay an extra week in Vail."

"I thought you called from Kansas City."

Gil held up his cell phone. "I work anywhere. Did you show any vacant stores?"

"There were no lookers. Good thing, you didn't tell me what rent to ask for."

"Tim, it's easy. Rent's what they'll pay. Ask them."

"You're kidding."

"It's fun. You ask them questions and find out how much they can afford. You convince them to pay it." Gil's eyes danced, "They know what they can afford. You get them to make that offer."

"We accept their offer?"

"We start with their offer. You dicker until it's as good as you can get it. When it is, tell them: 'I'll fight for my people to accept'."

"What do you mean 'I'll fight'? I can't tell them what the rent will be?"

"No."

"Oh, come on."

"No, seriously, you can't."

Tim looked around, "Who knows? Do you?"

Gil tapped his lips, raised his index finger to point to the ceiling and said in a spooky radio voice, "The market knows."

Tim's eyes swam, "God will tell me?"

"The god of supply and demand will."

Tim's jaw dropped.

"Tim, get them to tell you."

"That's crazy."

"They will."

"How?"

"You get to know them, find out how much they estimate their sales will be for a year." He paused to make sure Tim was listening, "They will never tell you a low number for fear you will turn them down as not strong enough."

Tim tilted his head so he would not miss a word.

Gil continued, "All rent is a percentage of sales. Usually 5 to 10 percent. So when they give you an estimate, they don't realize it but they have told you what they can pay."

Tim watched Gil run his palms on the Formica table, "Never, ever give a price first. Sometimes they'll offer more than we budgeted." The edge of his lips began to grin, "Once they give you an estimate, they are hooked. The game changes to how much more you can get."

"I haggle?"

"You pay attention. You watch their eyes, their face, their hands -- everything. Learn to read them. Soon will smell when they are at their top dollar. That's when you drop your head and slump a little so they feel they won."

Tim was stunned, "That's it? I am a damn hunting dog? And when I find a pigeon, I haggle?"

"Negotiate," corrected Gil.

"Like used cars?"

"Only it's real estate." Gil said.

"How can that be fun?"

"Because it's for money. You are a salesman at your core. I saw it in your eyes. It's in your genes. All salesmen tell stories to lead people to do what they want. Great ones seduce their target without notice."

Tim looked out the restaurant window across the interstate to the mall's drab buildings. "Polluted site, bad hotel, vacant stores and an empty office tower. Why did Malifer buy Cypress Tree in the first place?"

Gil whispered, "The price was right. Mr. Roy saw upside, he still does. We all do."

"But it is filled with problems."

"We knew about the asbestos," Gil said.

"Why didn't you make the previous owner take it out?"

Gil looked straight at him, "Tim, listen again, the . . . price . . . was . . . right, the bank was right, and the loan was right."

Tim exhaled, "So, it's ours."

8

Lesson In Negotiation

Back at the mall more antiques were being brought in and Gil said they should look at the antiques before it became crowded.

Tables filled the main hall and gave the impression the mall was filled with customers even though most were booth employees.

Cecil watched Pete Gravel was move tables behind masking tape marks on the floor.

"Cecil, you missed breakfast," Gil said.

Cecil pointed down the hall. "You'll be interested in what's several tables down."

Gil stretched his neck but didn't see anything. "What?"

"Go look," Cecil said, "you'll know when you see them."

They passed heavy furniture, shelves loaded with books and junk covered with attic dust. Tim slowed at the third table to feel a large glass bowl.

"Buying your wife something?" Gil asked.

"This is cheap pressed."

"Think so?" Gil picked up one, "How can you tell?"

Tim picked up a large bowel. "Check this one. It's heavy with lead, feel the sharp edges. It's cut glass."

Gil bounced it in his hand to gauge its weight. "I never knew that."

"This bowl is worth more than the rest of the table."

Gil's eyes roamed looking for what Cecil had found. All of a sudden, he froze. His hand laid on Tim's shoulder as he nodded toward a table loaded with hand tools. Stacked to one side were old beer cans.

That's what Cecil wanted him to see. He had been collecting beer cans for years. With his thumb and index finger, Gil twisted a make believe handlebar mustache. "Watch me vith dis rube, Mister Lichten. I'll teach vou to ne-go-ti-ate."

Tim bowed and swept his hand to open the way for Gil to lead then stayed back and moved to a nearby bench.

With hands behind his back, Gil meandered to the table and touched a hammer. He glanced at the booth owner in blue overalls.

"You've got some great stuff here," Gil said.

The old man's smile framed long yellow teeth, "Yeah, everyone says 'my daddy had one', But they don't buy."

Gil asked, "How much for this ax head?"

"It's marked $15," said the man as he coughed.

Gil moved past screwdrivers but stopped in front of the stack of beer cans. He picked one up then set it down to pick up another.

The vendor's bloodshot eyes followed Gil's fingers as they touched each can. "Found those last week in Parrot, Ga," he said leaning on his cane.

Gil pointed to a large wood comb-like contraption. "What's that?"

"Slaves used it before the cotton gin to take seeds out of cotton. I found it across the river from Vicksburg. I'll let you have it for $200."

The old man's eyes smiled as Gil eased back to the cans. "How much are these old cans?"

"How many do you want?"

Gil shrugged and lifted a cone top can. "Red Top, never heard of them."

A gray haired lady picked up a hatchet, "Just like my granddaddy's. My brother lost it when he was a boy in Selma." She held out twenty dollars.

The old man palmed her money. "I traded for that in Demopolis, It could be his."

"I want to surprise him."

"Yes'um," He put the hatchet in an old Target bag and flashed her a plastic smile. He then turned back to Gil, "Red Top's are from Cincinnati."

"Never seen a cone top," Gil said.

"Son, you got a lot to learn if you're going to collect. I sell every Red Top I find."

Gil pulled some cans to one side, "So, how much for these nine cans?"

"I'll have to look them up." The man sat down to pull out a box under the table. "You work in the mall?"

"In the mall office."

"I'll make you a deal." He gave up looking for the book. "What's your offer?"

"They're your cans. You need to give me a price."

The man grabbed his cane and mumbled to himself, "They haven't rusted too much."

Gil moved the Billy Beer out of his group.

The man's goose hand divided Gil's stack in two groups. "The last ones I sold in Memphis. Said he had a collection behind his bar."

"That's what I want to do."

The old man watched Gil hold each can.

"I want to scatter them on a bookshelf, you know, like they were left there."

Gil began to rock from foot to foot.

The man's thin smile agreed, "Good idea. Scattered like that will start people to talk." He moved more cans near Gil's group. "Big collections are worth gold."

"Is that so?" Gil picked a few more and reached for his wallet. "That's fifteen cans." Gil looked at the man. "How much?"

The man turned away.

Gil swayed and turned and winked at Tim. "Well, how much?" Gil asked louder.

The man continued to hobble around as he looked for more cans.

Gil turned to Tim, mouthed "I got to pee." Then turned back to the old man, "Tell you what I'll do. I have fifteen cans. I'll give you $45. Good, bad and ugly."

The man snorted, "Thought you wanted to buy some." He grunted, picked up his paper and sat on a wooden folding chair that swayed under his weight. "If you want charity, go to church." He began to read.

Gil slumped, leaned on one foot then the other. When he couldn't take it any longer, he put his wallet in his pocket and walked away. As he passed Tim, he said, "I'll be back."

Pete Gravel walked by Tim, "Is Gil gonna buy some of this junk?"
"He's teaching me."

"Garbage, it's all garbage," Pete said.

"But it's special garbage."

"Some people are crazy enough to buy junk."

"Pete, you know that insulation you put in your attic?"

"Yes sir."

"That was the mall's trash."

"Yes sir."

"Your knowledge gave it worth."

Pete grinned, "And I made gumbo."

"Right."

When Gil returned he stayed two tables away, but eyed his cans. The old man got up from time to time to talk with customers but somehow kept his back to Gil.

Gil sat with Tim for a while, but those cans were like a lodestone. They called like Greek sirens until Gil had again picked up one. His eyes were glassy.

When the can was placed back on the table it clinked. Gil froze like he heard the top of a cookie jar.

The old man nodded to Gil.

"Sixty dollars – but I get this one also." Gil added another and pulled three twenties from his wallet. He put his head down and waved the bills the way he fetched a dog with a bone.

"Son, I know when I am being played." The man put both hands on his cane, and stood to count the cans.

Gil's eyes jumped each time the man's boney fingers removed one. Gil studied the nine left, removed the Great Falls Select but put back the Narragansett and two German Balloon cans. "Eighty," Gil said.

The man looked at Gil's eyes as he removed one more can.

Gil added back four cans. "Hundred and twenty."

The man's thin eyes froze on Gil. Then the old man's empty left palm turned up to ask for Gil's money. His right hand reached for a used Wal-Mart bag.

Gil exhaled, counted out six twenty-dollar bills to the outstretched paw. "You win," whispered Gil.

Both men placed cans in a brown sack.

Back in the office Gil set the bag on his desk and asked, "Tim, what did you learn?"

Tim counted on his fingers, "Don't make the first offer. Don't let the other man control the process. Don't allow your emotions to pressure a deal. And for God's sake don't be afraid to walk away."

"You forgot the most important." Gil said.

"What's that?"

"Don't try to impress someone on how great a negotiator you are. That damn snake'll bite your ass every time.

Gil reached for a beer can price guide on the shelf behind his desk.

"Gil, there're fourteen cans. I thought you bought twelve."

"Well I guess someone put two extra cans in the bag. The rule is to always let the other man feel he won, but go away knowing you did."

"Did he give them, or did you take them?" Tim asked.

"What matters is he feels he won."

"Maybe." Tim said.

"In business you write the rules as you go."

"What about the golden rule?"

"If it gives gold, it rules."

The Hunting Dog

9

Lutz, Florida

Mord Doyle drove his pickup in the dark. He was careful as he rolled his sleeves above his forearm tattoos. Outside Tampa, where a small two-lane road from Lutz was being widened to four lanes, his pickup lights had a hard time staying on the road. At a crossroad, he turned into his construction site and parked next to where a building's foundation was laid out.

He grabbed the long flashlight to inspect the forms where concrete would be poured. When he found an area, he switched off the light, flipped his cigarette and pulled back the rebar. He raked gravel to one side, dug a shallow trench, returned to his pickup to lift a long stiff urine smelling black plastic bag wrapped with duct tape His tattooed muscles popped until he let the lump fall with a thud in the sand. He quickly replaced the rebar and gravel.

When he finished he lifted his cap, ran his fingers through his thin white hair, and clicked on the flashlight to inspect.

Mord walked to the pickup, reached for his thermos of coffee and lit a cigarette. Three pickups with Mexicans drove by. Birds chirped to announce the crack of dawn. It was 5:28. His crew would soon arrive with the concrete truck.

In the slow fuzzy light dew formed on the truck's dark green hood.

Mord liked these small construction jobs. They reminded him of years ago when life was simple. Today they would pour the wine store's foundation slab.

Ricco Marionetti sent his son, Tony, to an Australian University to study wine marketing. When he came home, Tony asked Ricco to back the wine store. This site was found, and plans were drawn. Tony left on a buying trip to Europe, and Ricco asked Mord Doyle to build it.

Ricco graduated top of his class from Harvard. When his father died, he became the family overseer of scattered real estate holdings.

Ricco trusted Mord because he knew what to do when needed. Mord respected Ricco's gut feel for the essence of business.

Mord once was a CPA. His mind loved to study accounting columns in search of investments. However, in prison, his body learned to love manual labor. His body craved to lift and hammer and build, but now it was worn and tired.

Whatever Ricco wanted, Mord Doyle would do. Ricco had given him a second chance when he got out of prison. Mord did anything for Ricco. He loved to help anyway he could; to find investments, suggest properties, cut costs or when necessary to mop up problems.

"Tony's Vino-Vino, what a stupid store name." Mord said out-loud to himself as the concrete truck pulled in. Behind was his brother's pickup with flames painted on it.

"Tony should work with me." Mord said, "I'd teach him business from the ground up."

10

Sales Calls

Soon Tim's daily ritual became prospecting for tenants. First breakfast at Star's with Cecil and Gil, then a walk through the mall to visit store managers.

He found these managers had no vision of how to grow sales. They saw their job only to keep racks straight and ring up sales.

Even Cyrus at the shoe store said, "Malifer is only interested in rent."

Luke Douglas had recently been made manager of the bank branch. He knew if Tim filled vacant spaces, he would get new customers, so he suggested leads.

Cecil advised Tim not to waste time downtown with Davis Street merchants. There had been bad blood between his late father and the Dabe brothers. So Tim ventured to nearby LaGrange, Peachtree City, even down to Macon and Columbus.

Tim avoided Atlanta because Gil said Atlanta's stores would expand inside Atlanta before Fenton.

Each day, he would make visits, send follow up letters and pin their location on his wall map.

Tim's mom gave him a framed needlework plaque when he got his first job. It hung to the right of his map on the bulletin board. "Tell them what you'll do – do it – then show them you did."

When Bobbie saw it, she gave him a framed cartoon of two vultures in a tree. One was saying: "Patience, hell. I'm going to kill something." Tim hung it below his mom's needlework.

Bobbie Malcour was Cecil's twin sister. They both were tall and played tennis, but she was not as flamboyant. Her bones were big. She accepted that her brother was the manager, but she was smarter. They both still lived with their eighty-year-old mother in the family antebellum home on the affluent end of Bluff View.

11

A Death at Home

Before going to work, Cecil went in the back yard and started digging in the rose bed. "Damn, Bobbie, you have done it this time. Momma will be mad as hell at you."

"It's only a damn dog, Cecil! Lighten up and quit being a wimp."

"But Fritz was Mom's dog. We got him to distract her from the scotch."

"Lot of good that did."

"Dammit, Bobbie, what will you tell her when she wakes up?"

"She won't be sober for a week; by then we will figure out something. Maybe put her in the hospital again."

"Bobbie, you don't have feelings do you?"

"I have feelings, but we have to see the world as it is." Her jaw began to shake.

"Maybe your medication needs to be adjusted."

Bobbie dropped dead Fritz into the hole as Cecil shoveled dirt. "Being twins doesn't mean we think alike."

"Bobbie, I'm keeping my promise. I will take care of you and Momma, as long as I live. Just don't blow up so much."

"Don't preach to me! I have had about all I can take!"

Cecil threw down his shovel. "Damn it! I don't need this shit! I am up to my ass with alligators. Gil tells Mr. Roy every move I make."

12

Dust From The Floor

Lamar Bashire was a short bald headed sausage of a man stuffed into overalls. He daily held court in his one man hardware store with or without anyone present.

In winter, he fired up a pot belly stove. In the summer, he would open both the front and back doors to let the slow thick Georgia air flow through.

Lamar's Hardware was in the old part of town and faced a park called 'The Old Courthouse'. An outlaw gang of Sherman's army burned the original 1840 Courthouse in the war. Today large live oaks stood guard around the former building's blood-red foundation bricks.

In one corner of the park was a gazebo and a marble monument to the Fenton men who died in the raid.

Locals still called the revered park 'The Old Courthouse' even though a modern one was built in 1883 on the hill above Davis Street. The new building was called the "Government Building."

After the war, northern "investors" came to town. They built a new business area on the higher part of Davis Street. The flood-prone Courthouse Square buildings soon became neglected.

Lamar's grandfather arrived in the 1920s. He purchased his first building at a tax sale for twenty-eight dollars. He picked up the adjacent buildings over time. Lamar rents one to Abe Zimmerman, the shoe repairman. Another to the Snodgrass spinsters who sell antiques. The limestone front building has sat empty since Dr. Julian retired and moved to Athens.

"Been no floods since the WPA dam was built," Lamar said.

When Lamar told a story, his slow rhythms and rich tones always haunted Tim. If he repeated local gossip, his stories became more bizarre, but somehow more believable.

Aimee told Tim that Faulkner, Welty, Robert Penn Warren and others didn't make up their fiction from thin air. They had stewed them from the gossip they heard, but the truth was always at their core.

There were several of these weavers of words in Fenton. They sat in beauty parlors, ate lunch at Star's or fished at the river. They all had a gift that bound Fenton with threads from ages past.

Lamar rocked back and forth as he blended fact with fiction for anyone who would listen. In his yarns were voices from England or Ireland, from Italy, France or Germany, all paced by an African beat into a verbal gumbo.

"Tim, people are crazy. Some of our local 'hysterical' ladies had my block put in a historic district."

"You can raise your rents," Tim said.

"Like hell. They just want to control my property."

"Lamar, you might be eligible for federal funds."

"Bullshit! They told the paper they wanted this area to have historic integrity. They want to make a tourist spot, but none of them live down here."

"But your property's value will rise."

"Which will raise taxes."

Tim waved off his objection, "You're against progress."

"Their art club bought the old fire house in the next block and made it their Saturday clubhouse. Now they want to control my block. A 'bunch of phooey about nothing.'" Lamar grabbed a hand full of peanuts out of the wood barrel next to his chair.

"You'll like it."

"If I want to paint my door, the damn color must be in their 'hysteric' guidelines."

"What color did they use in 1840?" Tim asked.

"How the hell do I know? This area has always been poor. They want us to use their 'Hysteric Fenton' colors. Their past crumbles on Davis Street!" He threw the shells towards the trash.

Tim shrugged.

"This area was downtown Fenton until their carpetbagger grandpas built Davis Street. It killed this area. They even tried to rename Davis Street as Lincoln Street. We stopped that foolishness in 1892."

People walked in from time to time but rarely purchased more than a few nails. They came to hear Lamar's gossip peppered with humor. Somehow, no matter how wild his story, its truth survived.

Lamar knew about everyone. He knew their memories. He knew the history they wanted to forget.

Lamar loved to come up with verbal pearls. He had a ledger on the counter where he would write them down. One day he planned to publish them. He would call it 'Dust from the Floor'.

"If you don't understand why, look for the money."

"A rich person is one who has an accountant out of town."

"He who doesn't read, doesn't think."

"Government doesn't give a dime unless a politician can make a buck."

"Lamar, I hear Sheriff Baker might have drug connections."

"Those who say that don't know anything. The real connection's Angelo Saulora, who lives on the street behind the Government Building."

"How do you know?"

Lamar smiled, took his bottom false teeth out to flick a peanut on the floor.

Tim asked, "Who's Saulora? I don't know him."

"He's about 75, short, pitch black hair which he loads with Vitalis. He combs it straight back."

"I didn't know they still made that."

"There's a lot you don't know. He has Greek black eyes. John the barber says he got his wooden leg because of a shooting. If you see him, his young Spanish wife with a cute dimple in her left cheek will be driving his Bentley."

Tim smiled, "What do you know about him?"

Lamar shrugged, "Last Wednesday, he had lunch with Mr. Reed, the bank president."

"He must be a big depositor."

Lamar shook his head, "He has a small account which is fed from a bank in Belize."

"Now how do you know that?"

Lamar's grin assured Tim that he knew.

Tim smiled, "Maybe you have an eye on his wife."

Lamar's eyes let Tim know that was out of line, "He's with Fishbone-Puxar."

"Never heard of them," Tim said.

"That's who sold the city the street bricks for the downtown remodel."

"Maybe he wanted to retire in Fenton."

Lamar looked over his glasses, "Maybe he wanted to hide."

"You're guessing about the drugs?"

"Why don't you ask Cecil? You know Cecil's on the bank's board. His grandfather started it. I bet he knows."

"I will."

"Shit, Cecil knows more skeletons than a graveyard."

"That's a good phrase for your journal."

Lamar reached for his notebook. "Believe what you want, but I don't trust him."

"Who?"

"Saulora," Lamar said.

Tim didn't say anything.

"Facts are facts." Lamar looked again at Tim, "There are people in Fenton under witness protection."

Tim waited for more but Lamar never told him who they were.

One day Tim asked, "So who's the richest man in town?"

Lamar rocked in his oak chair. "There are a good number that have their lawyers and accountants out of town." He rubbed his beard. "My guess is the mayor, Lex Canaglia. His company paves all the roads around here. He owns real estate. He even bought three empty factories for the land. His fingers touch everything. If you want his help, make him a partner."

Tim poured himself some coffee, "So, he takes bribes?"

Lamar's bottom jaw went back and forth, "No that would be illegal, but you might make sure you use his company to pave your parking lot."

"I'm sure he will be able to bid." Tim said.

"Bid? You did not hear me."

"Even the city puts things out for bid."

Lamar scrunched his lips. "To bid on city contracts, you must have a physical address in the Central Business District."

"Business people downtown make a strong downtown," Tim said.

"Well it's political manure," Lamar said. "Down the street is Donna's Interiors. She is the mayor's wife. You will be surprised how many businesses have "offices" rented in her back room. They get their mail sent to her and she forwards it to their office in the county."

"Is Lex an attorney?" Tim asked.

"No, not at all. Lex coached football at Fenton High, married the senior homecoming queen, had a son six months later which he named Lex. He lost his school job but started to make deliveries for his father's office-supply store. Somewhere in there his wife got cancer. While she was in the hospital, he pounded bimbos on his truck route."

Lamar looked at Tim to make sure he understood, "He did the honorable thing. He buried his wife. Then married Donna four days before his daughter was born."

"Good future government official," Tim said.

"What do you think Lex named her?" Lamar paused and looked over his glasses, "Lex!!! Fenton has three Lex Canaglias."

"Now, that's funny!"

Lamar held up his hand. "Wait, let me finish the story. The first Lex grew up and went off to some Minnesota Law School.

"Why didn't he stay in Georgia?"

"That's another story, but the daughter did. They both became attorneys. One day father Lex wanted to buy another vacant spinning mill and asked the oldest Lex to handle the deal. Well, Son played with the paperwork, and pocketed some major cash."

"Was that legal?"

Lamar's shaking hand let Tim know he was out of order, "Anyway, Daddy Lex got mad as a wild pig in a den of snakes and hired Daughter Lex, to sue his older son." Lamar smiled and made sure Tim followed, "The youngest Lex, who had passed the Georgia bar, became the old man's new attorney."

Tim got so excited that he spilled his coffee. "Lex #1 hires Lex #3 to sue Lex #2 for money Lex #2 stole from Lex #1."

Lamar held up both of his hands, "I need to tell you the best part."

"Excuse, me."

"Anyway, right before they were to go to court, a turned over rented canoe was found ten miles down river A suicide note was taped to Lex #2's mobile phone which he left on the dashboard of his black Lexus at the dock."

"Damn!"

"When your late father-in-law, Nick Maples at the paper asked the sheriff why they didn't have boats out looking for the body, he just said, 'He'll turn up soon enough'."

"Some lazy sheriff," Tim said.

"That never went in the paper." Lamar looked over the top of his gold wire glasses while Tim waited. "Weeks later the wife went in the bank and withdrew a sizable amount of cash and left town. The sheriff had attached a tracking device on the Lexus, so he simply followed her all the way to Dauphin Island."

"You mean the sheriff was right?"

Lamar slapped his knee, "Truth always comes out."

"Or in this case, follow the money," Tim said as he noticed Lamar waiting. "There's not more?"

"Well he served his time and came back to town, and everything was fine. Until one day, the Mrs. was out and saw his black Lexus drive into the Plantation Motel all the way to the rear cabins. She drove around the block to take another look. Sure enough there was his Lexus with its logo of William Mitchel Law School on the rear window."

"So what does she do? She parks behind some bushes and calls him and tells him she got a phone call he is with some bimbo at the Plantation. He denies it. She tells him she's going over there, and if he is, she will kill him." "In five seconds he leaves with a plastic trash bag over his head and jumps in his car and races off. Well, the wife takes out after him, and when he stops at a light, she rams him in the rear at about sixty miles an hour."

Lamar's cheeks turned red. He sputtered, spewed, sprayed and splattered mist everywhere. "He didn't know what hit him, and it put them both in the hospital for the longest time."

Tim laughed so hard tears gushed. He gasped for air.

In the middle of it all, the postman came in, set the mail by the register, and laughed at their laughing. He looked at Tim, turned to Lamar, "Lex?"

Lamar nodded, and the spray started again.

"How stupid can a man be?" the postman asked.

"It's sad when a man can't trust his son." Tim said.

"The moral of the story is when you wrong a woman, you better watch your back," the postman said as he walked out.

"Tim, know who you can trust. Look at their history. Sons follow fathers. Bastards breed bastards."

"Lamar, evil lusts for the hearts of all men."

"Yeah, but in Fenton too many folks already have carpetbag hearts."

"You think they're all crooks?" Tim asked.

"Their hearts are stained green."

Tim thought for a moment. "Lamar, lots of people came to Fenton to make money. That doesn't make them crooks. Look at your grandfather."

"My grandfather came looking for hope."

"Everyone needs hope, even crooks."

"Today greed rules."

"But the world's not about greed – yet," Tim said.

"Don't kid yourself."

13

Phone Call from Mike

A week later, Tim was on his way to the car when his phone rang. It was his friend Mike in Chicago.

"Tim, we got it!"

"Got what?" Tim asked.

"The bid! Our bid to make tri-color dimmable LED flashlights for the Navy."

"I forgot all about that," Tim said.

"I told you it would take months."

"Mike, I don't think I'll be able to help."

"No problem. They sent the contract! All we have to do is sign. They'll send us a check for start-up costs."

"Don't you think they will want to see our factory? Where did you tell them we have a plant?"

"They never look at these small bids."

"Mike, the bid was shy of a million bucks. That's big."

"Not to the feds."

"Well damn."

"I told you, Beth's Papa did it."

"You still think we'll get start-up costs?" Tim asked.

"You bet I do! They want us to rush this, so they had better send it fast. We asked for $450,000 start up."

"I don't feel right," Tim said.

"Once they pay, Papa will convert it, and I'll send yours."

"I don't . . . "

"Your share's $100,000."

"Shit."

"What's the matter?"

"I feel like I've hit the lottery with a stolen ticket."

"Not stolen, a found one because some bureaucrat lost it."

"I'm not telling Aimee."

"Don't tell anyone."

"You're sure this will work?"

"Tim, they dish out so many of these penny-ante candy contracts. They don't have time to track them."

"It's close to half a million! People go to jail if you rob a thousand from a bank."

"This is not a bank. We don't have a gun. We only want to start a small factory. A lot of new ones fail. They know the risks. They want us to try. We are helping a public servant get rid of budgeted funds. However, there is a difference."

"What difference?"

"It's going in our pockets."

"Mike, we have to give them a product."

"It cost me $5,000 for the prototype we sent. All we have to do is get their funds, so we can start the factory."

"Mike, you talk as if . ."

"Tim, you are only a consultant and have no exposure."

"Yes, but . . ."

"No buts about it. The feds are pencil pushers. To them this is small potatoes. If we happen to go belly up, it is easier for them to bid it out again and move on. Even if they do start looking, there are bigger fish in the pond. Our tracks will be cold. Besides, Beth's family has connections."

"You've got the contract?"

"In my hand."

"I can't tell Aimee."

"Don't tell anyone. It's an investment."

"Shit."

14

John's Barbershop

One day Tim headed toward Davis Street.

At the Pine Street stop light, he noticed a barber's pole in front of a shop he had missed. He pulled to the curb. A bell above the door chimed when he walked in.

A lone hunched man in a white smock sat in the last barber chair. The other chair was empty. An antique Philco radio was on.

"You open for business?" Tim asked.

"Yes sir, right on time." The man slid out of the leather chair and faced it toward Tim.

"It sure feels great to step right in."

"Friends never wait around here." The barber snapped his red University of Georgia barber's apron and wrapped it over Tim. He then rotated the chair to study Tim's head.

"Don't believe I know your hair. How do you want it?"

"Off the ears, not too short."

"We can handle that."

There were five empty oak captain's chairs with a long mirror on the opposite wall. The tall floor model radio had the morning paper on top.

"I haven't seen a tall radio like that since I was a kid."

"Dad bought it the day we opened."

"That wood cabinet has great sound," Tim said.

"I never turn it off. If the lights are on, it's on."

"No TV?"

"I can't cut hair and watch TV."

"I never noticed your shop."

"My pole fell some time ago. My son visited last week and put it back."

"Well, it found me."

"I helped Dad tile this floor when I was nine. It wasn't easy. We were both on our knees."

Tim closed his eyes, "I remember working with my father."

"Dad wanted the shop here because it would catch men on their way to work."

"Makes sense," Tim said.

The man stopped cutting Tim's hair, "Sorry I didn't introduce myself. I'm John."

"Tim Lichten. I lease Cypress Tree Mall. We moved from Chicago."

"You related to the owners? I hear they're all related."

"No, I don't have that kind of money."

"They sure threw a party last year when they took over. Were you there?"

"No, I just started. Was it good?"

"They sent engraved invitations. It was something else. A man from Kansas City with a bow-tie and a rose on his lapel." John pointed with his scissors to his lapel. "He made a speech in front of all the local owners, their employees, everyone. Got everyone in a good mood with jokes but ticked everyone when he said they were going to teach local merchants how they should sell in today's world."

"He said that?"

"Insulted everyone! Richard Dabe said he wasn't going to be taught anything by anyone with a foreign accent."

"You mean a northern accent," Tim said.

"Northern is foreign."

"That's what my wife says."

"You're from Chicago?"

"My wife is from Fenton. She's a Maples."

"Rose Maples daughter?"

Tim nodded.

"Her father was a good man, but the paper killed him."

"He was a reporter."

"Some say he was on a major story when he died."

"No kidding."

"He always told the truth, even when it stung."

"I wish they would today," Tim said.

"Today I don't think there is truth."

"What was his name?" Tim asked.

"Who?"

"The man with the rose in his lapel."

John paused to think, "I don't know, but he had red hair. After that party, local owners refused to talk to them."

"Maybe that's why I have a job."

"Could be."

"Has the fix up on Davis Street helped?" Tim asked.

"I fixed my dog, but it didn't help him either."

"You mean it's a dog?"

"I fixed my dog for my benefit, but the vet got the money. I would like to see where all the Davis Street money landed."

A bell above the front door chimed and in came two older men. "John, you have a packed house today," said the man using a walker. "Come on in Sy, plenty of room."

"Ed was kind enough to pick me up, so I could get a haircut. I appreciate it."

Sy went to the empty chair. Ed put a yellow Georgia Tech apron on him. Ed said, "Anything for a buck. Sy, God knows you have some."

John clipped his scissors in the air. "No business like mo' business. I want you men to meet Tim Lichten. He leases the mall."

"That's a full-time job," Ed said.

Tim's mind became numb with their rumors of the crooks downtown. They knew hidden money somehow showed up in pockets of contractors. "No one turns down found money," said Sy when they accused him of selling his condemned slum houses under the hill so the garage could be built. They laughed then gossiped more.

The radio interrupted "Now, for our morning obituary report." They all became quiet.

After the final ad from the Lone Cedar Funeral Home, Sy broke in: "You know we're in trouble when the highlight of our day is the funeral home report."

They all chuckled. John said, "But Tim's highlight will be his walk down Davis Street. He'll be awed by the sculptures and aromatic fountain."

"And brick street with Vermont granite curbs," Ed said.

"Don't break your neck looking at all the shoppers," Sy said.

"What a crock."

"What's wrong with them?" Tim asked, "I love fountains."

"You seen it?" Ed asked.

"Not on foot. But today I am checking every brick."

"The mayor's wife designed it all. She's an expert. She has a design business and graduated in primary art education," John said.

"She's a damn florist!" Ed said.

"The electric bill to run the fountain's pump was $45,000 first year, so the city gave it to the Davis Street Merchants Association, and they turned the water off!" John said.

"One sculpture's from Lubbock, Texas. The stone cannon is from Indiana. What do they know about Fenton or even Georgia?" Sy asked.

Ed broke in, "Thank goodness they didn't buy a third one. I heard it was supposed to be a pile of railroad ties from Chicago."

Sy turned to Tim, "You haven't seen our statues?"

"I'm going now," Tim said.

Sy said. "Use the four-story parking garage. Take it all in. Let us know what you think."

"You've got a deal," Tim said.

John handed Tim a mirror, so he could see his work. I'll expect to see you again in four weeks." John took his payment and made the change from a green bank bag. The cash register stayed silent.

Ed asked, "Going downtown?"

"I have to see those sculptures."

"Don't die laughing," John said.

". . . or crying," Sy said.

15

Davis Street

Davis Street was developed in the 1870s on the bluff above the river, about a half mile south of Lamar's.

Below the bluff sat Flood Street with the entrance to the parking garage that Sy talked about.

When Tim drove up, the booth that once held someone to collect the parking fee had a hand-written note on the cracked window. "Elevator out – park on 4th floor"

Tim drove up, past two empty floors. On the third were a few spots marked for bank executives and a law firm.

On the top floor in the sun, sat a pickup with three cars.

He stepped on the rubberized moving sidewalk, but it was turned off so he walked in morbid silence.

Davis Street's renovation was three blocks long. Both the street and sidewalks were paved with new brick.

Davis Street itself was blocked off with large yellow concrete pylons at both ends. Only delivery trucks were allowed. On the sidewalks sat huge brown pots with dead evergreens.

Tim looked at the store fronts. One had a single guitar in the window, another a display of shoes with a handwritten sign: Sizes AA to EEEE. Next door was the Missionary AME Church, which had about twenty chairs set up, but the lights were out.

A block away, an old lady pushed a grocery cart filled with bags. A small black dog ran around her feet. A waving newspaper floated across the street. The scene took Tim back to a Swedish movie he saw in college.

The cross street was closed off. What once was the street was now a park that ran uphill. In front of the new Courthouse at top was a canon sculpture and a small fountain. The water flowed downhill past shrubs and sculptures to a waterfall on Davis. Only, there was no water. Just concrete with a slime green puddle in the pool.

He took in the panorama: the dry fountain, the dead trees the stupid sculpture, named "King Cotton" that looked like a bronze basketball with brown leaves and puffs on it.

From where Tim stood, the cannon at the top looked like a giant single finger salute.

The men in the barbershop were right.

The next block did have two stores that looked alive. On the left was "Richard Dabe's Mens Store." The other across the street, was "Fenton Dry Goods," run by Richard's brother Jacob.

Tim aimed at Richard's store first. The modern bronze street windows looked out of place with its over-sized 1950's retro neon sign. When he opened the heavy oak front door, he found a showroom as up to date as any in Chicago. The stained wood mannequins showed off men's clothing under focused accent lights. However, there was no sound, no background music, no perfumed air. Only cold silence.

A single older man sat in the shoe department reading the Wall Street Journal. Tim walked around looking at shirts. When he felt the cloth of a maroon sport shirt, the man looked up, put his paper down and approached.

"Those shirts are the latest Cutter & Buck. They came in yesterday."

"I'm Tim Lichten and came to meet Richard Dabe."

The man asked, "I'm Richard. What do you sell?"

"I'm with Cypress Tree Mall. I came to introduce myself." Tim offered his hand.

The man did not offer his. "You people bought that mall from a damn thief."

Tim raised both his hands in defense, "I don't own it, I'm just trying to make a living."

"That bastard Canaglia stole the land from me."

"Who?"

"Our mayor. He's a damn crook!" Richard Dabe quickly walked past Tim to open the front door. He motioned with his left hand for Tim to leave.

Tim stepped back, "I came in to meet you, maybe buy something."

Richard sneered; his head motioned for Tim to leave. Tim's first reaction was to stand his ground, to make him physically kick him out. But he slowly moved to the door then pitched the shirt he was holding on a table of slacks.

"It is a pleasure to see how you treat customers." Out of habit, Tim held his hand out to shake goodbye.

Richard Dabe refused to remove his right hand from the door handle. "Son, go back north. We don't need your kind here."

Tim's rejected right hand floated up to give a silent weak wave. The door slammed behind him.

Tim stood alone on the street, "To hell with him, to hell with them all." He headed in long steady strides back to his car, but slowed at the fountain. "Richard Dabe's rudeness is Richard Dabe's problem. Why should I care?"

He looked back down the block. A tattered newspaper still danced on the brick walk.

"What a crock," Tim said.

He looked at Jacob Dabe's red-brick store. Over the third-floor windows, etched in stone was, Fenton Dry Goods 1882. All the old windows were replaced with anodized bronze molding and tinted glass. Tim might as well give Jacob a try.

16

Visit to Jacob Dabe

As soon as Tim stepped inside the store, his spirit lifted. The wide store's high ceiling was filled with light. Large antique ceiling fans turned fast enough to blur their brass blades. There was a balcony that ran across the back wall. Next to its rail, a grayhaired lady looked up as Tim walked in.

On the first floor, two men tagged slacks. The older pudgy man had a yellow cloth tape measure over his shoulders. The other man was in a silk suit and vest. His shoes were spit shined Stacey Adams.

The elder man looked over his glasses into Tim's eyes as he offered his hand, "I'm Jacob Dabe. How can we help you?"

Once Jacob understood who Tim was, he said, "Mr. Lichten, this is Horace Jesse Lee. He has worked for me for twenty years. If I'm not here, Horace will take good care of you."

Horace had the same 'dead fish' handshake that Pete Gravel used. He then returned to tagging slacks.

Jacob motioned to the wood stairs. "Mr. Lichten, let's go up to my office."

"Mr. Dabe, you've done an excellent job remodeling without killing this store's character."

"Some of my fixtures go back to the 1890s."

"The ceiling fans are amazing."

"They were the first electric fans in Georgia. When this store was built the owner installed a generator at the river to electrify the store."

Jacob lifted shoe boxes from an old oak chair so Tim could sit.

Tim looked over the balcony. "Man, you sure can see your world up here."

"What I don't, Irene catches. That's why she's on the opposite side of the balcony." She glanced at Tim through her pointy glasses, smiled, but continued to add figures on an ancient tape machine.

"Mr. Lichten, can I offer you a Coke?"

"That would be great."

Jacob walked to an old rounded top red Coca-Cola machine, turned the key, removed three bottles and locked it back with the key still in the door. He gave one to Tim, and walked to give Irene one before sitting at his desk.

"So, Tim, tell me about yourself."

"I recently started leasing Cypress Tree, which made my wife happy."

"Luke Douglas said you are from Chicago."

"My wife was a Maples. Her father was with the paper."

Jacob's clear eyes were friendly, "Nick was a good man. He always wrote the truth."

"I was lucky to get on with the Mall."

"The Maples family settled here before the war. My family came after."

"The War of Northern Aggression?" Tim asked with a smile.

"Around here we call it Sherman's Torrid Penetration."

"Wars may last a few years, but they take ages to overcome," Tim said.

"It was the first modern war about business," Jacob said.

"Not to free slaves?"

"Study your history. That's not why it was fought."

Tim had touched a sour topic.

Jacob continued, "But it put in place the enslavement of everyone."

Tim looked at him. "Are you serious?"

"The loss of cheap labor, forced the powers to enslave everyone."

"The powers?" Tim asked.

"All fights start with bullies stealing lunch money." Jacob's voice vibrated, "It's easy to rob from those who have little."

Tim flinched at Jacob's statement. "I'm going to have to think about that. You said your people came after the war?"

"My great-granddaddy came from Lebanon in the 1870s. His brothers sold dry goods from wagons they drove from town to town."

"Where did he live?"

"Camped out, for the most part. At one time, they had six wagons. He settled in Fenton and married the daughter of the man who built this building.

When her father died, he took over. His brother opened in Chattanooga, and a cousin in Birmingham."

"I understand that happened a lot."

"All over the South. He died with two stores and some rent houses." He nodded across the street, "When my father died, Richard got twenty of the houses and one haberdashery. I got this three floor department store and a few houses. My sister, Irene, had the children's store but came to work for me." He nodded to the gray-haired lady, "Irene and I now have nine stores."

"All in Fenton?"

"Three on Davis. My two sons run six out of town."

"That's what the tax man likes, successful businesses."

Jacob gave a half laugh, "I wish, but we barely break-even."

"Mrs. Maples said a lot of people respect you."

"Respect gives no profit," Jacob said.

Irene answered the phone and held it up for Jacob to see. He turned to Tim, "Excuse me while I take this." He motioned for Tim to remain seated.

"Yes Ben, what can I do for you?" Jacob listened, "Evict him today. Put his stuff on the street. His wife will move in with her mother."

Tim looked at the store below.

Jacob hung up the phone, "Rental property is one headache after another but that's where my profit lies."

"How many rentals do you have?" asked Tim.

"Hundred and eighty seven."

"That's some investment."

"Well, we sell clothes. Most of the time on credit." He nodded to Irene. "She runs my loan company. If customers don't have money, we give them credit. Over time, we end up with their house."

"And they pay you?" Tim said.

"Rent to stay."

Tim didn't say anything.

"When they pay in person, I give them a discount on clothes." Jacob looked at Tim, "which I sell on lay away. I cash payroll checks, find jobs for them, even put them in a larger house when they need one."

"One big circle," Tim said.

"Not quite."

"Their kids shop the mall . . . "

Tim smiled, "Then we should talk."

Jacob continued, " . . . and they buy drugs, which takes their money out of my control."

Tim waited.

Jacob leaned back in his chair, "I'm going in another direction. Did you notice the new construction down here?"

"The building going up?" asked Tim.

"Yes, condos. But we might be changing it. There are companies looking at small towns. We asked Larry Morgan, who has contacts, if he could lease some of them as government offices."

"That'll help downtown traffic."

"The mayor signed a document that made all downtown a Federal 'Enterprise Zone'. Federal agencies must locate in that zone if they need space."

"You're going in a new direction."

"I rent the land. If the developer doesn't pay my land lease, I can take over the improvements."

"Sounds secure," Tim said.

"You never know." Jacob leaned in, "The secret is to work with others. The bank tied us with a South American construction company. There are several others involved in this project, but I own the land."

"You are in control."

"Some control with money, others with connections, but I use property."

"Your brother said he once owned the mall's property."

"Richard has never been a happy man."

"It shows," Tim said.

"He's my brother, but he stole that land from a widow, sold the timber for more than he paid her, set up a creosote plant which dumped toxic chemicals on it. The feds wanted it cleaned up. He refused, had the plant file bankruptcy, and he walked away."

"He told me the mayor stole it."

"That's not true. It sat with uncollected taxes for years. When the Fenton by-pass was rumored. He ran to the tax office to pay the back taxes only to find Canaglia held the title, free and clear."

"Ouch!"

Jacob shook his head, "Tim, there's never enough money to feed the greedy."

Tim glanced over the rail at Horace arranging dress shirts. "He seems to be a good man."

Jacob leaned into Tim, "Horace would get drunk on Saturday night. The Sheriff would put him in jail and call me to bail him out. I did that a few times. Suddenly one night in bed it hit me like a brick." Jacob slapped his fore head. "I wasn't helping Horace. The next time I got a call, I told the Sheriff: "Horace doesn't work for me anymore."

"You fired him?"

"Right there on the phone."

A twinkle came to Tim's eyes, "You cut off the Sheriff's donut money."

Jacob slapped a stack of invoices, "Horace wasn't arrested anymore! Know what else?" Jacob glanced to see where Horace was, "Horace became a man. He did not have a job. When he found out no one would hire him, he finally came to see me. We had a real long talk."

"Tough love," Tim said.

"No one would hire Horace without calling me."

"It was a good lesson for him," Tim said.

"People change. Companies change. Towns change all for better or worse."

"Even change changes." Tim said.

Jacob nodded agreement, "It's a constant struggle. If you can't get cheap labor, you buy machines. When the mills moved overseas they sold the machines also. Now we have no jobs."

"No money feeding the town."

"Today, if you build a house in Fenton, do you know who builds it for you?" Jacob paused. "Mexicans!" He shook his head. "You know their papers aren't legal, but we look the other way."

"They're hard workers," Tim said.

"Labor is a commodity like cotton or cows."

"That you buy?"

"That you rent, as cheap as possible."

Tim looked to see if Jacob would crack a smile, but he sat stone faced. Tim asked, "Do you know what you're saying?"

Jacob whispered, "There's not a dime's difference between slavery in the 1800s and the way some companies treat employees today."

"Damn, you're serious."

"Tim, there's a hog farmer who lives near here. He makes sure his hogs have the best of care. He feeds them until they are stuffed. He has a vet check them every week. He even plays music to them! And he's going to kill them!"

"What's the solution?" Tim asked.

Jacob tapped his pencil on his desk. "Education on several levels. People don't see the size of the problem, but it's more than that. There's no leader free enough to lead."

"Free?"

"From the profit virus."

"Why do you call it a virus?" Tim asked.

"It eats souls."

Tim sat silent.

"Like the wasp that lays eggs inside a caterpillar. They suck the host until maggots eat their way out like fads."

"But . . . " Tim stopped.

"Fads make people sheep," Jacob sighed. "Fads to put profit in pockets of business."

"Who?" Tim asked.

"Liberals, Conservatives, fundamentalists, political demigods of all types."

Tim couldn't speak.

"Anything that dulls creative thought leads to a blindness of the soul."

"But they are sincere." Tim squirmed in defense.

"Tim, in a cage with a cobra you will be damn sincere also. Remember, greed blinds."

Tim didn't say anything so Jacob continued, "Problems always arise when others follow profit in blind obedience."

Tim listened to the slow grind of the ceiling fans. "But it is all legal."

"But not right."

Irene picked up the empty coke bottles.

"Tell me about your company?" Jacob said.

"They want to turn Cypress Tree around."

"Some say they're crooks."

"Well, that's not true. I checked them out before I started. They are respectable."

"The best criminals are always respectable."

"Respectable criminal, isn't that an oxymoron?"

"Sad to say, no." Jacob raised his finger in a question, "Do you know how evil controls?"

"How?"

"By the ultimate power of persuasion."

"It kills?" Tim asked.

"No." He tapped his finger on a stack of invoices, "Evil takes control of your free will, of your ability to make a choice. It backs you into a corner so you must choose it, so it controls your soul."

A chill ran up Tim's back.

"You do what it wants," Jacob whispered, "of your own free will."

Tim gritted his teeth, "A slave?"

"To evil," Jacob said, "you become a willing slave."

"Where's the line?" Tim asked, "Where the evil begins?"

"It's like a fog. It's always there. Large companies divide making profit into a hundred simple acts. They say to be more efficient. It is really to hide each person's small theft. To take away their guilt, so they don't care."

Tim said, "They are free."

"They think they have free will – but they don't."

Tim rubbed the back of his neck. "And their humanity withers."

"We all learn to lie a little each day."

"Mr. Dabe, when I came, I didn't know we'd talk about these things."

"Neither did I, but they bother me. I hope they bother you."

Tim thought a moment, "Does evil lurk in everything?"

"Even religion," Jacob said.

Tim looked in Jacob's eyes, "That's scary."

Jacob spread his hands, palms up, said nothing.

"Profit is more desperate than I realized," Tim said.

"Tim, soon the air you breathe will have a charge."

"How will they do that?"

"They already do. When I was a kid, water was free and pure," Jacob said. "There's a point where profit changes to greed. It sucks life . . . " Jacob tapped his pencil on the desk. " . . . so much so that accountants with sharp pencils squeeze juicy money like pythons." He snapped the pencil point.

Tim sat silent.

Jacob said, "We all wait for a new Messiah, to throw the money changers out."

An hour after Tim got back to the mall office, FedEx delivered a shoebox size package that Tim had to sign for. It was from Mike in Chicago. Tim signed for it, shook it but didn't open it. Instead, he went to see Luke Douglas at the bank and rented a safe-deposit box. He locked it away without breaking the seal.

17

A Minor Change

Gil came into Tim's office with a copy of a lease, "Did you see the change the home office put in the lease?"

"Where?"

"Page thirty-three." Gil gave him a Xeroxed copy. "Two new words. See if you can find them."

Tim looked puzzled.

"That Paul is one sharp attorney. No one's going to notice."

"Why not?" Tim took the new page and started to read. "Where?" He held it so the light made it easier to see. He reached for Gil's copy of the old lease and put them side by side. None of the lines ended with a different word. None began with a new one. None had more words per line than the previous copy.

"Can't find it can you?"

"Wait a minute." Tim went over it again.

Gil smiled, "Paul will earn his pay this time. The two word change will put seven percent on our bottom line."

"Don't tell me, I'll find them."

Gil left saying, "Call me when you say uncle."

Tim started to read every word, slow and out loud.

18

The Chamber Drive

Each spring, members of the Chamber of Commerce would dress in bright neon-green sport coats, and blitz the city to recruit fresh members. The big award was for the team that signed the most new members.

Car salesmen found it a great day to bird dog for leads as they drove around in their flashy new models. Insurance agents liked to show clients they were good citizens. CPA's pushed junior accountants out but most soon returned to hide behind their desks. However, everyone showed up at 4:00 P. M around the keg of beer in the Chamber Office.

When Tim walked by the mall's bank, Luke Douglas said, "Tim, I want you to go with me next Thursday for the Chamber drive. Old man Reed is on my ass to get more new deposits in the bank."

"Sounds like we both could win," Tim said.

"I have a list of fifteen cash businesses I need to develop as customers. Most don't bank with us, and all will be fun to visit."

"Great. Do you think I might find a tenant?"

"Maybe down the road."

"Never underestimate the power of a journey."

"Last year I signed Bodkin's Bikes. Then they filed bankruptcy the next day. The guys made fun of me for a month. This year I want to win the 'Golden Retriever' award for most new members."

"I love awards."

Luke explained, "I want to stay out until we hit my whole list. Maybe until the party starts at 4:00 p.m."

"Thursday is yours."

Thursday morning, after a pep talk at the Holiday Inn, they were sent on their way. Luke pulled out a hand-drawn map with notes, "Tim, you drive, and I'll navigate."

Their first stop was B. D.'s, a small corner grocery two blocks north of Old Courthouse Square.

Luke pointed to a fire hydrant. "Park there, right in front, it's O.K. We will only be here a minute."

They walked past the rusty screen door with a faded Wonder Bread ad, past the half-empty meat cooler, past cans of beans, corn and tuna, into a back room filled with cigarette smoke.

B. D. was at the pool table focused on his next shot. The electronic slot machines sat silent. Several men watched the table.

Luke and Tim stood in silence.

B. D. mumbled through his hanging cigarette, called his shot with a tiny nod like a hidden bid at an auction. He missed the shot, glanced at Tim, took a drag on his Camel, "Whatcha' want Luke?"

Luke pulled out a brochure on the Chamber and started to explain that B. D. needed to join.

B. D. butted in, "What makes you think I'm interested?"

Luke smiled but continued the robotic pitch. When he took a breath, B. D. turned to Tim. "How much will it cost to shut him up?"

Tim smiled, "Dues for a year is one hundred bucks."

B. D. put his cigarette in an empty bottle of beer, reached in his front pocket, slapped a hundred-dollar bill into Tim's hand, "Now, get out'a here."

The next stop was May's Emporium of Junque & Bric-a-Brac. Her store was once the "Shady Rest Side Motel" on the old Atlanta Road which died when the Plantation Motel put in color TV's.

May had her unshaven son, Clement, cut down the hedges that hid it from the road. Then he took out the walls between the rooms to make one long showroom.

On Saturdays he would offer to haul away leftovers from local garage sales for twenty-five dollars. Once the leftovers were on his truck, May had new inventory and Clement had beer money.

Men's, women's, children's, books, bikes, tricycles, TV's etc. If you needed a chair, a lamp, or a waffle iron, you only needed to look until you found one to your liking. Three children's car seats had each been resold a dozen times.

Miss May shuffled around in a red-striped house-dress with a green fanny pack on her hip. A large purple plastic Dorothy Lamar flower was set to distract from her white roots. Her runny lipstick reminded Tim of Bette Davis in 'What Ever Happened to Baby Jane?'.

Her flip-flops popped as they unstuck from the vinyl floor.

"Miss May, how's Marsha?" Luke asked.

"She's in Nashville, Luke. You should have married her."

"Yes'um, but she ran off to sing. She sure had a voice."

"She's in a band on weekends. Works at a Waffle House where all the stars go."

Luke added, "She'll get discovered one day."

Tim pulled out a Chamber pamphlet. "Miss. May, we want you to join the Chamber of Commerce."

"That bag of crooks? Why?"

"Because Tim and I are in a contest for a trip to New York City."

She twisted her long ebony cigarette holder and took a drag off her Lucky Strike. "How will that help me?"

"I'll bring you a T-Shirt," Luke smiled. "Miss. May, dues are a hundred a year. You can afford it."

Tim's head bobbed like a parrot, "You need to join."

Luke handed her the leaflet.

She puffed her cigarette and posed like Dorothy Lamour as she tapped ashes to a marble ashtray by to the antique RCA TV. "Marsha's going to make it big someday, I really think so."

"She sure had a voice in our sophomore choir. Didn't you play the piano?"

"I haven't touched it in years," she turned to the music corner where an old upright hid under stacks of sheet music.

She opened her neon green fanny pack to pull out a roll of bills wrapped with a salvaged celery rubber band. She counted five twenties.

Luke started to write a receipt.

"What you writing?" she asked.

"It's so you can take it off your taxes."

"Oh, bullshit."

Back in the car, Luke said, "When the motel died, May converted it to a second-hand store."

"I'm more interested in the trip we might win."

"People like to help you. It makes them feel good."

"So there's no trip?"

"Nope, we just sell hope," said Luke. "Everyone needs hope. If they have no hope, they want you to have it."

Luke motioned for Tim to turn past the railroad track, then enter the gravel parking lot on the left.

"Pull over to the right where those men are sitting under the tree."

He parked next to a small wide flat-roofed building, with a large rusting tin sign, "King Cotton Cigars — Leader of All." Under the massive oak tree, about twenty feet from the building, sat seven black men. Between the tree and the building, four posts held up a rusted tin roof over a Bar-B-Q smoker going full blast.

On the cook's long canvas apron were faded broad red letters "King Cotton." He was a thick necked, dark bull of a man with a boxer's nose. He forked a slab of pork ribs, threw them on his butcher's block and chopped with a cleaver. Another man swabbed sauce on slabs in the smoker.

"Mr. Lukes, what can I do for you?"

"Cotton, we came for ribs."

"That's not why you's here, Mr. Lukes. You knows it's too early. But we can take your order."

One of the men on the bench grinned, and slapped his leg. "Cot, they look like bill collectors."

Someone else said, "Money men, these are money men." Everyone laughed. "Grab your roll Cot, grab your roll and run."

Luke took center stage, raised his hand and announced for all to hear, "Cotton, we're here to invite you to join the Fenton Chamber of Commerce."

Cotton's large ivory eyes rolled on Luke, "Wha'cha talk-en about? That's a white man's club Mr. Lukes."

"It's for business people. Chu's Grocery is a member. May's Emporium just joined. You own a business. We're here to invite you to join."

Cotton looked at the jury sitting on the old church pew. He squeezed his chin, raised his eyebrows and nodded. "They's money men all right."

Tim said, "Luke says you make the best Bar-B-Q in Georgia. If you join, more people will find you. You should join."

"I don't go to meetings, 'cept church when someone dies."

"No problem," Luke said.

Cotton winked to the bench, "Okay money men, what do the dues do?" Cotton's eyes searched for smiles as he repeated, "What do the dues do?"

"They'll help bring new businesses to Fenton. The more that come - the more people have jobs, the more Bar-B-Q you'll sell," Luke said.

The jury waited and watched.

Cotton turned to a thin blind man who sat in a purple vinyl chair at the trunk of the oak tree. "Pops what'd you think?"

Everyone leaned in to hear his frail voice, "Cot, you have da best Bar-B-Q. You should be in da Chamber. Potius sero quam numquam. Better late than never."

"Will the Chamber buy my Bar-B-Q for some of their parties?"

"We'll start today!" Luke said.

Cotton turned to Luke, "How much are dues?"

"A hundred a year. You'll get listed as a member. You will be invited to various functions."

Tim broke in. "And you'll get a brass plaque to put on the wall."

"For true?"

"With your name engraved and everything."

Cotton's eyes popped, "The high-sheriff can see it when he picks up his Bar-B-Q."

"Amen," voices echoed.

Luke said, "Maybe a food critic will come from the New York Times. All kinds of tourists will follow."

"You might become as famous as the Varsity in Atlanta," Tim said.

Cotton reached for his chain guarded billfold, found two fifty-dollar bills, then with a certain bravado gave them to Luke. "Be sure to get me that plaque for the 'high-sheriff' to see."

When they drove off, Luke said, "That thin white-haired man was his father."

"He sure had their respect."

"He used to teach Latin."

"The blind man?"

"They claim he knows all of Cicero and Livy by heart."

"Wow!"

"In Latin."

"Damn."

Gil went on to explain that Cotton couldn't have a liquor license because he had been in prison, but each week one of Richard Dabe's men filled the shelves under Cotton's bar with unlabeled pint bottles of moonshine. Once a week, Cotton stopped by Richard Dabe's with a plate of Bar-B-Q and cash to settle up for the bottle filling service.

A few years ago a drunk man was shot in the parking-lot. The Snodgrass sisters wrote a letter to the paper that the sheriff should check if Cotton sold liquor. Sheriff Baker assured them that he had ribs there at least once a week without ever seeing the first sign of any spirits being sold.

Storage of gifts under the counter was legal. Nor was there a law against giving someone a gift. No one had a problem with the empty bottles saved for Dabe's delivery man. Everything was legal.

Luke said, "When Cotton gives Sheriff Baker free ribs, it's as close as he gets to paying taxes."

"Well, he got closer today."

'10-10 Berry Street' was a large two-story red-brick house built in the early 1900s. It had a long porch in front. The right yard had a seven-foot brick fence that enclosed a small swimming pool. From the street, you could see the tops of five patio umbrellas.

"This is Rose Marie's. She rents rooms to young single women," said Luke. "After work the living room doubles as a private club, if you know what I mean." Luke pointed to her driveway, "Turn here, park in back."

Tim parked next to tall oleander bushes. On the screened back porch, Luke yelled, "Rose Marie!"

"Come on in," a whiskey voiced female answered. Rose Marie was behind the bar dressed in a pink housecoat with a red feather boa. Her make-up looked as if she had just come from Merle Norman.

She came around with her arms opened wide. Luke hugged her.

On the bar sat empty bottles of Usher's next to full but open bottles of Chivas. Between two couches on one wall sat a juke box. In the corner was an ancient wooden telephone booth. The air was stale with cigar.

"Rose Marie, this is Tim Lichten. Tim, Rose Marie is a Fenton institution."
She hugged them both.
"Luke you should have brought him earlier. He hugs so good."
"I bet you say that to all the men," Tim said.
"Only the rich ones."
"We want you to join the Chamber!" Luke said.
Her eyes sparkled, "I have been asked to do a lot of things, but no one's asked for that."
"I'm serious, if you join the Chamber you'll get a brass plaque. You can put it over the bar."
Her eyes turned to the stairs, "The girls might like it on the landing as they go to their rooms."
"It will impress," said Luke.
"They can throw away their etchings," said Rose Marie.
Tim glanced at Luke, "She's going to join." He handed her a brochure.
"She knows a good deal," Luke said.
She glanced at the leaflet, "You two are one hell of a sales team," she reached into her bra and pulled out some bills. "The more I think about this the more I like it. We need a Chamber's seal of approval. How much?"
"One hundred a year," Tim said.
She peeled a hundred-dollar bill from a stack of several. "Can I pay for more than a year?"
"Sure." Luke elbowed Tim.
She counted four more. "Make sure I get all the bulletins. I want to be listed in every Chamber publication."
Luke started to write a receipt, "How do you want to be listed? Rose Marie's? The Boy's Club? The 10-10 Berry Club? What do you want to call it?"
She slumped on a stool, "My place never had a name. Hell, I don't even have a business license. It's called '10-10 Berry'." She practiced a few names. "The Office . . . The Camp . . . The Deer Camp . . . D-e-a-r Camp."
Luke said, "My dad always said he had to 'See a man about a hunting dog' when he didn't want us kids to know where he was going. Maybe you should

call it 'A Hunting Dog'."

"That's good," she looked around the room, at the tables, the oak floor, the large dark oil painting one man gave her. "I've had a blast with this place. I've loved every minute. God knows how many girls have lived here."

"You've helped them a lot," Luke said.

"I'm proud when they leave. Several married very well."

"Wasn't one a governor's wife?"

"Now Luke, that's her business. I never tell names. When they move out, I'm proud as a peacock."

"They graduate." Tim said.

"Sometimes I'll get a letter, or a Christmas card. Still, I give them privacy."

"Rose Marie, how long have you been here?" Tim asked.

"Thirty-two years. One of my first customers bought this house. He set things up so I could rent it for $25 a month, as long as I live."

"Is that still the rent?" Tim asked.

"It can't change. I pay the whole year at once. The trust he set up takes care of any repairs, paints, even puts on a new roof when needed." She looked at Luke, "Thanks to you."

Luke looked down then turned to Tim, "Our bank's trust department is her landlord. Her man was on our board until he died."

She started to cough, "I've got to stop smoking." She coughed some more, "That man was a saint. He helped so many that others would not." She turned to Luke, "Call it: 1010 Berry, that's it, '1010 Berry'. It's time this place gets respect."

Luke gave her a receipt.

"Luke, why did you stop coming around?"

"I got married."

"Come see us sometime. Give that wife a rest. You're probably shaking her bones to death." She smiled, "And bring Tim with you . . . you won't get in trouble. Tell your wives you're looking at a hunting dog."

They drove off in silence. Tim waited for Luke to say something, but a block away he could not hold it any longer, "Damn, Luke! She paid for five years! Amazing, abso-fuckin-lutely amazing!"

"She's a trip. That's for sure."

"How do you know these people?"

"My father owned Fenton Distribution. They put the records in her juke box. He took me there for my 18th birthday."

"Damn, she treated you as family!"

"Everyone is family," said Luke, "everyone."

"Rose Marie listened to everything we said. She actually paid attention."

Luke bit his lower lip, "Everyone needs to be heard. If you respect people's words, they will give you their trust."

"Today's been an education," Tim said.

"I wanted you to come with me because you percolate trust."

"That's what salesmen do."

"Tim, turn left here. I want to show you something."

Tim drove until Luke pointed out a tall granite mega-church. "I've learned to follow the cash."

"I think they have it."

"Rose Marie's rent goes to that church. The church pays for the upkeep of her house."

Tim had a puzzled look on his face, so Luke added, "Peccatum Tacituritatis."

"What the hell does that mean?"

"I have no idea. I must Google it someday. It is the name of her trust. Apparently, it was a favorite saying of the man who set up the trust." Luke smiled, "You'll be amazed what you learn if you follow cash."

"Is that your church?"

"That's where I was married, and where half of the bank attends."

Tim slowed as he looked at the new brick construction. "Will that be a gym?"

"Family life center. It will make the 'YMCA' look like a toy box," said Luke.

"Amazing."

"It's one of the richest churches in Georgia. The man Rose Marie talked about was their head deacon. His son is TV's Rev. Channing."

"Small world," Tim said.

"Some think he is the holiest man in America."

"From the diamonds his wife flashes I'd say she is the most showy."

"God has blessed him," said Luke.

"One doesn't equal the other," Tim said.

"But Channing's father still takes care of Rose Marie's girls."

"Luke, what do you know about Saulora, Angelo Saulora?"
"He moved here while I lived in Macon. I think he might be a retired banker. He lived in South America. He's an investor."
"I thought he might be on your board."
"Someday maybe, but that's not my call."

After eleven new members were signed, Luke and Tim drove by Cotton's and picked up ribs for the party.

Wanda Morrison, the Chamber manager called Luke and Tim "Legends" as she gave them the coveted "Golden Retriever Award."

Luke passed around several pints that Cotton had donated.

When they started to leave, Wanda said she could take Luke to his car back at the Holiday Inn as it was on her way home.

At a quarter past one in the morning, the police surprised Luke and Wanda, in the Chamber's parking lot. They were drunk in the back seat of Wanda's red Cadillac.

19

Follow up from Mike

"Tim, did you like your 'birthday present'?" It was Mike in Chicago on the phone.

"Mike, great to hear from you! Yes, all securely delivered by FedEx. How's working for your father-in-law?"

"It is amazing all the ways he comes up with how to make a buck. He respects how you helped."

"Mike, I didn't do that much."

"Much more than you realize. When he gets to feeling better, he wants a factory in Georgia."

"You're kidding?"

"We might want to expand a "paper stretching factory" there."

"You guys are something else."

"But you liked the package?"

"Oh yes," Tim said, realizing he had put it unopened in the safe-deposit box.

"What did Aimee think?"

Tim stammered, "Boy - did it - surprise her."

"You didn't break your teeth on the peanut brittle did you?"

"No, I liked the — divinity the best, reminded me of some mother used to make."

"You sound like you are not in a position to talk."

"You guessed that right. Let me call you after I find answers. We have an office building that would make a great office if you do come."

When he hung up, Tim left for the bank.

Inside the sealed FedEx package was a brown paper wrapped block. He ripped it open and there were five banded stacks of hundred-dollar bills with

"$10,000" on each band. There was also a small jeweler's velvet bag with about fifty cut diamonds. Two Rolex boxes with his and her matching gold watches. He took the two watches and put everything else back in the vault.

20

The Jeweler's Gift

Andre Falconi waved from the back of his jewelry store to Gil.

Gil waved back, but stayed across the hall.

Andre again waved with his long thin hand for Gil to come. "I need to talk to you." He rushed to the front of his store, "Did you have a good weekend?"

Gil crossed over to talk. "Excellent weekend, Andre, and you?"

"Mr. Gil, may I offer you some coffee?"

"I hoped you would." Gil glanced at his watch as he followed Andre to the back office.

"Mr. Gil, that's a beautiful maroon silk shirt."

"Thanks, Aimee gave it to me."

"Well she has exquisite taste."

Andre poured two cups. "Did she tell you she came in Saturday with her mother?"

"I know they went shopping."

"She has an amazing eye." After they both sipped their coffee, Andre's face got serious, "Mr. Gil, I'm afraid I cannot stay open much longer."

"Andre, you're a survivor."

"Mr. Gil, I need a short term break in the rent."

"Andre, don't ask. Cash flow is tight for us. They'll never approve."

"Could you tell Mr. Roy my cash is all tied up in inventory?"

Gil shook his head, "This is not the right time."

Andre's baggy dark eyes begged, "Mr. Gil, please, ask the man. He'll remember me. Please tell him I need help. I'll show you my books." He reached for a ledger behind him.

Gil held up his hands. "I believe you Andre, but these are hard times."

Gil looked toward the front of the store, "Andre, I don't think . . . "

"Mr. Gil, come, let me show you something." Andre stood up and snaked through the glass cases until he stretched into the front show window. "Did Miss Ford tell you the ring she wants?" He pulled out a huge emerald-cut diamond ring.

"We have talked, but I don't think we are at that point."

With his left hand, Andre turned on a ceiling spot light for these presentations. "She showed this one to her mother. If I know anything, I know she loves it, believe me."

Andre turned it and watched the glisten in Gil's eyes. "Mr. Gil, you like?"

"I'm speechless." Gil glanced for the price, but Andre hid it under his thumb.

"Mr. Gil, I trust you as my son. Do this for me. Show it to her." He removed the price and placed the ring in a blue velvet box. "If she likes it, we will make a special price for you."

Gil felt the sharp edges of the diamond. They were hard and cold. Susan had mentioned the ring, but didn't suggest he get it. It was spectacular.

"How many carats?"

"Four point twenty-three."

"Andre, I don't think . . . "

"Please, take it to her, if she likes – we will talk about a price. Please."

Gil's eyes danced as they took in the diamond. "This is too much." He closed the box and handed it to Andre, who wouldn't take it so Gil placed it on the counter and backed away.

Andre rushed around the counter to block Gil who had begun to edge toward the store's front. When Gil stopped, Andre slipped the royal blue box into Gil's coat pocket. "Show it to her, if she likes – it's my gift. If she doesn't, bring it back, no problem. Listen to me, I trust you."

Gil knew Mr. Roy would not reduce Andre's rent. He reached in his pocket and stroked the silky velvet case. It felt so smooth, "I'll see what Susan says."

"Thank you, Mr. Gil. You will make her most happy." Andre took Gil's free hand between both of his and shook, "Thank you, Mr. Gil."

21

The Party

Tim and Aimee picked up the map that came with the invitation, and dropped the kids at her mother's. They made the longish drive to Callaway Gardens, a 6,500-acre resort in Pine Mountain.

When they entered Callaway's, Aimee pulled out the map that directed the way down the narrow winding roads, past the golf course, the cabins, until they arrived at the large villa where the company party was. Several couples had flown to its private airport from Kansas City early to play golf.

The grand room had a high ceiling with a large chandelier. It opened onto a slate patio that overlooked the lake.

On the right side of the stone fireplace was a table loaded with appetizers. Huge gulf shrimp, steak tartar and various trays of rare imported cheeses.

At the grand piano sat a 50-year-old tuxedoed man who played and sang. His smoky French voice sounded like a blend of Charles Aznavour with Frank Sinatra.

Gil was introducing Susan Ford to everyone.

When the piano player took a break, Mr. Roy and his wife thanked everyone for coming. When he finished, Gil and Susan took the floor. His mother took out her smart phone to record the event.

Gil held up his hand, "I have an announcement," he paused to let the crowd settle down. "Earlier this week I asked Mr. Ford for the hand of his daughter, Susan Perkins Ford, in marriage." All eyes were on Susan.

"I am happy, MOST HAPPY, to report that Mr. Ford approved, and Susan has accepted." The room exploded in applause. Gil held her hand up as she made a curtsy to the crowd. "So ladies and gentlemen, I introduce you to Miss Susan Perkins Ford." There was more applause, and Susan curtsied again. "To seal this occasion, I want to present Susan with a symbol of my love."

Gil reached into his pocket and brought out the deep-blue box from Falconi's. When he put it on her hand, thousands of chandelier lights flashed. Aimee gasped as the glitter stunned the room. Susan held her hand high for all to see.

Mr. Ford took the stage, made a toast, and thanked Gilbert Armstrong Palm. "I am proud to approve such an arrangement."

Gil's father made a similar response and toast.

A long round of toasts began, and at the end someone would say "Hip-hip" and everyone responded "Hooray."

Mr. Roy made a toast. His wife gave them a Rembrandt etching purchased at Sotheby's.

Then Cecil said, "To the fairest lady to grace the earth, except for my mother." Everyone laughed but still gave the mandatory "Hip-Hip, Hooray."

When the toasts died down, the piano player started to sing from the doorway. "I'm going to love you like nobody's loved you." When he paused to set down a glass of wine. Mr. Roy's wife, Carol started to sing from the other side of the room, "Come rain or come shine."

The duet moved to the piano. When they finished, the crowd exploded with approval. Carol said something to the singer. He nodded and together they sang, "You make me feel so young." Everyone began to sing.

At the singer's next break, Susan's brother sang an Irish ditty. Her father pulled out a fiddle and played "Fire on the mountain, run boys run." The party turned into an amateur hour with various solos, trios and community sing-a-longs.

■

Mr. Roy walked around with a silver goblet of scotch. Behind his shaded aviator glasses, he spotted Tim with Aimee, "How are things?"

"This is the best party," Tim said.

"Is there progress in Fenton?" Mr. Roy asked.

Tim smiled, "I pitch every day, even in my sleep. If I shake enough hands and nod my head with a smile, we will get them to say yes."

"That's a good attitude. You have to invite them in the door." Roy Parino turned to Aimee, "Do you enjoy being back in Fenton?"

"Love it, Mr. Parino but I wish Tim could come home when supper's hot."

Mr. Roy frowned, but with a twinkle in his eye, turned to Tim, "I don't want you to work past midnight anymore."

"Yes sir."

Mr. Roy put his hand on Tim's shoulder. "Tim, our better employees go home for supper." He smiled at Aimee, "You might make her think we're ogres."

"It's better since you took Gil's bullwhip away." Tim said.

Mr. Roy smiled, "He gets out of hand." Then his smile dropped, "Do you ever work on the office tower?"

"No sir, Louie does all that."

Louie heard his name and walked into the conversation.

"You talking about me?"

"Tim tells me you still work alone on the office tower."

"This is a great party," Louie said.

Mr. Roy turned and squared off in front of Louie, "Tell me about the tower."

Louie looked at the floor, "No one comes in. The phone never rings."

"And the solution is?" Mr. Roy asked.

Louie froze, "But . . . but . . . "

"Louie, what is the solution?"

"But Mr. Parino, the economy is bad. Things will get better."

Parino's glass eye glared through the sunglasses. "It's your job." He poked his index finger like a knife into Louie's chest, "It's your fucking job." He smirked, turned and walked away.

Louie was flush red. Tim glanced at the floor. Aimee grabbed Tim's hand.

■

"Jane, such a striking dress."

"Thank you, Carol, I heard your Eakins retrospective at the Museum is exceptional."

"You and Zack must see it."

"We must, but he's always out of town."

"Will you be able to help us with our Charity Auction?"

"I'd love to. You should also get Susan involved."

"Great idea! Now that she'll be part of the family. Maybe she can get us a Howard Finster."

■

Roy Parino walked to Zack Palm, "Louie concerns me. He has no ownership of his job, no spark. Last time I saw him; he was the same."

"Gil thinks he'll come around."

"Gil's wrong. The tower is 90% vacant. We need change."

Zack looked around the room until he eyed Gil and waved him over. "Gil, tell Roy about Louie."

Gil sipped his drink, "He'll be fine."

Mr. Roy swirled his goblet of scotch. "Tim needs to also be on the tower. When he learns the ropes, cut Louie." He turned to Zack, who nodded. Mr. Roy punctuated his decree with the bob of his head, like a judge does when he signs a death sentence. He raised his silver goblet in a silent toast, turned and walked away.

Zack stood alone with Gil. "I guess we have our orders."

"I'll talk to Tim," Gil said.

"Tonight would not be too soon."

■

Jane Palm came over to talk to Aimee, "I'm glad to hear you could move back home. Zack and I have always lived in Kansas City. I don't know how I could exist away from family."

Aimee smiled, "Family has good and bad points."

"But it's good to have them near."

"Sometimes they want to control too much," Aimee said.

"That's how they show their love."

"I understand you and Mr. Roy's wife go way back." Aimee said.

"I interned with Carol at the Art Institute in Kansas City. We introduced Roy to Carol at our house."

.

Zack came up behind Tim and put his hand on Tim's shoulder and leaned to talk in his ear. "Mr. Roy and I think you should help Louie on the office tower. Learn all you can."

"No problem."

"Good, keep up the good work."

.

A short, older dark-haired man with a young lady in a red dress came over to Carol Parino, "Carol, your voice was mag-nig-fi-co, like when you sang at Geno's funeral in Miami."

"Thank you, Angelo. I don't think I've seen you since then."

"Carol, may I introduce Salma Mele Blanco. She cooks and drives for me."

"Delighted to meet you, Salma. I understand you're from Columbia."

.

Cecil Malcour saw Gil alone. "We need to talk. The CPA dropped off some figures. They refute ours."

"Damn, I told that fart to use our numbers."

"Gil, what should I tell the bank?"

"He didn't copy them did he?"

"No, but Reed will call me asking for them."

"I'll talk to Dad. Maybe he or Mr. Roy can come up with something."

.

"Tim, we've been thinking. You should start helping on the tower." Gil said.

"Your dad told me."

"Good, you know."

■

22

The Ride Home

At midnight, Aimee and Tim said their good-byes and walked toward his new Infinity. The diamond-studded black sky hung high over the lake. Muted conversations and music danced between the trees.

Tim stopped and turned, "Listen." There was a distant frog croak. "When did you last hear one of those?"

"Not since I was a girl."

"And that smell reminds me of New Orleans."

"It's sweet olive," Aimee said. "It might be a block away."

Tim opened the car's moon roof. It was that kind of night. "So what did you think?" Tim asked as they started the trip back home.

"It was fun. One wine was an expensive South Australia Cabernet Sauvignon," she said.

"I noticed the Scotch choice was Chivas or Glenfiddich."

"No one noticed my new Rolex." She held it out in the moonlight.

"Be thankful our little business with Mike had a good Christmas on the carts."

"Bobbie can't stop her tongue once she has some wine," Aimee said.

"Like I told you, she has her moments. Gil said she was a top tennis player in college."

"She told me Cecil gets bonus checks from the trash company."

"I don't know about that. Sometimes in the office she is in another world."

"That's true about you at home."

He cut his eyes at her, "What'cha talking about?"

She smiled.

Tim said, "Be careful, both she and Cecil will fish for information."

"Women think they must play a part." Aimee said.

"Aimee, we're all actors."

"But it's a man's play."

"Men don't see life that way." Tim said.

"Women do."

Tim thought a moment, "But something does bug Bobbie."

"Gil's hair is too long." Aimee said.

"Well, at least it was in a pony tail."

"Susan looked so good," she paused, "Who was the short old man with dark hair and thick black-rimmed glasses? He had a gorgeous Hispanic wife. He looked familiar."

"I think he's a relative of Carol Parino's."

"Zack Palm said he wants me to help lease the office tower."

"Instead of vacant stores?"

"No, along with the stores," Tim said.

"Good, you're moving up."

"Maybe, but I don't know if that's good."

"Why not?"

"Louie came over with his girlfriend. He smiled, raised his drink and said in my ear: 'They will suck you in, and you'll never get out.' I thought it was about his girl, but now I'm not so sure."

"Did he say anything else?"

"His eyes did."

"With you on the tower, you should make an effort to know Louie better."

"Good idea – but he keeps to himself."

"Cecil loves praise doesn't he?"

Tim rolled his eyes, "He soaks it in like a sponge. I saw him being schmoozed by the old man and the Hispanic lady in red."

Aimee mulled, "He looks so familiar."

Tim smiled, "Maybe you like his wallet."

"I don't think his nurse in red would let me."

"Good."

"Gil once told me Cecil's father committed suicide."

"When?"

"Years ago when Cecil was a teenager."

"That's too bad. However, you're right, Cecil's one of a kind."

"All he could say was 'Yes sir, Mr. Roy.'; 'Good thinking Mr. Roy.'; 'Couldn't have said it better myself, Mr. Roy.' I can't stand people like that. I want to whack them in the back of the head," Tim said.

"Mr. Roy's a class act," Aimee said.

"His wife also."

"Bobbie doesn't think so," Aimee paused, "After Carol's last song, she turned to me and said: 'Cecil can't stand the bitch!'"

"She did not!"

"Did so! And her eyes popped!"

"Maybe . . . " Tim said.

"If he hates her, why doesn't he quit?"

"Maybe he . . . "

Aimee interrupted, "Life's too short to hate."

"Maybe he can't."

"Quit? Why not?"

"I don't know. Maybe he likes the soft feel of wealth."

Aimee hummed, "Or maybe he's a prisoner of it?"

"Or blinded," Tim said.

"Maybe he doesn't think."

"A lot of people get used to being fed." Tim said.

"But the party was great." Aimee said.

"It was like they were all relatives."

Aimee looked out at the stars, "They aren't family. They're a company, and it's a business."

When they got home, Tim turned off the car, "You think a business and a family are opposites?"

"Family is warm and about love. A business is about cold profit."

They were both quiet for a long-time. "Money measures in unemotional numbers. So why do they use . . . "

Aimee finished, " . . . family? They want employees to feel warm and cozy, like a family. They don't want them to see the truth."

" . . . like?"

"How they turn it into cold greed."

"That's a crazy statement," Tim said.

"But true."

"Why?"

"It's the way men sell everything."

23

Louie Vicks

Monday after the party, Louie Vicks didn't come into the office until about 1:30. He poured himself coffee and downed a cellophane packet of imported vitamins.

Tim walked over, "Louie, I haven't had lunch, want to join me?"

"Let's go. You just saw me have breakfast. I need some real food."

"Did your team win yesterday?"

"My bookie's not happy."

"Good for you."

"I'm still digging out of the hole."

Outside, they walked toward Louie's red Corvette parked away from other cars.

"You sure parked in the south forty."

"Don't want to get pinged by some mother's door."

"Even past Bobbie's Land Rover."

"You should have been here when she got it." Louie pointed to a pinkish Lincoln. "Cecil picked up his light rose Lincoln one morning after breakfast. She didn't know he was getting it. Damn, she charged out and came back with a blood-red Rover."

Tim grinned, "She can spit nails at times can't she?"

Louie started to laugh, "One day Gil came in the office and walked right by Bobbie as she opened the mail. He didn't even see her. Bobbie turned and said, "Well, Good morning big-shot." But Gil didn't hear her and kept walking. She turned and threw her letter opener at him, and it stuck in the back of his head. He bled like a pig, blood everywhere. She fessed up, apologized, helped him wash off. She felt so bad she bought him a silk shirt."

"Is she nuts?"

"Not really. She blows up once in a while. Goes to Dr. Monish in the tower once a week to control her moods. Later that day, Gil brought her a dozen roses and said he was sorry." Louie paused to think, "Yeah, she can be something else, but down deep she's O.K."

"Looking at these cars, you guys make a lot more than I do," Tim said.

"Cecil and Bobbie have family money." Louie opened his Corvette door, "Dad gave me this when I landed the job. He said I needed to look successful."

Tim said, "So how did you get the job?"

"I was Gil's roommate at Emory. My dad's a broker and heard Malifer was buying the mall. I called Gil, and they hired me."

"So you like it?"

"Hell no, but it's a job. It's such a bad economy."

"You don't feel guilty when you come in late?"

"Tim, none of them work. They hire us - to feel important. If you try too hard, Gil will say 'slow down'."

"I don't believe that."

"Tim, the mall's a cash cow. Malifer's milking it dry, and all I want is some of the cream."

Louie parked at Red's Truck Stop. "So, Tim, what do you think of Cypress Tree?"

"I don't understand Cecil."

"I think someone made them hire him. I don't know why. He can't manage squat. Gil's here to watch Cecil."

"Maybe watch us all."

"Cecil's first secretary walked out on him after three days, went home got drunk, fell and hit her head. Bobbie thinks it might have been suicide. Anyway, Cecil hired his twin sister, Bobbie – the bomber bitch."

"She is different," Tim said.

"She's weird at times, always drinking grapefruit juice. Sometimes she'll surprise you. Says Cecil made her crazy."

Tim smiled, "At least she knows she is. Most don't." They both laughed.

"You know Zack is Gil's father."

"Yes, but are they related to Mr. Roy?"

"No, but like family."

"Like?"

"They're very close."

"What about Cecil?" Tim asked.

"Is he family?"

Louie thought a second, "No, but knows something."

The waitress poured coffee.

"Tim, don't forget your weekly written report. Make one up if you must. They go bonkers if you don't send one."

"Gil said his dad reads every one," Tim said.

"They're too busy counting cash, but Zack logs everyone." Louie threw up his hands and shook his head hopelessly.

Tim looked at the occupied booths. Each had old dial pay phones next to the paper napkins. The truckers were all using mobile phones. Others spread trip logs on tables and finger pecked information into iPads and laptop computers.

"Louie, look around. These cowboys are computerized, but Malifer wants written reports. I think we should get with the program."

"Don't think. That will get you in trouble."

Tim held the headset of the phone at their table. "Why does this place still have these?"

"All change comes slow but moves fast," Louie said.

When the food came, Louie cut up his sausage patty and fried eggs, then mixed them in with the thick grits.

"The sausage and eggs need an iron skillet." Louie said as he buttered his biscuit. He picked up the sorghum pitcher, "Soaked with sorghum and washed down with black gut coffee. Tim you should try grits, sausage, eggs - you'll never eat better."

"For now, this hamburger and sweet tea are close enough."

"Louie, tell me about Cypress Tree."

"It's a can of worms."

"Why?"

"Bobbie's a bitch. Cecil's a joke. Pete knows his job but doesn't do much but turn a screwdriver. And between you and me, Gil can't decide."

"Why not?"

"No balls."

"You didn't say that! He's why you have your job."

"Look, I like him a lot. I drink with him. My girl introduced him to Susan. He's a salesman, a damn good one. But he freezes and can't make up his mind."

"He's our boss!"

"But he can't piss without asking Dad."

"But he's boss."

"Look at his eyes, they're frozen."

"What about Cecil?"

"He knows something."

"What?"

"Shit, I don't know. Except he's a blackmailer."

"About what?"

Louie shrugged, "Smart ones never tell what they know. They let you know that they know."

"Are you a blackmailer?" Tim asked.

"No, but I think I know what Malifer's up to."

"What?"

"I'll tell you when I'm sure."

"What about Mr. Roy?"

"He's a collector. Gil says he has a Henry Moore in his back yard."

"Henry Moore? The sculptor?"

"He met him in England and helped him carve it. Gil says it looks as if stone termites ate it."

Tim smirked, "Modern art."

"I don't like modern art," Louie said.

"A lot of things are too hard to understand," Tim said.

When they arrived back at the Mall, Louie said, "Tim, I'm not feeling well. Tell Gil I'll see him tomorrow."

Tim opened the car door, "When will you tell me what they're up to?"

"Well, here's a clue," he took a breath, "it's all about money."

"Money?"

Louie repeated, "It's only about money."

·

Three weeks later at 2:15 on a Tuesday afternoon, Tim was with Gil when they drove by Shady's, a small bar with a gravel parking lot. Louie's red Corvette was under the oak tree. Gil's fists clinched the steering wheel so hard they turned white. Two blocks later he shouted out, "Damn-it, son-of-a-bitch. Some people never learn."

At the next stop light, Gil hit his horn. "Damn, lazy son-of-a-bitch."

The Hunting Dog

24

Archie

Several weeks later, Tim walked up to Archie and Izzy by the mall's fountain. "Archie, I thought you two found a new office."

Archie smiled and slapped the roll of paper in his hand, squinted his eyes, and adjusted his checkered hat. "I recognize your voice. It'll come to me . . . "

Izzy said, "Tim."

"Yes, Tim . . . Tim Lichten," Archie said.

"You remember!"

They all shook hands."

Izzy said, "We have both been in Florida, trying to sell his condo."

Archie said, "I once had a clear mind, passed my CPA at 18 on the first try, but now Izzy helps me."

"You both sound good to me."

"Tim, are you running this place yet?"

"I'm still getting my feet wet." Tim said.

"Don't get muddy. There are pot holes."

"I let Cecil play with those." Tim said.

"He makes them. He doesn't fix them," Archie paused, then said, "That's one mixed-up family. His father was the same way." Archie clapped the rolled paper in his hand. "You know, I was the manager of this place, even had a minor ownership."

"That's what I understand," Tim said.

"At least I got a pension out of it." Archie whacked the paper again. "Tim, can you help us?"

"How?"

"We both tried to read this article about Georgia trying to get water out of the Tennessee River, but the print is too small." He showed Tim the article, and Tim read it to them.

"Thanks, I need to get my eyes checked. Think, think." Archie muttered.

"Think? About what?" Tim asked.

"I was just reminding myself to think. At my age, I have to remember what I want to absorb." They all chuckled.

Izzy said, "I go with the flow."

"But sometimes I get flooded." Archie said.

Archie reminded Tim how his own grandfather would sit on the front porch and tell story after story about what happened seventy years before. He would then turn to Tim and not know him. Archie was almost there.

Izzy Stone was Archie's stockbroker. His shoes were shined, his white shirt always held a wide tie in a half Windsor. "I sold him his first shares of McDonalds, and he still owns them."

Archie laughed, "Remember you didn't want me to buy them. You tried to get me to invest with you on three Frostop locations. Don't take credit."

Izzy said, "Well, I always liked their root-beer."

Archie said, "You should travel more Izzy. You would learn something."

"You should find a girlfriend and enjoy yourself already."

"I'm looking. I look every day I walk the mall."

"Such a deal." Izzy pushed at the air in Archie's direction.

"I feel fine now, but electricity be the death of us."

Archie grew more like Tim's grandfather. A strange mix of logic and visions.

"Bunch of crooks," Archie said. "The 'electrics' make the weak pay through the nose."

"Archie, they justify their rates."

"They all cook profits. We're falling headlong into a dark age that will last a thousand years."

Sometimes, on Archie's worst days Tim would walk away, but he always later regretted it. He would then try to remember every word because somewhere in the fog of Archie's mind was a kernel of corn.

25

Cecil's Gold Star

Every morning Bobbie opened and stacked Cecil's mail in the center of his desk. This morning, she left on top the sealed FedEx envelope. It was marked "personal" and from Mr. Roy Parino.

She dusted the small bronze bust of grandpa Malcour, straightened the framed watercolor Cecil had painted, and picked up papers in Cecil's 'out' box.

"Good morning, C. C."

"Good morning, Roberta." He always returned her first greeting, 'C. C.' with 'Roberta'. The rest of the day she was Bobbie and he was Cecil.

"Cecil, there's something from Mr. Roy."

"Oh, hell, what's the old goat want now?"

Bobbie went to the coffeepot, picked up Cecil's Havilland cup, and brought his coffee. She glanced at the FedEx envelope still sealed on his desk. "It looks important."

Cecil put on his gold reading glasses, picked up the envelope, looked at the front and back, but placed it to the side. He glanced at the rest of the mail, picked up the morning paper, and walked to the rest room.

When he returned, the unopened envelope was again on top of the stack in the center of his desk.

Cecil said to himself, but loud enough for Bobbie to hear, "Oh, I forgot to look at Mr. Roy's." He opened it and removed a sealed white envelope marked "Personal For Cecil." He took his letter opener, extracted the sanguine bordered hand-written note with a flourish. He glanced to make sure Bobbie watched.

Cecil read, paused, took a deep breath, and glanced to make sure she saw him dial the mayor's office.

"Marge this is Cecil Malcour with the mall. I need five minutes with the mayor sometime today if it is possible . . . I promise it won't take two minutes . . . That should work. Thank you, Marge."

Cecil went to the corner of his office and picked up his grandfather's cane. The fox head handle was carved ages ago from apple wood. It fit well in his hand as he walked around the office. He opened the bottom drawer of his desk, removed a clean handkerchief and dusted its hickory shaft. He caressed every notch and furrow as if it held some power.

He closed the door to his office and called Doctor Markham Chantage. They both were in high school with the mayor. When he hung up, he stood, looked in his mirror, straightened his coat and tie, picked up the cane and walked out.

"Bobbie, I am on my way to breakfast at Star's and then to see the mayor for Mr. Roy."

"How long will you be?"

"As long as it takes."

"Take your phone," she said.

He reached for it but replaced it in the charger, "Tell anyone I will call when I get back."

"I may not be here. I have a doctor's appointment."

Cecil walked into Star's Cafe. When he saw the others, his chest went out, like a peacock. He released Mr. Roy's handwritten note about six inches above the table and let it float to the surface. Everyone knew the maroon border. He held tight to some legal forms like they were gold.

MALIFER

Cecil --- Gil and Tim have asked the mayor to sign papers, so we will be eligible to lease to the Federal government. The mayor has stalled and stalled. He must sign. Do what you must, but get his signature. Attached are copies if the mayor has lost them. Get updated by Tim and Gil. It is now your turn to get his signature on these papers. ---

ROY

To help decaying towns the Federal Government recently required all Federal offices to be located in a city's declared Enterprise Zone. Mayor Canaglia made sure all Fenton's downtown offices were approved Zone.

Several landlords made requests to get their office buildings also in the zone. The mayor always refused because they were not next to the city council's established area.

At a Chamber meeting Tim cornered the mayor and told him a federal agency had approached his home office in Kansas City for space in Cypress Mall's Office Tower. The mayor tried to find out what agency. Tim did not know, and wouldn't tell if he did. So nothing happened.

Cypress Tree was four miles from Fenton's Enterprise Zone. Mayor Canaglia had the authority with his signature to enlarge the zone, but by law, any expansion had to be attached to the existing area.

Paul Daniel, Malifer's in-house attorney had come up with a creative way that would fulfill all the concerns of the law. Papers were drawn up and delivered to the mayor.

The expanded zone would look like a dumbbell. Downtown would be at one end, and Cypress Tree at the other with Chestnut Boulevard's tree-lined middle median holding the two together like a thin four-mile ribbon. The design followed federal rules, but the mayor refused to sign.

Malifer tried everything. Gil made an unsolicited generous donation to the mayor's campaign fund. Cecil had the mayor's wife draw plans to remodel Cypress Tree's office. The plans were paid for and stood rolled up in the corner of Cecil's office. They had even started talks with the mayor's paving company about the parking lot. Still no signature.

Cecil finished breakfast, stood up, looked at his grandfather's antique fobbed pocket watch, straightened his coat, grabbed the cane and said: "Wish me luck. I am off to sing an opera."

He didn't explain why he was so sure, or how he would persuade the mayor. When he left, Gil sat silent and a chill ran up Tim's back.

What Mr. Roy saw in Cecil, Tim could not understand. It seemed to defy logic. Tim came to the conclusion that Louie was right - Mr. Roy was a collector. He collected art. He collected real estate and he collected employees. However, Cecil's value was a mystery to Tim.

When Cecil knocked on the front door of Dr. Markham Chantage's home, his wife had their five-year-old son, Randy on a chair in the front room. He was dressed in his light-blue Easter suit and yellow tie. His shoes shined. His hair was brushed.

Cecil, with Mrs. Chantage and her boy went straight to the mayor's office. Miss Marge, the receptionist asked them to sit on the long leather couch. Cecil gave the boy some papers to hold and rehearsed with him what he was to say.

Soon they were escorted to the mayor. Cecil said that Dr. Chantage could not make it, but he sent his wife and Randy to represent him. The boy handed the papers to the mayor, bowed and said the line Cecil had told him.

The mayor showed no emotion. He apologized for not getting the documents back to Malifer sooner, smiled, signed and passed them to Miss Marge to notarize. Miss Marge took their photograph.

The whole affair was over within three minutes.

After Cecil drove the two back home, he went straight to the mall. When he walked into the office, Cecil picked up three chocolates from Bobbie's candy jar. Gil was out, so he went straight to Tim's office.

Cecil put the papers on Tim's desk and gave a weird smile, "Tim, I told you it was not who you know but what you know. It is also important the way you let them know that you know what you know."

Tim's stomach churned. Whatever Cecil possessed worked.

"Be sure to tell Gil to call Mr. Roy," Cecil said.

"He'll give you a gold star, Cecil."

Tim looked over the document. It was all there, the map that showed the two areas linked by a ribbon of the road. It brought the art of the gerrymander to a new level. The mayor's signature slithered around the signature line.

He tried to wipe off a spot of chocolate with Cecil's fingerprint, but it only got worse.

Tim reached for the phone, felt queasy, rested the phone and took several slow breaths. He stood up, tried to take another deep breath, and rushed to the restroom where he barfed up his breakfast.

26

Kansas City Meeting

Over the next few months, Malifer purchased two strip centers in the Nashville market and a failing office tower with retail on the main floor in Memphis. They also hired two eager men to lease them.

Gil was on the road a good amount. He had to make sure Memphis understood Malifer's way of working. He was also picking their brains for ideas. "It is amazing what they will tell you about their old company."

Tim grinned, "Industrial spying."

Cecil said, "Power is what you know about who you know."

"When Roy approved Bill, the new man in Memphis, he said to pick his brain fast because he is a job hopper."

Louie broke in, "What did you learn from me?"

Without looking up Gil said, "Patience."

A week later, Mr. Roy told Gil in his weekly phone call that the leasing team should have a meeting in the home office.

"It will be good for team building. Maybe we can come up with fresh ideas before the convention in New Orleans," Gil said.

Cecil said, "Tell Mr. Roy the bank is starting to give me grief."

On the 5th of the month, the company plane stopped to picked up Gil, Tim and Louie on the way to Kansas City. Zack Palm and a few others were already on board.

The plane had large curved leather seats. At the rear of the plane was a small, well-stocked liquor and sandwich bar.

"This is the queen of air yachts!" Louie said.

Zack told a joke. He was on a roll - batta-bam-batta-bing. His red hair vibrated and everyone said he should be on TV.

Soon Gil told one, then Bill from Memphis, Harry from Nashville and back to Gil and Louie. Tim laughed, but could take only one joke home to Aimee.

In Kansas City, they went to Rami's Royal Steakhouse. Outside, waiting for them was Mr. Roy with Rami, the Lebanese owner.

Rami led them past the crowded tables, past the packed bar, through the kitchen, then down steps into a vaulted wine cellar.

In that candle-lit sanctum, Rami told them they could be as loud as they wanted because the dusty bottles were sworn to secrecy.

Tim ordered a Chivas and water from one of the jacketed waiters and met the new faces from the home office in the rows of dusty wine bottles.

Once everyone had a drink, Mr. Roy made his way to the head of the table. Everyone else settled behind a chair. Tim counted thirteen people.

Mr. Roy, wearing tinted glasses, started to speak, "Gentlemen, we welcome our three new members. Let's be thankful we have endured."

He raised his glass in a toast. In a low, deep voice he began to sing. Each note rich. Zack, Gil, and others joined as the volume grew.

"We were dirt of the land
We were dregs of the pile.
But in sin and with friend
we made all worthwhile.
We will grow as we stand,
with our heads we prevail
and not quit to the end."

Words vibrated like Russian choral music. Tim soon sang harmony at top volume.

"and to hell with poverty
and to hell, and to hell,
and to hell with poverty,
and to hell WITH --POV--ER--TY."

The tones bounced off the ceiling and vibrated the candles. Dust fell from bottles as echoes hid in dark corners.

Everyone lifted their glasses high and suddenly shouted "Hail, Hail, Malifer."

Mr. Roy cleared his throat, "Let's sing one more time – only this time with spirit."

This time they all started in a low deep whisper, and slowly raised the volume as some harmonized. Water in the crystal glasses shivered. Tim's forehead started to vibrate, and tears without warning fled down his cheeks. The final loud notes lasted slow and long. The crystal hummed until it faded to a whisper.

The next morning they all took the short walk across Brush Creek to Lingua Towers. Malifer owned the building and occupied the top floor, but Mr. Roy named it after the largest rent payer.

They stepped off the elevator to see Malifer's bull head logo etched on the glass entrance. Inside the foyer of the office, a thick Persian carpet lay on the black marble floor. A copy of 'Architectural Digest' with Lingua Towers on the cover was framed at the reception desk.

The wall held a framed large sketch of the same bull's head logo signed by Picasso. Next to it was a photograph of a young Mr. Roy when Picasso gave him the sketch.

"It is a sketch Picasso gave Mr. Roy when he met him," said the tall blond receptionist. "The bull is different in the final Guernica version. Even so, we are proud of it."

She gave them each a magnetic pass key which allowed them in the door behind her.

Gil showed the new hires around accounting, human resources and other support staff. Tim enjoyed meeting Paul Daniel, the attorney, and Lucy, his paralegal. He had talked to both several times, so it was good to meet them in person.

They strolled down a hall filled with photos of company events. "Our wall of history," Gil said. Scattered throughout were small bronze sculptures and large oil paintings.

The glass room where their meeting was held had a huge marble slab table that could seat twenty. On the walls were large framed prints.

A few minutes before the hour they poured themselves coffee and took a chair in the board room. At 9:00 A. M. sharp, Mr. Roy took his position at the head of the table. Behind him was a large modern print of a blue man who stood in front of the Sphinx.

Tim's eyes roamed the other prints in the room. Behind Gil was the same blue man in a maze of red-brick towers without windows. In back of Tim's chair hung one of a squarish blue man with red arrows that flew every which way around him. Tim leaned to read the artist's signature – Folon.

Tim jotted down the name. He didn't like modern art, but these images haunted him.

"Falconi's sales have dropped like a brick. He gets no traffic," Gil said.

"Damn, he signed a contract," Zack said.

"Tell him to advertise more," a voice on the left said.

"Profit is a bitch to be married to, but that's our lot in life," Mr. Roy said.

"She who must be obeyed," answered Zack.

Everyone moaned.

"Falconi's has no cash flow." Gil said, "Can't we cut his rent now and let him double up when business comes back?"

Louie said, "He might close if we don't reduce his rent."

"That's blackmail!" Zack said.

Heads turned to Mr. Roy, who sat stone faced behind his sunglasses.

Zack whispered, "We never lower rent."

"Andre Falconi's the last good, local tenant in Cypress Tree." Gil pleaded.

"Local jewelers sell as much out the back door as they do the front. He has cash, and he can pay the rent." Zack slapped the table with his left hand.

Louie popped off, "Some say his diamonds are hot."

Mr. Roy removed his glasses, "I don't want gossip. Show proof. Only scum accuse with gossip." His glass eye now pierced like a sword.

The room became quiet and still, and the air turned cold. Some sipped coffee trying to think what to say.

Zack broke in, "Should his bad luck affect our income?" He looked at the group and paused, "Of course not."

In one last gasp, Gil said, "We have to look at the big picture. If we help him, it will benefit us."

Mr. Roy's index finger started to slide around the top of his coffee cup.

In a soft, firm, clear voice, he said, "We have a problem in Fenton. It's bad, and it's worse because of the bank we used to finance. Every day our ship sinks deeper." He paused, and his tongue licked his upper lip. He took a sip of coffee. "We went to bed with the wrong bank." We got over-extended.

He turned to look at Zack Palm, "As you say: The lady looked good in the bar last night, but this morning she has fangs."

Zack blurted, "And she's bald!"

Everyone exploded with laughter.

Mr. Roy waited for silence, "The bank we used for Fenton is choking us. I'm personally in the deal, my art collection, my home, my wife's diamonds, even part of other properties. All I have is now on the line." Then in a whisper, "I brought you here to tell you as clear as I can. If we don't solve Cypress Tree's money problems, it will bring down Malifer. And we'll all be on the street."

No one moved. Silence haunted the air.

Mr. Roy sipped his coffee, "How will we get out of this?" He looked at Gil, "At least Cecil knew how to get the mayor to put Cypress Tree in the enterprise zone."

All sat still as stones.

"I'll kiss a snake to get free of this." Mr. Roy stared at Zack for a long time as his bottom jaw moved left to right chewing thoughts into words. "People have not listened to me." His glass eye looked at Gil, "We had a discussion at your party. I want it done." Gil slumped, nodded his head and glanced at Louie. The silence shouted volumes.

Mr. Roy pulled out a maroon bordered notepad, wrote something on it. He held the folded note up until Zack took it to a secretary.

The Hunting Dog

27

Conversation with Aimee

At 2PM, someone delivered a tray of sandwiches from Panera Bread. When 8:00 P.M rolled around they all walked back to the hotel bar. Tim ordered a scotch, then made his way to his room, ordered room service, and fired up his computer.

Aimee saw he was on Facebook and started a conversation:

AIMEE: How is Kansas City?

TIM: The main office is very nice. The meeting was tense at times.

AIMEE: Will you be back tomorrow?

TIM: We land at five. Louie said he would give me a ride home.

AIMEE: Supper will be ready.

TIM: I emailed your joke to several clients.

AIMEE: I thought you said Malifer didn't like email.

TIM: That's just Mr. Roy and Zack.

AIMEE: You would think they would like its speed.

TIM: Speed goes both ways.

AIMEE: What's the problem?

TIM: Too much information.

AIMEE: Did you finish Fahrenheit 451?

TIM: Almost, It is too real to think about.

AIMEE: It's science fiction.

TIM: But true.

AIMEE: Novels make you think.

TIM: I want it lite. Escape think. Not THINK think.

AIMEE: That's what good novels do.

TIM: Maybe.

AIMEE: Really? Reading exercises thought.

TIM: I read, so I think, therefore, I am?

AIMEE: You are what you think.

TIM: I watch TV. I know enough.

AIMEE: That kills thought.

TIM: And truth, like war.

AIMEE: You should write a novel.

TIM: Fat chance.

AIMEE: You could make a fortune.

TIM: Chet Quinn made peanuts on his novel.

AIMEE: He did OK.

TIM: Not for all the work put in.

AIMEE: So, how's work?

TIM: Gil's worried about something.

AIMEE: Do your job.

TIM: Sometimes I wonder what it is.

AIMEE: ????

AIMEE: Let me go see why the boys are fighting. Bye. XOXOXOXOX

TIM: Bye XX

28

Pressure

Back in Fenton on Monday morning, Cecil was late for breakfast. When he did walk into Star's, he placed a hand-written note in the middle of the table. Gil and Tim recognized the maroon border stationary Mr. Roy wrote on in the Kansas City meeting.

"It came as I left." Cecil said. "What's it about?"

Tim picked it up, read it and passed it to Gil.

MALIFER

Cecil,

Congratulations and THANKS with the help to get the Mayor to sign. Good Job!!! That should help with cash flow. However, at the party at Callaway Gardens, I suggested changes, but NO ONE listened. Am I to move to Fenton myself? Please find what's going on and let me know.

Roy

Gil froze. His eyes did not blink. His mouth dropped. His cheeks turned blue-white. His hand trembled.

"Are you OK, Gil?" Cecil asked.

He nodded, "He wants me to take care of something."

Cecil asked, "What should I tell him?"

"Tell him it has started. Tell him I will finish next week after we get back from New Orleans."

Tim talked about the plane trip, the meal in the wine cellar and about next week's convention. Nevertheless, inbetween topics the note on the table screamed for attention.

"Mr. Roy doesn't understand!" Gil said.

Cecil and Tim sat frozen.

Gil said, "We need to expand our search for office tenants. When Louie gets in, I'll tell him to contact brokers in Atlanta. We can't let his dad have an unwritten exclusive anymore."

Tim and Cecil nodded, as Gil regained his color. "Cecil, who should Tim see about getting state offices?"

"Perkins dishes out offices. Tim needs to go to the State Office of Space Resources." Tim jotted the name.

Gil said, "Damn Cecil, I cannot tell you how important the mayor's signature was. Mr. Roy mentioned it several times in our meeting. If you hear of any leads at the bank, even a whisper of one, let us know!"

When they all stood up to leave, Gil walked over to Ruby and slipped her a twenty-dollar bill. "Happy Anniversary."

"Mr. Gil, how did you know?"

"The rose in your lapel."

"Thank you sir."

When they returned to the mall, Tim followed Cecil in and asked him for directions to Mr. Perkin's office. He ended by repeating how Mr. Roy praised Cecil's power to get the mayor's signature.

"Tim, it is not who you know. It's not what you know, but how you use them." Cecil's eyebrows popped up as he smiled. Tim smiled back but quickly looked away.

Tim found the office on the second floor of the state's office annex. Erma Gilmore, a hefty woman with a forty year old hairstyle sat alone in the large marble walled office. Her flower-print dress and hair style shouted her age.

At first, she quizzed what he wanted, why he wanted it, what company he represented. When she heard Tim was from Fenton and Aimee was the former Aimee Maples, she realized she was classmates with Aimee's mother. "My goodness, Rose married Nick, a cub reporter for the Fenton paper."

"I've heard that."

"And he was a jewel."

"Well they're not rich."

"Respect has nothing to do with money," she said.

"I thought money had to do with everything."

Erma stared at him until he started to feel uncomfortable. When she saw his jaw tighten, she changed the subject. "Our board approves state office leases the first Tuesday of each month."

"Even in State-owned buildings?" Tim asked.

"All leases. Agencies rent space from state owned buildings, as they do from the private sector."

"So, the state is in the real estate business."

"Most agencies want to be in state owned buildings because that is where the action is. But we lease from the public all over the state.

Tim smiled, "So if we want to lease to the state, what's the procedure?"

"By bid," she said.

"We just have to be the low bidder?"

She looked over her glasses at him and lowered her voice, "You do understand politics?"

"But on the surface, a low bid will win?"

"If someone bids lower, the board would squirm to keep it out of the press. That's for sure."

"So we have a chance?"

"That depends. You must find an agency that wants to move. On the other hand, Fenton is not that far."

"Maybe we can get the rent right," Tim said.

"And the board approves." She reached for a long index card file, like Tim used in high school. "These are our leases. You're free to look any time."

The green box held one dog-eared index card for each state agency. It showed their address, sub offices, total square footage each office had and when the present lease ended. It also gave the contact's name and phone number.

Erma reached to a stack of papers. "This is an agenda for our last meeting." She handed him a copy. "We email it the Wednesday before the meeting."

"Can I get on the list?" Tim handed her his business card.

"Sure. Our meeting is public and in the next room. If you come, pick up an agenda at the door. We always have last minute additions."

She typed on her computer, and the printer started. "I'll give you a list of leases that end in the next six months."

"Is that the same as the index file?"

"Yes, but my computer's more accurate. Anybody can go in that box. Cards have been known to vanish. I password protect my files." She looked at him as she gave up the list. "You understand I can only give you public information."

"Erma, you're a whiz on that computer."

"I'd be lost without it. Mr. Perkins doesn't know how much it helps."

"I bet he thinks it's only a fancy typewriter."

"He insists on the green box. I use the computer." She took a deep breath and sat up straight.

Tim took the hint and sat at the table and started to flip through the cards.

Soon she was chatting again. "My uncle, Colonel Lee Jenkins, ran this office. He died two years ago, and the governor appointed Mr. Perkins."

"You must know everyone."

"They all would visit my uncle."

"He ran the show?"

She nodded. "Today the governor tells Perkins what to do. If I didn't know so many people, they would get rid of me. I can retire next year."

"You don't look busy today."

"It's never busy until Thursday before their meeting. Friday morning they line up in here to get on the agenda. Mr. Perkins has Tina help for a few days," she smirked.

"Who's Tina?"

"Contract labor," she scoffed, "and personal friend."

"Girl friend, part-time work?"

"Little work. Full time pay."

"Oh."

"The rest of the month it's only me."

"Where's Mr. Perkins now?"

She rolled her eyes, "He's out inspecting real estate with Governor Walls."

"Well at least he's at work," Tim said.

She groaned and shook her head. "Tim, anyone can rent to the state. Big companies and individuals, but for some it's their means of support."

"I guess they're lucky to own property?"

"Property is power and power is money." She bit her lip as if she had said too much.

"It's always who you know," Tim said.

"Thirty years ago, things were different."

"How?"

"We've always let relatives of politicians rent to the state. Many were widows and without leasing to the state, they would not have survived."

"That still happens?"

"Of course a contribution is expected at election time. But now it's out of hand, way out of hand."

"What do you mean?" Tim asked.

"Local politicians get tied in with foreign ghost corporations and get rent way above market. When I check who the owners are, it's impossible. Mr. Perkins says if they are legally registered, not to worry about it."

"You smell a fish?"

"A rotten one."

"What can be done?" Tim asked.

"If Nick Maples were alive I would tell him about it. Today newspapers don't investigate squat."

"What can be done?"

"Someone else can solve the problem. I just want to retire." She waited for Tim to comment, but he didn't, so she continued, "I'm taking notes. I might even write a book."

"People want to know how government works."

"It will make them sick."

"I'll be your agent. We'll get rich." They both laughed.

"If not killed." She took her glasses off and cleaned them. "You know, I get rent from the highway department," she paused and glanced at Tim. "When I first started here years ago, the highway department needed five acres south of Fenton. I mentioned our family farm, and they gave us the bid." She smiled, "That was before momma died, and it was all on the up and up, for only a year while they widen the road."

"I understand."

"Mom was paid a hundred dollars the first year. The lease was extended again and again, and each time a small increase. No one ever bid against me."

Tim thought only a fool would bid against the lady who types the agenda. "How much is the rent now?"

"Today it renews every three years for more than my salary. The highway department rents it, in case they might need to store something. Which they do every few years."

"I understand."

"And my brother still raises cattle on it."

Footstep echoes came from the marble stairs. Erma stood up and busied herself with some files. Tim sat at the table and pulled some more cards out of the green file box.

A fat man in golf clothes charged in, "Any calls, Erma?"

"Only Tommy Ray Blass."

"Did you tell him to stop crying?"

"I told him you were with the governor."

"Good."

"Did you have a good game?" she asked.

"The governor beat me again. Larry Morgan and his partner choked on the back nine, so they lost big." The man's bulging pig eyes rolled to Tim but silently questioned Erma.

"Mr. Perkins, let me introduce Tim Lichten with Cypress Tree Mall in Fenton. They might want to bid in the future."

They shook hands. "Good to meet you, son. What agency wants your space?"

"None right now. I came to learn the process."

"Well, Erma's the right person."

"Yes, sir. She's let me look at the file." Tim lifted the green file box.

"That's where you'll find what's available."

"Do you know of anyone that might be interested in our office tower?"

"In Fenton?"

"Yes sir."

"Not off hand, but I'll keep you in mind. One never knows." He turned to Erma, "Erma, come in my office a second."

When the door reopened, Erma didn't say anything, but her eyes said it was time for Tim to go. She wrote a quick note, folded it over and slipped it in Tim's hand. Tim slipped it into his coat pocket without looking, nodded and left.

At his car, he looked. "Go see Tommy Ray Blass."

The next morning Tim pulled out the note and gave Erma a call. "This is Tim, from yesterday. Can you talk?"

"I'm sorry about yesterday, but Mr. Perkins told me to get rid of you. I must tell you about Mr. Blass. Perkins wants them to stay where they are. They've treated Mr. Blass wrong. It's not right."

"Tell me about them."

"They are in an old K-Mart building, on the road to Fenton. Tommy Ray has the only office in the place and wants out."

"Maybe we can help."

"Just keep me out of it," she said.

"I will."

"Tommy Ray Blass has been banished for years. But Fenton might work for them."

"I appreciate your help."

"Tell Rose I said hello."

Tim hung up, started to call Blass, but remembered his mother's sales lectures, "Meet a client in person, listen to their concerns, read their emotions…" He put it on his list to do first thing after next week's convention in New Orleans.

29

Bobbie Visits Doctor

The doctor's office was on the sixth floor of the tower. The inner door was open, so Bobbie stuck her head in.

"Are, you back in town?" she asked.

"Is that you Bobbie?"

"It's me."

"Come in and close the door." The doctor moved to a high backed chair across from where she sat. "Bobbie, I'm sorry I wasn't here last week. How have you been?"

"I felt abandoned."

"I was at a seminar in Aspen."

"Well, I was annoyed." Bobbie stared into his eyes.

"Do you realize this begins our fifth year?" He picked up a file and pulled a pen from his pocket, "How do you feel about it?"

"Do you want to get me mad?"

"I only asked a question. That's what I do. Besides, I thought we already addressed your anger. Are you still mad about what you can't control?"

Her nostrils widened. "Why is it when you leave, things flare?"

"There is always change - accept it and move on," he said.

Bobbie's cheeks turned red, "I don't know who I am. I wish I were a man. I should be Bob."

"You aren't."

"I'm nothing."

"You said you were Bobbie. Be the best Bobbie possible."

Her jaw locked, and she glared. He answered her stare with silence. For thirty minutes, she sat and glared in anger. The doctor sat like a stone as he waited. Will against will.

She shrieked, "You bastard! You pompous ass bastard! You're supposed to make me better. You don't know what it's like." Tears ran, "You don't know what change does!"

She reached over and picked up a small bronze bust of Freud. Her eyes focused on the doctor. Her teeth clinched. She glared. He sat steadfast until her flush melted and she put the bust back.

"I'm listening," he said.

"You're so smug. You have yours with all the money it brings." She started to cry.

"Bobbie, only you can make yourself better."

"Life's a bitch."

"Play with the cards dealt. You are in control. You can decide."

A small chime pinged. The doctor wrote a note and handed it to her. "Bobbie, I'm changing your medication." He handed her the prescription. "Have a good week."

She went to the elevator and pushed the button to the top floor. It was where vacant posh offices once held silk suited attorneys. At the end of the wide hall she unlocked a heavy oak door and entered. On the parquet, a lone leather wing chair sat next to glass windows overlooking Atlanta's far off skyline.

This place was where she could be alone. She would read poetry or talk to herself. Most of the time for a few minutes but sometimes for hours. It made things better.

30

Finding Happiness

When the plane started to descend and lean right, Tim got woozy. The early sun danced on Lake Pontchartrain. He saw the thin straight line on top of the water. It was the twenty-mile causeway that runs across the belly of the lake from New Orleans to Covington. Cars looked like ants crossing a tight wire. Tim wanted to see the Super Dome, but laid back and took some deep breaths.

He adjusted his earplugs, turned up the volume, closed his eyes, and hoped his queasy stomach would stay down. He took another deep breath and held it until he felt the wheels descend. He kept his eyes closed as he took one final serious breath. The jets roared off the ground as the plane bumped the tarmac. They landed.

As he walked off, hot humidity slapped his face. The smell of mildew reminded him of his college locker room. It had been twenty years.

Tim searched for a familiar face but only recognized the sheen of sweat on everyone's face.

The car rental lady looked like Betty, who helped him with statistics. She gave him the rental agreement.

He walked ten feet, turned back to ask if she might have had a daughter in his class, but she was on to the next customer.

Driving on I-10, he saw new office buildings were now between old landmarks. Tim couldn't remember what they replaced. His mind played tricks. Things were the same, but different. Houses seemed smaller. Trees had grown taller. "Damn, why didn't I pay attention when I lived here?"

It was 9:45 when he turned onto Carrollton heading under the oaks toward the University Section. He drove past Xavier then at the Camellia Grill he turned left down St. Charles until he was in front of Tulane and

Loyola.

Tim slowed the car and looked at the cracked sidewalks he had walked years ago.

He parked, and started to follow memories that meandered around the campus.

The air had a hint of azaleas and new magnolias, but the brick and limestone were the same. Tim's shirt became heavy and limp with humidity as he walked. Students looked like grade school kids.

Columned houses leaned like tombstones in the morning sun. Shadows danced on their white wood walls under the trees. The antebellum mansion Music School was replaced with grass and modern architecture.

He remembered one night in the vanished building music students sat around and talked. An older suited man came up and listened. One of the students stood and offered him a chair. The man nodded, sat and listened.

"Bach, Beethoven and Debussy talk to the listener but Dixieland is more," said one student.

"Dixieland is only a regional folk music," Tim remembered saying.

"Mozart is like a stone sculpture. When we play Dixieland, we are the art, as much as the color in a painting by Matisse," answered a girl.

The students nodded in agreement and turned to the old man. He smiled and turned to Tim, "Son, just listen to it."

The students all grinned.

"Go to Preservation Hall," the old man said as his fingers tapped on the table like he was playing notes on a piano. "Close your eyes and listen. Don't try to analyze or break down the music, just listen to the instruments. Don't philosophize, don't talk, just be quiet. You'll hear them talk. They'll interrupt, answer back and sass one another. In Dixieland, the music talks and you become part of it and it will give you its life."

He looked around the table and leaned towards Tim, "Dixieland, like all life, communicates in a conversation." He tapped on the table with both piano hands. "Son, it's alive."

His hands stayed firm on the table in a final chord. His white eyes roamed their faces. All were silent.

When he stood up to leave, he raised his hand and made a long slow pass through the air as if some ancient decree had been given.

The debate was over.

"Who was that?" Tim asked.

"Professor Marsalis. He teaches piano."

"That's not all," Tim said.

Time crushes memories in its march. Tim looked back at the new music building and hoped time had not crushed the man's lesson.

Tim returned to his car and headed to the Camellia Grill. The gas station on the corner was gone. The drug store was no longer, but the thick cream white doric columns of the Camellia Grill called like Greek sirens. It was a small diner, always open, with a maitre'd to assign you a counter stool.

Four people were in line outside the front door. Once Tim was inside, he was assigned a place on the bench up against the wall. There he would wait for a seat at the counter.

Bacon sizzled. Glass clinked. Black men in white uniforms darted behind the counter. A thin film of grease still covered the pink walls. It was all the same, even the gray-haired lady at the cash register. Tim sat on the wall, leaned back and closed his eyes. The voices, the smell of slow coffee and chatter of dishes had not changed.

"Sir, over here," someone said.

He pointed Tim to a stool at the counter.

"Mornin' sir, you want your usual?" a waiter asked.

"What?"

The waiter smiled, "It's been a long time. Do you want something special or your usual?"

Tim looked at him. "You remember me?"

The man's eyes smiled. Tim glanced at his name tag, Owen.

The man rolled his pencil in his fingers, "I remember you. You used to come in here late at night. You were a student that lived nearby." He rubbed his chin and asked. "You found happiness since you left?"

"You don't remember me," Tim said.

"You all come in, look around, smell the coffee. You are all the same." He leaned over and whispered, "Your name is . . . Tim, and you studied philosophy to find happiness. So I ask, you found it?"

Tim's eyes popped. "You do remember!" He didn't know what to say. "I'm still on the search. I'm married, two boys and a good job but still on the search."

A steel spatula clanged on the griddle.

Owen leaned in and said, "Remember what I told you last time."

For the life of him, Tim couldn't remember the waiter or what he had said. "How do you remember me?"

Owen tilted his head, "You came in because you remembered something special about this place. God lets me remember everyone who comes here. When you first came in years ago, I asked you questions. Your answers gave me memory tags. They told me what made you special. With that, God let's me remember everyone."

"OK, Owen, what do I order?"

Owen stood up straight and grinned, "Most times, one burger with cheese, extra pickle, no onion but an order of onion rings, one chocolate freeze. You always end with cheesecake and black coffee."

"Damn, you're good."

"And you never forget the cheesecake." As he checked off the items on the order ticket, Owen repeated the order louder so the cook could hear, and the cook echoed it back.

"Is the cheesecake the same?" Tim asked.

"Beauty never changes. What makes you think the cheesecake changed?"

"OK, but don't forget the coffee."

"No cream."

"Right."

Tim watched as Owen made the chocolate freeze and put it in front of him. Owen picked up a straw, opened the paper cover, and with a certain panache, presented it to Tim so he could remove the straw. When Tim pulled the straw, Owen said, "It comes from inside."

Tim loved that place.

Tim finished the cheesecake, took out ten bucks for a tip and slipped it in Owen's jacket pocket.

"Don't forget where to find happiness," said Owen.

Outside, Tim turned to the right and walked the short block to the top of the Mississippi levee. He was shocked how high the river was.

Aimee's uncle claimed silt had settled so much over the years, that the Mississippi river bed was higher than surrounding land. He swore someday a behemoth flood would happen. When it did, Katrina would look like a puddle. Tim knew that wasn't true. If it was, someone would do something about it.

Tim walked down the levee and called Mrs. Bourgeois to make sure she was home. Soon he was in front of her house. It was a long narrow 'shotgun' house common in New Orleans. They all had a front porch, parlor, formal dining room, kitchen and a bedroom in the back. All one room behind the other without a hallway. Because houses were taxed on their width at the front, over the kitchen an upstairs bedroom or two would sometimes be built in the "untaxed zone."

Mrs. Bourgeois closed off the upstairs bedroom and installed exterior steps to the second level. That's where Tim lived when he was in college.

Since her husband died, Mrs. Bourgeois rented the upstairs to boys from nearby Tulane and Loyola. She felt secure with 'her' boys in the second-floor apartment.

There was a large oak tree in a small front yard. Huge azaleas guarded the screened porch. In the rear, a ten-foot high brick wall protected a magnolia tree and private courtyard.

When he drove up, Mrs. "B" was on the front porch watching TV. It was in the parlor, but angled through the long plantation windows, so she could see it on the porch. When his car stopped, she stood up and pushed the screen door open and waited on the top step. She was now past eighty, but walked with only a slight limp.

She kissed him, and with her thumb wiped her lipstick off his cheek.

"Tim, I'm so tickled you came." She hugged him again, "Sit down and tell me how you've been."

Tim took a deep whiff. "That's Jungle Gardenia."

"Did I use too much?"

"Oh, no. I love it."

A slow fan moved the lazy porch air back and forth.

"You still watch your soaps?"

"My show's on. You don't mind, while we talk?"

"Not at all."

She focused on the show. "That's Bob with the broken arm. He's playing around with Judy. How's your wife and boys?"

"Fine."

"They looked great in your Christmas card. One's named Tim Jr., and the little one is - Ray?"

"That's right."

She turned to look at the TV, "Judy's had one affair after another. She's now back with Bob. Why are you in town?"

"I have a convention at the Monteleone."

The phone rang. She kept her eyes on the TV as her right hand picked up the phone. "Yes Ethel, I'm watching, but guess who's here. Tim! You remember Tim? . . . Yeah, Judy's back with Bob, surprised me too, but you know how she is. She has to have a boy toy . . . " She held the phone away from her ear, "Ethel wants to know: how long you'll be in town?"

"Two days."

"Couple of days Ethel, busy with meetings . . . At the Monteleone . . . Yes, I'll be waiting . . . Okay, bye." She hung up the phone, stared at the TV for a few seconds, "Tonight, Ethel's picking me up to play Bingo at the Legion Hall - Oh, my goodness," Mrs. B's hand slapped her jaw, "Did you see her hit Bob?" She started to dial the phone.

"You play Bingo often?" Tim asked.

"Once a week," she returned to make a call. "Mabel, guess who came to see me: Tim, remember him? . . . Yeah, that's him. The one you made gumbo for when he had the flu . . . Tim, you remember the gumbo she fixed?"

"The best!"

"Mabel, he remembers. Oh, yes, real successful, even has a gold Rolex."

Tim glanced at the time.

She hung up the phone. "Mabel and I watch the same soap. Ethel watches another show, so I have to tell her what happens on my show."

"You talk to them a lot?"

"No, not much. Maybe, five or six times a day."

Her world was filled with virtual TV characters, phone calls, neighbors, and memories. Somehow she talked, held one eye on the soap opera, and conversed with Tim in a tightrope of reality.

"You want some coffee?"

"What about your show?"

"Mable can tell me."

He followed her through the house. She pointed to a lamp her daughter made and then to photos of her grandchildren with her late husband, Jerry.

"See your picture?" she smiled at faded framed photos on the dining room wall. There were twenty-six photos. Each year, she took at least one photo of the boy who rented her apartment.

"Three of them are me!"

"I still remember taking them."

"You still rent the apartment?"

"Oh, yes. Jesse Cross is number sixteen. He's studying architecture and works. Never comes home until 7:30."

She turned on the drip coffee pot and sat at her white enamel kitchen table.

"Want some King cake?"

"Oh, Mrs. B, I just ate."

"Good, you need dessert."

The kitchen phone rang. Without moving from her chair, she reached behind, picked up the phone and announced, "Ethel, we're having coffee. I'll call you back."

She hung up, went back to the coffee and said, "Maybe fifteen or twenty."

"What's that?"

"Maybe we talk twenty times a day. I told you five, it was more."

She reminded him that he had trimmed her bushes and helped her move some furniture.

"Tim, the best thing you did for me was your party. It made me feel young again."

"Mrs. B, I have a confession. I had invited so many people. I wanted to use your court yard, so I invited you. To my surprise, you accepted, and you were the hit of the party."

"I'm so glad you did. That was one of the highlights of my life," she said.

"You played the ukulele, and sang. What was the one about the flounder flapping?"

"Jerry learned those in the Navy."

"You were something else."

She blushed, "We had fun, didn't we?"

"And you told the wildest stories!"

"God loves you, Tim."

"Everyone begged me to have another, but I never did."

"You should have." She shuffled over to a bookshelf with a row of green journals and pulled one down. "You know I've always kept a diary." Her red fingernail followed the ink as she read the notes.

"Here we go, 'March 21, Dear Jerry' – Jerry was my husband you know - Last night Tim threw a fantastic party. There were 35 well behaved college kids. I played your old ukulele and sang those songs you used to sing on ship. I felt so young, like I did when we were in Hawaii." She whispered to herself, "I miss you, but I'll be fine."

"Mrs. 'B' you should take those notes and write a book. I'd love to read it."

"People don't read anymore. Anyway, they don't want to read some old lady's stories."

"You never know. People need stories to help them remember their own dreams."

She thought a second, "Well maybe someday. When I can find the time."

They drank coffee and had a piece of stale King's cake as she peppered him with questions. "How are the children? How's your health? Are you happy with your job?"

The lace curtains glowed when lightning flashed, and thunder bounced around the clouds. Her eyes sparked as he talked. The phone rang, but she let it ring. "Hell, make her think I'm in the bathroom." She paused, "I bet we talk fifty times a day."

When the sun came out, Tim walked over and opened the back door. "The air smells so damn fresh."

"Gentlemen don't use damn."

"Sorry."

Tim looked at his watch. It was after four. "Mrs. B, I need to be on my way."

"Tim, I have something for you." He followed her to the front room where she opened a cedar trunk and removed a multicolored crocheted wrap. "It's an afghan. I work on these and give one to all my boys who qualify."

"How does one qualify?"

"You come back to visit."

Tim brought it to the porch, so he could admire the explosions of color.

"Well, thank you. Aimee will love it."

"Do you have room for it? I could ship it?"

"I'll take it. I don't want to lose this in the mail."

She folded it and handed it to him. "You're sure you have room?"

"If not, I'll ship my clothes back. I'm not letting this out of my sight."

He leaned to hug her good-bye. She grabbed on to him and held so tight that she pinched his arm.

"Tim, is your mother alive?"

"Yes, Ma'am."

"Go see her."

"Yes, Ma'am."

"Loneliness has no laughter."

"I know."

The sidewalk was damp, and acorns cracked beneath his feet. When he drove off he wondered why he had to visit her. She was only an old landlady who once came to a party. Someday, he hoped to pass on what she gave him.

31

New Orleans Adventure

Tim drove toward Canal Street and the Monteleone Hotel. Gil and Louie would be there with the others he met in Kansas City.

He checked in and found the phone light blinking in his room. It was Gil. "Tim, come up to my suite. It's at the end of the hall on eighteen. You got to see this place. Everybody's here. We have beer, liquor, chips, whatever."

"Ok, as soon as I get a shower to get rid of this damp sweat. I'll be up in fifteen minutes."

When Tim got off the elevator, he heard Louie's voice. The suite door had been left ajar, so he walked straight in.

"There he is!" Zack said as he saw Tim.

"So what's the agenda?" Tim asked.

"We're working on it," Zack Palm said. "Some want to eat at Manale's and others want to find a place in the Quarter."

Louie held up a slip of paper, "I want to find a woman."

"If you can't find one in New Orleans, you're in big trouble," Tim said.

"That puts you in the Quarter," Zack said.

The large hotel room had two levels and a ceiling two floors high. The first level was great for business entertaining and overlooked the Mississippi River. The loft level held the bedroom and second bathroom.

"Where's Gil?" asked Tim.

"He's in the shower. He thinks if he takes a shower, he can get rid of the humidity," Zack said.

Tim smiled, "Makes perfect sense."

"Wait until you see his new gold Rolex Explorer. He picked it up this afternoon."

Louie held the note in his hand not holding his beer. "I understand some fun can happen in New Orleeens."

"Louie, it's New Or'luns . . . not New Orleeeens," Tim said.

"Yes, you better say "Or'luns"," Zack said, "or she'll think you're an invader from up 'Neeoourth'."

Tim pointed to Louie's loafers, "With tassels on their toes."

Louie smiled, "The bellhop gave me a name of a place." He waved his folded slip of paper. "We're going on an 'add-VEN-ture'."

Tim shook hands with co-workers he met in Kansas City. They were all negotiators, who always first took control to sell the fine points in a lease.

This was free time before the big event tomorrow. It was a time to open a beer and build teamwork. But they jockeyed to show dominance. They joked. They drank, and they punched with facts about clients or competition. It was their convention pre-game ritual.

Some rounded their shoulders as if they were bears, others foxed their eyes. They slapped backs, laughed, and exchanged war stories.

Salesmen always have new tricks to close a deal. Tim stood back and watched like a hawk to hone his craft before the convention began.

Tim would test his ability to control by manipulating them to the restaurant of his choice. Maybe Tortorici's or Tujague's. No one knew either place. He would try for Tortorici's, but that meant he would need to control what exit they took from the hotel.

Gil came from the upstairs bathroom with his hair slicked back. His silk shirt and tan set off loose gold jewelry.

Tim shook hands, "You look good."

"I'm ready for a steak," Gil said.

Tim said, "Our plan is to head out and find something to surprise ourselves." Others overheard and started toward the door.

"Gil we have a special occasion tonight," Zack said.

"What's that?"

"A bachelor party for Louie."

"He's engaged?"

Zack smiled, "Not yet. That's why we need the party. Maybe he'll find somebody."

Louie smiled and waved his note in the air. "Ad-VENT-ure."

"Let's eat first," Zack said.

So far, so good, Tim thought. "Onward Malifer Properties!"

"A toast to Louie's party," Gil said.

They toasted and were off down Royal Street. They stopped across from the Wildlife and Fisheries Museum, to read the menu posted outside Brennan's.

"Menu looks good," Zack said.

"They are great for breakfast," Tim said. He walked away, others followed. The humidity changed to a light mist. On the next corner was Tortorici's Italian Restaurant. Tim took the lead and stopped to look at the menu posted in the window. "I smell veal parmigiana," Tim said.

Zack stepped inside to check it out. Tim said, "I love Italian sausage."

Zack popped out the door, "They'll have a table in five minutes. The place is small, so I told them we'd stay outside the front door."

"Been open over a hundred years, and I've never heard of this place." Gil said.

Tim backed away as others crowded to read, "Looks like good Italian," Louie said.

"I'm hungry," Tim groaned.

It started to drizzle so they gathered inside in the small vestibule.

The drizzle became heavier, so Tim ran to get under Tortorici's leaking awning. As soon as he nudged into the back of the pack, the rain started to pour.

The maitre'd turned to them and waved them in, but no one moved.

"The man said to go," Tim said. The maitre'd started towards the table. They all marched past uniformed waiters and sober diners.

They were led to the back of the restaurant to a long table ready for them. Everyone sat, ordered a drink and started to joke and talk about Louie's 'ad-ven-ture'.

Tim caught a man at the next table who glared at them, but Tim looked away. Another table talked to the maitre'd, who came and talked to Zack Palm. Zack with the raise of his hand told all to lower the volume.

The loudness hushed, but the ribald jokes continued as other patrons turned to stare.

Tim turned to Gil on his left, "I'm embarrassed."

"You know anyone in here?" Gil said.

"No."

"Do you plan to come back?"

"After this I don't think they will be open much longer," Tim said.

"Then relax."

"A toast to Louie's future wife, whatever her name will be," Gil said.

"To all our kids!" Louie raised his glass.

Once food arrived, the drunken jokes died.

Later, the waiter asked, "Does anyone care for dessert?"

Louie said, "Make mine Chivas straight." He smiled with a glazed look.

"Sir, do you think that is a good idea?" said the waiter.

Zack added, "Louie, you might be at your limit."

"Limit? If I had too much, could I do this?" Louie stood straight up, steadied himself, leaned forward so his head was waist high. Then in one abrupt move he did a back-flip to land on his knees. He staggered to his feet, looked at the waiter and saluted. "Chivas and water, sir."

Zack stood up, "Let's take this party elsewhere."

The tab was quickly in Zack's hand. Zack signed the tab, palmed a hundred to the maitre'd and followed the pack out.

The rat pack stopped on the wet street and gave "high five's" as they aimed for the lights of Bourbon Street.

Louie sang in front with his small note high for all to see. "Now for the Pirate Trap."

"Where the hell is it?" Zack asked.

Louie said, "It's in the high-class section of Bourbon Street."

"That's a sight to see," Tim said.

"Past the strip bars," Louie said.

"Is it 'spectable?" Gil asked. "I only go to 'spectable places."

"It's reee-spectable and reee-asonable," Louie said.

"Prices, or reputation?" Tim asked.

Louie grinned, "It's got reee-spectable drinks and reee-asonable women."

Everyone laughed.

"They have so much class, they don't need respect," assured Louie.

"Good. I don't want to see some dogs," Zack said.

"No dog's in this place," Gil said. He 'meowed' as he staggered.

Passing strangers laughed.

At Bourbon Street, the drunken pack turned right and snaked through an onslaught of tourist gawkers. They glanced past each doorway barker for a flash of flesh. Happiness was there somewhere. They would find it.

"Thar she blows!" Louie shouted pointing to a corner building. A carved wood sign hung with 'The Pirate Trap' in gold letters. A purple haze glowed from an inside neon sign. They all cheered. One by one they paraded past the doorman's eyes.

The bar was filled with white smiles and eyes that watched. Above, large framed mirrors hung tilted to show squirming bodies below. Two bartenders poured drinks as sweat dripped from their ebony brows. Tim ordered scotch.

A blond batted her eyes, "Welcome to "Nu Orluns."

"Well, thank you," He paid for his drink and turned to see her point to a table in the corner. When he sat, she squeezed in, to his right. Another female slipped in on his left, so close their thighs touched.

Tim eyed one, "My name's Tim."

"I'm Flower."

"I'm Bell, you going to buy us a drink?"

Over her shoulder, Tim saw Louie walking upstairs behind a red dress. He held a bottle of Champagne and two glasses. Tim waved, but Louie was focused on the dress. At the top of the stairs was a back-lit stained glass of a rising sun.

"Wha'ca lookin' for?" Flower asked.

"Friends. Where'd they all go?"

"I think they all bought Champagne," said Flower.

"Get some Champagne and we'll go upstairs," Bell said.

Tim looked around, "This place is too noisy."

Bell leaned over and said in his ear, "Its quiet upstairs."

"How much?"

"Quiet."

"No, how much will it cost?"

Flower batted her eyes at him. "What do you want?"

"Champagne, how much will it cost?"

Bell's mouth tightened, "Two Hundred."

Flower puckered her lips. "And we'll be really friendly."

The three sat in silence. Flower looked around the room and tapped on the table. "Well?"

Tim shook his head, "I came in for a quiet drink with friends."

Bell batted her eyes, "We'll be friends."

Tim sipped his thin drink.

Flower stood up, and without a word walked away.

Bell moved her hand up Tim's arm, "Why don't you buy me a rum and Coke."

"How long have you lived in New Orleans?" Tim asked.

"Three years."

"Where are you from?"

"Suck Creek, Tennessee," she looked at his drink and licked her lips. "Will I get a drink?"

Bell saw his eyes search, so she turned her head to give him one last chance to inspect. He looked at her straw hair, at the dark rings under her eyes, at the cracks in her lips and at her milk-white neck with Wal-Mart pearls.

Tim stood up. "I need a better place."

"Where're we going?"

"Not we, me. I'm leaving."

32

Songs of Preservation

Outside, off to the right, Bourbon Street was coated with a sheen of light from the distant bars. His hand automatically felt for his wallet. After a few steps, he turned to make sure no one followed. He crossed the street to head straight toward the river.

He stepped over a dead bird on the curb, walked fast under balconies and past a sleeping man next to steps. At Decatur, he turned to go over the flood wall and train tracks at St. Phillip. He soon was on the levee and "The Moon Walk", a long narrow public park on the top of the levee. He sat on one of the benches under a lamp post and watched the slow ferry move cars. A loaded ship went by. Blurry lights glittered in the dark water.

Years ago on one crisp spring morning, he and Aimee went to the Mississippi's headwaters at Lake Itasca. There the water was clear and fresh and clean and only twenty feet wide and a foot deep. They both took their shoes off and waded from one side of the Mississippi to the other.

Tonight that river was almost a mile wide and dark and thick and muddy. The air smelled sour with fumes of oil.

He figured he was ten blocks away from the hotel. Suddenly he knew where he had to go first. Tim got up and walked past all the couples on benches. He gave the saxophone player a dollar and continued towards Jackson Square.

Cafe du Monde was open, and the area around the square was filled with walkers.

At St. Peter's Street, he saw the green and white Pat O'Brien's sign. Next door onlookers peered into the windows of Preservation Hall.

He entered the antique carriageway and on the left, stepped into the back of the small packed room.

People sat on the floor in the first row, then benches for a few rows. In the back, everyone stood. Tim walked past them all to the back wall where he found his private niche, an empty ledge of a bricked up window. He stepped on the ledge, turned to face the band. His right hand reached up to grab for the long nail he had found years ago. It was exactly where he remembered. True anchors never change.

In that nook, Tim had learned to listen as Dixieland instruments chatted and yakked and argued for hours on end.

Up there, above the packed room, he could see the band and the eyes in the windows behind the band. What did he seek? What did they seek? Why did he come to this music grotto? What did everyone find here? The walls were filled with dark painted icons of Dixieland's saints. From the ceiling hung a chain with a single light bulb.

Tim watched floor dust rise like incense in the rays of light. Somehow he was tasting honey.

After five songs, his raised arm started to ache. Tim stepped down, sat on the floor and closed his eyes. The beat of the drum spoke to his chest, the banjo to his hands, the clarinet to his soul. The spirits danced around him and touched him and became one with him. They sang and bickered, and cursed and Tim listened while dust kissed his face.

33

Tommy Ray Blass

On the Monday after he returned from New Orleans, Tim picked up the note he taped on the back of his chair to visit the state office in the old K-Mart building. It was the lead Erma had given him.

Tommy Ray Blass had three ball point pens in the pocket protector of a wrinkled white shirt. His glasses and short haircut said he had been in the army.

"Mr. Lichten, this dump leaks every rain, has since they built it. When K-Mart closed, the governor's brother-in-law opened a recreation hall for Vets. The IRS got the owner for tax evasion." He leaned toward Tim, "It was a casino. Why he thought he could get away with it, I will never know."

Tim's eyes widened as if he had been told some CIA information. "I never heard that."

"There's a lot you've not heard."

"Mr. Blass, who owns this building?"

"A company in Belize."

"In Central America?"

"Yeah, and Governor Wall's in bed somehow."

"What makes you say that?"

Blass glared at Tim, "They've never put one dime in the building. The roof leaks, we park in pothole hell. Toilets don't work, but the state always pays the rent."

"This is a big building. You must have a lot of employees."

"Only eighteen. We are a small division of Labor. But we pay for the whole 150,000 square feet."

"Meanwhile your people are upset," Tim said.

"We closed off this area with offices, but we still have to walk 200 feet to the only restroom that works. I will escape this rattrap or Sixty Minutes will get the story. Go back and tell that to your Mr. Perkins!"

Tim held up his hands, "I don't work for Perkins. I've met him once, but he has no idea I'm here."

"He didn't send you?"

"No, not at all." Tim repeated his opening introduction, "I'm with Malifer Properties. I came because I overheard a conversation."

"You're not a consultant for Perkins?"

"No, and from what I hear, Perkins wouldn't want me here. Malifer owns numerous properties. Our largest here is Cypress Tree Mall." Tim handed him another business card. "I thought you might like our office tower."

Tommy Ray's ears perked.

"If you only have about twenty people, I think 3,000 square feet is all you need."

"That's what I tell them, but they make us lease the whole thing." He took a breath and in a softer, voice started to explain the history of his situation. "One of the owners is Fishbone-Puxar, a company out of Belize. However, don't ask me who else. All I know is Fishbone doesn't fix problems."

Tim said, "I assure you our roof won't leak."

"I asked Larry Morgan, a local realtor, to find us something. He thinks he has space for half what we now pay."

"Where?"

"The city wants to sell the old library, so he is looking for tenants."

"Then you are set?"

"Not exactly, it has asbestos, but the city said they will clean it. Morgan's working on the details."

"Sounds like he wants to line up tenants so a buyer will pay more."

"Exactly. If he gets the city to pay to clean it up, and the state to give him tenants, it will be a sweet deal."

"As long as he doesn't sell to Fishbone."

Blass rolled his eyes.

Tim said, "They'll need a year to get ready."

"Maybe, maybe not."

"It sounds like a white elephant," Tim said.

"All I need is 3,000 feet. With that we can use my budget for what it was intended." Blass gave a sheepish smile. "I hate politics. I want out!"

"Sounds like you are Wall's bad boy."

"I didn't back him in the election. So old cross-eyed Governor Walls forced this location on us to pay off his rat pack. We might like Fenton, being away from the capitol odor."

"I'd like to know more about Fishbone-Puxar."

"Mr. Lichten, you already know too much."

"You may be right."

Blass smiled, "I am, and those alligators bite."

"Do you have an obligation to Morgan?"

"We went to grade school together. He likes to think he knows the right people." Blass shook his head and chuckled. "When Perkins hears about you, he will be pissed, but he's already pissed."

"The worst case is they might let Morgan move you."

"Let's see what you can offer," said Blass.

"Fair enough. Now show me your office."

34

Louie Goes

When Tim got back in the office that afternoon, there was tension in the air. Bobbie said Zack Palm had called Gil, and they had a long talk. "What went on in New Orleans?" Tim shook his head that he didn't know. "Well something happened. Gil tried to call Louie, but he didn't answer."

"Where is he now?"

"I have no idea. He hasn't come back since lunch. Maybe he went to find him."

The air was still and heavy, like an ax.

Louie must have known something was up because he did not come in Monday. On Tuesday, he showed for a few minutes when everyone was at Star's. Bobbie told Louie that Gil needed to see him, but he still stayed out the rest of the day. Wednesday Louie called in sick and Bobbie told him again. Thursday morning Gil did not go to Star's. When Louie dropped by to check his mail, Gil marched him into his office.

"Louie, have a seat." Gil closed his door and sat at his desk. "Mr. Roy and Dad both have questions about your job performance. And dammit, Louie, it's one thing to get drunk, but Dad was with us! If Mr. Roy were there, you would have been fired when you did that back flip in the restaurant. The whole industry is talking about it. On top of that, around here you don't even try to work. What in hell's the matter?"

Louie rolled his head from side to side, "Oh, come on Gil, you've said yourself, have fun to keep up spirits. This economy has no prospects."

"But you don't try to find any. Some days you don't even show." Gil waited for Louie to look at him, but Louie only gazed at the floor. "Louie, my ass is on the line."

Louie scanned Gil's bookcase, counted the photos and softball trophies, looked at the Ping golf clubs in the corner. He had received this 'ass chewing' talk before, This time Gil's voice was at a higher pitch, and Louie noticed Gil's right hand shook.

"Mr. Roy has told me..," Gil's throat thickened and his voice froze.

Louie broke in, "I promise Gil. I'll change. I'll put in more effort . . . " He glanced to the shut door.

"Louie, I'm serious. If you don't change, you're gone."

Louie's shoulders slumped, "I'm sorry." He tilted his head and glanced at Gil's eyes long enough for Gil to see his glazed eyes, "OK?"

Gil didn't answer.

Louie stood, "Gil, I'm sorry. I'll do better." He turned for the door, and when Gil said nothing, Louie turned the knob, opened the door and left.

Gil sank deep into his chair and turned so his back was to the door.

Louie showed up early Friday for breakfast. It was the first time in weeks. Cecil and Tim both made the comment that he seemed back in his groove.

But something gnawed at Gil. He ate little. He looked sick. He said he did not sleep much and felt like he had an ulcer or something. He left to see a doctor.

Monday morning, instead of Zack's usual call to Gil, it was Mr. Roy, who phoned. "So how did it go with Louie?"

"I gave him one hell of a 'Dutch Uncle' talk." He waited for a response but there was only silence, so he continued, "I know I put the fear of the Lord in him."

"GIL! -- that's not what I want to hear!"

Gil hunched over and sat closer to his desk, "I talked to him. I thought . . . I mean he deserved one . . . "

"Gil! WHAT — MUST — BE — DONE?"

Gil's eyes searched the ceiling. "But . . . but . . ." He couldn't talk. All he could see was Mr. Roy's glass eye aimed at him.

"Damn, Gil, do it!" Mr. Roy slammed down the phone.

For the rest of the day, Gil waited for Louie. Bobbie called and left a message that Gil wanted to see him, but no response.

That night, Gil took out his phone several times to call Louie, but never dialed. Instead, he waited for Louie to call. The phone didn't ring.

On Tuesday, Louie strolled in at 11:15. Gil waved him into his office.

"Louie, shut the door and sit."

"I'm sorry I'm late this morning. I promise it'll be the last time," Louie said.

Gil turned over a document that was face down on his desk. "Louie, we'll pay you for 120 days. Start today to look for a job." Gil held the document until Louie was forced to take it. "This needs your signature." Gil held out a pen. "It will be better for you, if you resign rather than we fire you."

Louie looked at the pen, but didn't reach. Gil set it on the desk. Louie's hand shook so hard he laid the letter on the desk.

"Louie, we wish you the best. You'll find a job." Gil again offered him the pen. "You need to sign." Louie took the pen but had to steady his right hand with his left.

"If you get a quick job, you'll get 'double pay' for three months."

Louie's bloodshot eyes became watery, and he quit reading. He tried to swallow but could not. Gil's desk, golf clubs, photos all turned to blurred patches of color.

"Gil, are you serious?" he whispered.

"Sign the letter."

"Damn, Gil, why didn't you hit me in the back of the head?" He picked up the letter, signed it and slammed the pen on top.

Louie stared at the scribbled signature for a second, then stood to look at the picture of their softball team. He moved to the door, and squeezed the knob in hopes it was a dream. Without turning around, he said, "So it's over."

"Yes, Louie, your time here has ended."

"Fuck, Gil, why didn't you warn me?"

"I'm sorry."

Louie opened the door, but his hand froze on the knob.

"Louie, clean out your office and go home. It's for the best."

Louie half-turned toward Gil but still could not look at him, "See you."

He went to his desk, gathered things into a box, and left.

Bobbie picked a potted plant from her desk and followed fifteen feet behind him all the way to his car. They talked for a few minutes. She gave him the plant, and they hugged. She stood in the parking lot to watch until he drove out of sight.

Gil sat with his office door closed for a long time. He had met Louie in college, rented an apartment with him, personally recommended Louie to Mr. Roy. Now the office knew. His father knew. Most important, Mr. Roy knew. Gil had failed.

35

Success

"Good morning Bobbie!"

"Great necktie, Tim."

"Thanks. Glad you noticed."

"I like bright silk colors," Bobbie said.

Tim walked tall and proud, "I'm celebrating."

"Did you sign a lease?" Bobbie asked.

"Close."

"Who?"

"It's a regional office of Homeland Security."

Gil heard them and asked, "How much do they want?"

"Most of the sixth floor."

Gil slapped his hands, "Hot damn!"

"And they'll want more later." Tim said.

"Looks like Dad's golf games with a certain former senator will finally pay."

Tim looked at Gil, "What did he have to do with this?"

"You would be surprised."

"Gil, you should fill me in on things."

"Sometimes it is better not to know."

"It's always good to know the truth," Tim said.

"Focus on your job. We still have vacant space."

"Gil, in this economy they might stay that way."

Gil's eyes sharpened, "Tim, don't cast blame. We are all in this together."

"Don't blame me."

"It's all of us," Gil said.

"Whatever," Tim said.

36

The Incantation

A week later Tim got out of his car. It was cold. The morning air promised snow.

On most days, Tim parked out from other cars so he could get in a brisk walk as he approached the office. Today, he parked closer on the back side of the mall. He would walk through the mall instead.

The mall stores were not yet open, but a few managers were unlocking their doors. As Tim approached center court, he saw an old unshaven man in a tattered long coat. The man's hair looked as if it had been sucked by a rat. His boots were unlaced. When the man leaned over, Tim thought he was looking for coins in the fountain. The man raised a frayed green ledger, muttering something.

Fifty feet away a girl watched as she opened the gate for Footlocker. She was ready to run if the man looked her way.

"Where's security? Why haven't they come?" The man smelled like a wet dog. "Archie?"

The stranger chanted in a low monotone. "QUA-ER-E-VER-UM . . . RA-DIX-OM-NI-UM-MAL-OR-UM-EST-CU-PI-TAS."

The old man lifted his faded journal toward the fountain, bowed low as he chanted to his ghosts, "QUAE-REN-DA-PE-CU-NI-A-PRI-MUN-EST . . ."

Andre Falconi, came out of his store, "Archie's been here for ten minutes, I called security."

Tim turned to Falconi, "It's Archie?"

Falconi shrugged, "He needs help." Waved his hand in disgust and walked to his store.

When Tim turned back, Archie was face down on the floor. "Archie you OK?" Archie stood back up but continued to chant.

Tim turned to the office. Each click echoed faster as he walked.

Tim walked into Cecil's office. He was hunched over a spreadsheet. Tim waited for him to finish. Cecil glanced at Tim's shoes but said nothing. Tim sat in the office chair to wait.

After what seemed an eternity with no recognition, Tim whispered, "Cecil, we need to talk." Cecil hummed something, but continued to check off each number on the printed spreadsheet. "Cecil we need to talk."

Cecil ignored him.

Tim stood.

Cecil calculated.

Tim moved closer to the desk. "Archie has gone nuts in the mall."

Cecil held up his hand and hummed.

"Cecil, Archie's gone mad. He's chanting some witchcraft gibberish at the fountain."

Cecil finally put his pencil down, squished his eyes, adjusted his glasses and picked up another pencil.

"He's gone bonkers," Tim said.

Cecil didn't flinch.

Tim stared at Cecil.

Cecil finished another row.

"Cecil, this is insane!" Tim folded his arms. Bobbie came to the door, but Tim waved her away.

Finally, Cecil pulled a clean handkerchief from his desk drawer and cleaned his gold framed glasses. He wiped his hands, "Tim, they don't give a damn. They don't care about you or me. All they care about is their return on investment. If that's all they care about, it's all I care about." Cecil gave a strange weird sneer. "And, Tim, so should you."

37

The Big Refinance

Cecil and Tim followed Gil to his new Lexus in the parking lot.

"This will be quite a treat," Cecil said.

"It's has over four hundred horses under the hood," Gil said.

Cecil's fingers felt the smooth seat, "This leather smells rich."

Tim smiled, "It's from Corinthian pedigree cows."

"Did they give you matching Italian shoes?" Cecil asked.

They laughed.

"The engine makes my car sound like a tractor," Tim said.

Gil let them get the feel of the ride. "I've got some news. Mr. Roy wants to put Cypress Tree on the market. But we don't want anyone to know it's for sale."

"Yeah right," Tim said.

"Seriously, we don't want anyone to know," Gil said.

"How will he sell it without saying it is for sale?" Tim asked. "If we don't tell we'll never sell."

"That's just it. We never sell," Gil said, "We refinance."

"But the truth always escapes." Tim said.

"Not until we close," Gil said.

"We never sell," echoed Cecil.

"Why?" Tim asked.

"The new owners will want stability," Gil said. "The staff, maybe also the local merchants will fear any unknown owner."

"Some will think it's a chance to escape their lease," Cecil added.

Gil said, "That's what happened when we bought it. The old owner was local. He bragged he was going to make a mint when he sold. Tenants felt used and began to skip their rent. Each time Mr. Roy had more leverage to buy lower. He picked it up for a song."

"So why do you tell us?" Tim asked.

"Because when people come to check for the refinancing, you two will be key salesmen," Gil said. "Besides, refinancing says we must be making money."

"But Cypress Tree is dead in the water." Tim said.

"The point is, you sell profit potential," Gil said. "We always sell dreams not facts."

"They'll look at the books," Tim said.

Gil said, "People always want what they can't have."

"So Cypress Tree will be entertaining investors, but not for sale?" Tim asked.

"But we'll look at any offer." Gil said.

"Also called the best offer." Tim joked.

"Cecil, this means you don't tell anyone. Even Bobbie." Gil said.

"I understand."

"We sell sizzle."

For the next week, everyone was on a high state of alert for any visitors. First rumor was a major store coming with Mr. Roy. Pete had the housekeeping crew wash the plastic trees and dust store signs for spider webs.

However, no one showed.

After a few weeks, Tim questioned if any prospect would ever look at the property.

Cecil let slip at his bank board meeting that serious New York money would soon refinance the mall.

Though Zach Palm called and assured Cecil that wheels were moving, Tim saw no evidence. Cecil told Tim that Zack was Mr. Roy's 'go to man'. He was doing the actual search for someone to refinance. He said Mr. Roy used Zack for all kinds of projects. "He will wash his car if Mr. Roy asked."

He explained that Mr. Roy liked loyalty and trusted Zack with his most sensitive missions. "Zack is like a Las Vegas hotel 'glad-handler'. He's damn good at schmoozing."

One day, two young accountants showed up from a New York company. They were putting the financial package together to send to investor prospects. "It's like selling a piece of real estate," one of them said. "Only we sell the refinancing of the property. We spent a day in Kansas City and now must make an actual walk through."

"We can't look at pictures. They want to know it is real," the other said. "In Dayton, someone signed off for an apartment complex. The new owner discovered there were only 300 apartments. It was supposed to have 388."

"No one counted?" Tim asked.

"Even bankers take short cuts. Now we must check everything," said the little man. "They make us count the bricks if necessary."

A week later at Star's, Gil announced, "Dad called last night. He will be in early Monday with a Mr. Mord Doyle from Marionetti Enterprises."

Cecil and Tim rolled their eyes.

"Dad's known him for years."

"Is he the president?" Tim asked.

"No, but Mord is his left hand."

Their eyes waited for more.

"Marionetti's a small investment company that puts money in real estate," Gil said.

"Never heard of them," Tim said.

"You don't run in those circles. Dad said they are big enough." Gil sipped his coffee, "One other thing. I will be out next week."

"Where you going?"

"Florida. Mr. Roy wants me to check out some of Marionetti's properties. If we do a deal, we might take a trade."

"So what do we need to do?" Cecil asked.

"Dad will take the lead. You can answer questions. Be honest, but don't volunteer anything." Gil looked at Cecil, "Make sure Archie takes one of his month long visits to the psycho ward."

Cecil took a paper napkin to write a note to himself.

"And make sure trash is picked up outside," continued Gil.

Cecil wrote another note.

Zack Palm flew in from Kansas City and met Mord Doyle from Florida, then drove to Fenton. At exactly 11:00 A. M. Monday morning they walked in the door.

Mord's leathered skin draped on his face. His hands were callused. His right fingers stained with nicotine. A pin striped suit hung on him like he had lost weight.

Zack acted like they knew each other for years. Mord said he grew up with Mr. Roy in Atlantic City.

When Mord went to the restroom, Zack said, "Mr. Roy knew the Doyle family, but doesn't remember Mord. He thinks Mord may have been a caddy at their country club." Zack looked to make sure he was out of ear shot. "Mr. Roy says Mord's father was found dead under mysterious circumstances."

"Murder?"

Zack shrugged.

"Gil said you have known him for years."

"When I was in my twenties, he lived in the same building I did."

"Funny how small the world is," Tim said.

"Never burn bridges."

"Mord acts like you are best friends."

"Until we make a deal, I am."

Tim smiled.

"That's what sales are about, old memories that help make a new deal today."

"It's all about today's deal," Tim said.

"Tim, don't burn bridges. Old friends can become future prospects."

The four spent the first day nosing around the property. By Tuesday afternoon, Cecil started taking turns with Tim to babysit them. Mord smoked, so he spent a good bit of time checking the roof or the parking lot.

Late Tuesday night Zack called Cecil at home. Mr. Roy wanted him to meet with JPMorgan in New York, Wednesday morning. Mord would be left with Cecil and Tim.

Mord spent Wednesday, and most of Thursday locked in Cecil's office. When Cecil opened his door, smoke bellowed out. Cecil would run to find some file, quickly return behind the closed door. Except for a short lunch, Tim never saw them.

At 4:15 on Thursday, Mord Doyle appeared in Tim's office. He asked Tim if they could meet in the bar at the Plantation Motel.

Mord looked around, then said to Tim loud enough for Cecil to hear. "That damn Cecil, he's an encyclopedia. I tried to find one thing he could not answer. He knows it all."

Cecil popped out of his office to ask Bobbie, "What did he say?"

Mord smiled, "I asked Tim out for a drink. After you danced around the books all day, I have to relax."

Cecil rolled his eyes. When he saw Mord's back was to him, he fisted his right hand and gave the Italian 'up yours' response.

Mord heard the slap of Cecil's arm. Under his breath added, "Jackass." He lit another cigarette. "Tim, I'll see you at 5:30. If you want to bring Cecil, bring him."

As soon as Mord left for his hotel, Tim went to Cecil's office, "How did things go?"

"He drove me crazy."

Pete Gravel walked in with a box fan. "You want me to spray some of that orange smelling spray?" Pete asked.

"Gawd no!" Cecil looked at Tim, "Zack did not get called away. He ran from Mord."

Tim smiled, "He does get old, but he holds the gold."

Cecil picked up a section of the day's paper to fan the air, "If I had a gun, I would shoot him before he kills me." He adjusted the box fan.

Tim said, "We're meeting for drinks. Why don't you join us?"

Cecil looked over the top of his gold reading glasses. "No. Not NO, but Hell NO! He's a damn walking chimney! Besides, he wants you to verify what I told him."

"What did you say?"

"I showed him the books, went over leases and pitched the Zack line – we need cash. With it we would be able to redo the parking lot, attract some great new tenants. You know, the regular bull."

"You ought to join us."

"No, when I drink I say too much." Cecil paused, "I always get in trouble when I drink."

"It's going to be a long evening if I have to drink with him by myself. If you come it'll be a party. I know you love parties."

"Three's a crowd. Besides, I hope I never see him again."

Tim laughed.

Cecil held his arms as if he was begging, "Tim, please get him out of town before he kills me."

38

Raven's Den Meeting

Tim parked under the pecan trees in front of the Plantation Motel. Last year the owners had remodeled again, but never returned it to one of the finest motels in the South. Years ago it was a hidden political hot spot.

Each cabin had a porch out front with two rocking chairs. Most guests entered through the side door in the covered car port.

It was one of the first places in Georgia to be called a 'Motel', the first to have a television in their lounge, the first with a color television in every room, and the first direct dial telephones.

Salesmen who stayed three days, received a cash refund of one day. The ability to bill the company and pocket a third of it in cash kept the motel full most nights.

When Tim got out of the car, he glanced to where Lex's wife had rear-ended Lex's car.

Tim thought, "I need to instill urgency, so they will act fast." He took deep slow breaths. "What if they offer me a job. I must be careful not to oversell. If I go to work for them, I don't want my words to come back to haunt me."

A salesman is a hunter. He goes where the prey feels secure. He sets his trap and waits. A salesman with crafted words and patience can win. Time is always on the side of those who can wait. But Malifer didn't have the leisure of time.

"How can I get Mord excited? How can I catch this fish?"

It was 5:35 when Tim walked to the lobby. On the right was The Raven's

Nest. Mildew pinched Tim's nose, but the twang of a jukebox pulled him into where deal makers once squeezed the weak.

Mord sat alone at a table past the juke box. His sleeves rolled up to show a tattoo on his left forearm. His hand waved at Tim.

A lone thin blond waitress behind the bar, asked as Tim passed, "What do you want honey?

"Gin and tonic."

From across the room, Mord held up his empty glass, "Mary Lu, another for me." Cigarette smoke floated through the rays from the jukebox.

Mary Lu filled two glasses. Tim brought them past vacant tables.

"My treat," Tim said.

"Thanks, but I hate to be indebted."

"Looks as if we own the juke box."

Mord raised his glass in a toast. "Here's to a win-win deal."

"You think there's a chance?"

"It depends. Roy Parino is a great man," Mord said.

"They're all good people."

Mord went over his review of the property, more to remind himself what he would report. He gave the history how he started to work for Ricco Marionetti. Finally, he asked, "You know this 'refinancing' might turn into an outright purchase. How would you feel about that?"

"I want to see enough cash, so we can turn around."

"What about the local staff?"

"They're okay."

"Cecil?"

"He knows people."

"He bothers me." Mord said.

"Why?"

"He's not a manager."

"He knew how to get the mayor to help us, isn't that management?"

"I think he's weak. His secretary, she's too horsey for me."

"Bobbie? That's Cecil's twin sister."

"She mothers' him; I thought she was his wife. I can't believe Roy would let a sister work in the same office - besides . . ."

"Besides what?"

"Blood will kill profit." Mord said.

"Nepotism, the evil a family always finds an excuse for," Tim said.

Mord's eyes nodded, "Blood is strong."

"Mord, be careful. Gil, Zack and Mr. Roy don't like her, but she's still around. She's not that bad."

Mord leaned on the table with both arms, "Tim, let's get to the bottom line. Zack said they want to refinance, but led me to believe it could be bought. Cecil talked only of refinance. Will they sell this mall?

"I suppose so, for the right price."

"Or is Roy on an ego trip?"

"What do you mean?"

"Some want to know what their toys are worth."

"That's what makes Antiques Roadshow."

Mord waited.

Tim sipped his gin, "I think Mr. Roy would sell."

"Why?"

Tim put his drink down, and bit his index finger while he thought. "Cash is tight, sobering tight."

"I saw that in the books."

"It's a fact. Mr. Roy wants out."

"Do you see panic?"

Tim wouldn't look in Mord's eyes.

Mord asked again, "How tight is money?"

"How can I know that?"

"Have they laid off staff?"

"No, Cecil got our line of credit raised twice at his bank. Cecil's good. He's on the bank's board and has some kind of control with them. Although he can't do it much longer."

Mord took a long drag on the cigarette and let the smoke crawl out and around his face. "There are a lot of reasons why people are on boards."

"His dad started the bank."

"So they have family money?"

Tim thought a second, "Maybe. He plays a great shell game. Pay part, pay late, pay with an unsigned check. If he gets a bill for $912, he'll pay $9.12. I give him credit - he always comes up with new ways to stall."

"Roy has money."

Tim whispered, "But I don't think he has cash. He even put his art collection in hock to keep us afloat."

"So there is panic."

"Say a frenzy to sell, not panic."

Mord's eyes watched as Tim wove his tale. "Some want to sell another property, maybe one of Malifer's smaller properties to get cash."

"Why don't they do that?"

"Some think it has merit."

Mord nodded, "I think it might."

Tim shook his head, "But at a meeting we had at the home office, Mr. Roy made a snap decision."

Mord slapped the table, "He always was impulsive. Il papa dicit, finito."

"What does that mean?"

"The old man's spoken. It's over."

"Mord, you're a real Renaissance man."

"It's a quote from Ricco's father."

Tim smiled, "Mr. Roy has these knee-jerk reactions, but he'll cool down and become rational."

Mord got up to put some change in the jukebox. When he sat back down, they both sipped their drinks and listened to Willie Nelson sing "Blue Eyes Crying in the Rain."

Tim said, "I wish he would come to his senses soon."

Mord looked straight at Tim. "Why do you think the mall can survive?"

Tim started counting reasons on his fingers. "It's a damn good location. It's on the bypass. The downtown merchants don't trust each other. The mall is near a college. It is far enough from other malls. But we don't have . . ."

"Cash?" Mord said.

"We don't have Mr. Roy. When the head man wants out, it's over. Even if Elvis came in the door." Tim watched Mord's eyes, "Mord, when I played football, the most fun was to pick up a ball someone fumbled and make a touchdown." Tim saw Mord's eye spark, "But our coach wants to quit."

"That's Roy! If he couldn't win, he always folded the cards. He could never bluff."

"I think you're right."

Mord took a drag then asked, "Does Roy's brother still own an art gallery in Palm Beach?"

"I didn't know he had a brother."

"Roy and his wife were investors in it."

"I know they like art."

"Big time."

"Why did you bring up his brother?"

"Ricco collects art."

Mord smiled, and his head swayed. He rubbed his tattoo and started to wave his drink, "Tim, I want to grab that football and run! We'll put flags on the roof, maybe rent one of those big searchlights. And shine it all night!"

"Now you're talking!"

"We'll need to pave the parking lot."

"It's a mine field. I wish we had money to patch the pot holes."

Mord's scotch along with the music pulled at his mind to slow his tongue. Tim saw it was time to fish.

"How did Ricco get into business?"

"When he finished at Wharton, he did books for his father. When his father died, the clients were his."

"What was the business?"

"Family. Extended family investors."

"Like a family stockbroker?"

"Yeah, they don't trust banks, so they set up their own. The uncles moved over after the second world war to South America, Belize, Mexico and the States."

"Ricco's their private banker?"

Mord nodded, "He's the smartest man I know, a genius on tax laws. He has connections in the Cayman Islands, the Cook Islands, Costa Rica and Belize, even on the Isle of Man."

"Where do you fit in?"

"Special projects. Sometimes I clean up a mess. Sometimes I investigate people or research investments like Cypress Tree. In between, I deep sea fish or work with my brother in Tampa. He's in construction."

"So you are an independent contractor?" Tim asked.

Mord nodded, "I only work for Ricco. I know how to look for problems when he buys a project. From the roof to the basement and the books in the office. I'm not a CPA anymore, but I can read figures."

"Like the old TV show?"

"What's that?" Mord asked.

"Have Gun Will Travel."

"Well, I don't have a gun, but I get the job done."

"Does Ricco make money?"

"Making money is easy. What's hard is to keep it." Mord lowered his voice, "And if it doesn't have respect, Ricco gives it respect."

"Is it dirty?"

"Money's never dirty, money's green. Some want bribes that if you don't pay they call it dirty. Ricco doesn't like bribes even when called taxes. He's a tax law expert and pays as little as he legally can."

Tim said, "So he invests the family money."

"Tim, most world leaders do anything for power. Ricco sells, trades, reinvests the family's assets. His money's green, and clean."

Tim nodded, so Mord continued, "If you don't know your business --BAM!" Mord slapped his hands, "Some government thug will steal it."

"The big club takes the gold." Tim said.

"Governments have the big guns. Taxes are a racket run by bureaucrats."

Tim smiled because Mord sounded like Lamar. "And Ricco protects from taxes," Tim said.

"Tim, the United States is the hardest place to protect wealth from tax thieves."

"How does he do it?"

"He keeps profits offshore. Plays with them so their value can't be tracked. But still he must bring some cash onshore to deliver payments to his uncles from time to time."

Tim smiled, "If I was one of the family I would want to know I could trust the man with the keys to the bank."

"I assure you he can be trusted."

"If it was my money, I would be afraid the banker would, you know — would fudge fees. Who would know?"

Mord took a sip of his drink. "Tim, Ricco never takes a fee. They are family. Wall Street is where the crooks are."

"Why does he want the mall?"

"We need to rearrange our portfolio. Cypress Tree might be today's solution."

"I don't get it."

"Bureaucrats are rats. They go back to where they found the last cheese." Mord's eyes glowed in the dim light, "Roy has no link to our previous deals."

"So the feds won't snoop."

Mord stood up, "I'm going to the restroom, order us another round." He bent down and grabbed Tim's tie. "Tim, Malifer must - do - our - deal."

Tim waved to the waitress. She pulled away from the counter TV and came to the table. "Your friend okay? He's had a lot to drink."

"He's fine. He doesn't need to drive."

"Another round?" she asked.

Tim motioned for her to come closer. "Give him another, but I have to drive. Make mine a 7-Up with a lime." Tim looked at her name tag, "Mary Lu, I need your help. Mord works for a Northern company and wants to get information out of me. If I give it to him, I'll get fired. Whenever I order, no matter what I say, give me 7-Up with a lime and charge for a gin and tonic."

"So that's why he gave me $20 to double all your drinks."

"Now you know."

She put her hand on his shoulder, "Call me Belle Boyd."

"Thanks, I'll tell General Lee of your help."

She asked, "Another round for both of you?"

Mord came back, picked up his drink and walked over to the jukebox. Cigarette smoke slithered out his mouth to encircle him. When Patsy Kline started with 'Crazy', he returned to his chair.

"Tim, I'm not sure they will want our deal."

"Damn, they either do or they don't."

"How do I know?" asked Mord.

"It's like meeting a girl in a bar. If you make her an offer, she might say 'no' but won't let you leave."

Mord's eyes flashed. His tongue licked his thin smile. "I only have to keep talking."

Tim said, "I know one thing, the bank wants to steal it."

"Our deal will be unique," Mord said.

"How?"

"Can the hotel be part of it?"

"That's no problem."

"Good, but Marionetti needs something in return."

"He will make a ton of money."

"Is cash their bottom line?"

"We need cash."

"Marionetti needs to rearrange assets."

"Like trade properties? You need to talk to Mr. Roy about that."

Mord didn't move. His eyes only reflected the darkness behind Tim. "I'm going to show you how our deal will work." Mord took a deep drag, stood and grabbed three glasses and a candle from an empty table. "Think of our table as the U. S. That table is offshore - napkins are businesses, the glasses and candles are assets, now watch."

His hands flew like a card impresario in Times Square, "We'll trade this property for these two offshore." He set down a new napkin. "This one . . .," he put out his cigarette and lifted up the ashtray, "for cash." He reached for two glasses, "in exchange these two . . . then this one for these."

He laid out two more napkins. "This company is in Belize and this one in the Cook Islands." He picked up two beer bottles and set one on each. "These are now new companies. We'll trade this company in Belize to a company in the Cook Islands." He moved bottles, glasses and ashtrays from one napkin to another. He threw an empty napkin on his shoulder. "We dissolved that company." He picked up an ashtray full of cigarette butts, "Now we take this cash in the Cayman Islands and trade for a horse farm in Kentucky."

Mord Doyle was the culmination of every greasy-haired-fast-talking-carnival-barker Tim had ever seen on Bourbon Street. He lifted napkins, moved bottles, combined ashtray 'cash' until he finally said, "Now we trade for Cypress Tree." Mord gave Tim the ashtray filled with cigarette butts and took Tim's half empty 'Cypress Tree Mall' glass and sat it on Ricco's napkin.

Mord picked up the empty napkins, clapped his hands to show his magician's bare palms. "Fait accompli."

Tim sat mesmerized but reached for his glass of 7-up. "That's the most complex version of three-card-Monty I've ever seen," Tim said.

"It will be unusual, but it's legal. Governments make deals complicated. Most people give up and pay taxes. Ricco knows paths around taxes."

"All that to evade taxes?"

"Not evade, avoid! It's illegal to evade, but everyone has a right to avoid unnecessary taxes."

Tim bit his lip. Everything Hitler did was legal. "Loopholes," he said out loud.

"You can call them loopholes, but they're in the law, and they are legal. Maybe inserted to help a specific friend of a senator, or a relative back in their home state. Even so, available to all. Ricco only takes advantage of what they pass."

"I'm numb." Tim said.

"But now you know."

Mord sat down and waited.

Tim's thoughts screamed to express themselves, but silence was now his strongest friend.

Mord's hand started to swing. His arm swayed. His head bobbed, soon his whole body moved. "Families will come to see what all the action's about – the lights, the flags."

Tim asked, "How much will Ricco pay?"

"Enough." Mord held up both their glasses and ordered another.

"Tim, sometimes things require blind thought."

"Blind thought?"

"Religion calls it faith. People call it trust. I call it 'blind thought'. Sometimes with friends you have to look the other way – to be blind."

A waiter from across the street came in with their food. Mord started to eat as if his was the last Reuben sandwich on earth.

Tim said, "You're sure it's legal? Each step is clean?"

"Why do you think tax laws have so many pages?"

Tim was silent.

"It's to explain the exceptions." Mord said.

"Ricco simply follows the steps?"

"Word for word, because in the words are the secrets."

A light went off in Tim's eyes, "Their meaning hides the law's true aim to give exceptions."

"Now you understand. That's also why wording of our contract will be so important. Each iota must be precise."

"But is it legal?" Tim asked.

"If the intent is legal, and the words are legal, then the act must be legal."

"Two rights can't make a wrong."

"We'll exchange property in several countries. Ricco will sign documents to avoid each country's taxes. And he's smart enough to do it all under the radar." Mord leaned back, and his leathered tattoo glowed in the neon light of the juke box.

"Mord, tell me more about his clients."

"They're cousins and uncles, all business people who don't want attention."

"Business people appreciate attention."

"You're thinking of the Buffalo Bills, and the Donald Trumps. The loud mouths, the circus acts."

"So who are his clients?" Tim asked.

"They're hunters. They make big money, but when others come in their field, they leave for greener pastures."

"They don't like competition?"

"Cash is like smoke. It attracts people to things that aren't their business."

The juke box became silent. Tim looked at his watch. "Mord, its time I go. But to answer your question, if your deal is legal and Malifer ends with cash, I think they'll do it."

"Good." Mord raised up both thumbs.

Tim went to Mary Lu, paid the bill, and slipped twenty bucks in her hand and whispered, "Thanks Belle Boyd."

She answered loud enough for Mord to hear, "Do you want me to call a cab?"

"I'll be okay," Tim said.

Mord sat in the dark.

Mary Lu walked over, "Honey, you need anything?"

"No, I have an early flight."

"It's time to kick you out."

"Mary Lu, the world is changing. I don't know how many more of these deals I can put together. Computers are two-edged swords."

"Yes, sir," She put her hand on the back of a chair. He motioned for her to sit, and she did.

"I used to do business with cash. Now it's all done on computers."

"It's a different world," she said.

"My memory's getting fuzzy. Now I have to check everything three times."

"We all change."

He offered her a cigarette. She accepted.

39

Good News - Bad News

MONDAY MORNING

"Gil's back in town!" Tim said as Gil walked up to the table with a big smile, "Good news! It looks like we did it! Maybe it was good I was not here."

"What have you heard?" Cecil asked.

Ruby poured coffee.

"Mord told Dad he thought it is a good deal. They were on the phone three times over the weekend. It's looking good."

"Great!" Tim said as he gave both a "high five."

"Ricco Marionetti will meet Mr. Roy in person. He has some needs."

Tim asked, "Can we tell everybody?"

"No, not yet. Wait until we get the letter of intent signed."

"How long?" Tim asked.

"Ricco will visit Kansas City Wednesday to hammer out details. Once a letter of agreement is signed, attorneys will write a contract. We must get our lenders to sign off. That will take another week." Gil threw up both hands, "Four weeks, six at most."

"That's not fast." Cecil said, "The New York bank may try to foreclose."

"Once we show a letter of intent, they'll wait."

Tim said, "I think Ricco might be under more pressure than us."

"I can't imagine that," Gil said. "We've started the paperwork. He only needs to get his side to approve."

"I thought he was the man," Tim said.

"He is; that's why Mord says it'll go through," Gil said. "We have bankers. He has clients, but he's the man."

Tim nodded, "Mord said he's a genius."

"Well anyway, we're close. In fact, Tim didn't you want a break?"

"A few days would be great," Tim said.

FRIDAY MORNING

"Ruby, where's Gil?" Cecil asked.

"How do I know? All week he's been here early. Today he musta' slept in." She poured their coffee. "Maybe he went to get a haircut. He needs one."

"He could afford one," Tim said.

"I bet he stopped by a Realtor to put his house on the market," Cecil said.

"I guess we'll both be moving."

"Not me." Cecil placed his palm down on the table, "If the new company doesn't want me, I know enough people."

Ruby brought their breakfast, "Mr. Tim, you have your trip planned?"

"We're off to the beach."

"Pensacola?" Cecil asked.

"No, Aimee found a Bed and Breakfast north of Jacksonville."

Cecil pointed out the window. "Here comes Gil. He looks as if he lost his wallet or something."

Tim stretched his neck, "He's dragging."

Gil went straight to Ruby. "A cup of coffee, please."

"That's all? You must be sick."

"That's all." He sat and waited for her to leave.

Tim asked, "Damn, Gil, what's the matter?"

Gil whispered, "Marionetti crawfished."

No one said a word.

"Dad said he flew to Kansas City with Mord. They spent Wednesday on details. Things were fine. Everyone shook on the deal." Gil paused, "But last night Mord called Dad and said the deal was dead." Gil's bloodshot eyes watered, "I couldn't sleep after Dad called me."

"What happened?" asked Cecil.

Gil shrugged, "Mord's to get back with Dad after he talks to Ricco."

"Damn," Tim said.

"It's a pisser all right," Gil said.

Cecil asked, "So what will I do now?"

Gil raised his empty hands, "I guess we'll keep plugging. Hope for the best. Find someone else. Hell, I don't know."

Ruby came up, "Lordy what's happened to yall? You look like you've been slapped with a dead fish."

40

Mr. Marionetti

TUESDAY MORNING

"Mr. Lichten, this is Ricco Marionetti. Mordie Doyle said I shoulda call you. I'm a flying into Atlanta tomorrow, can you a picka me upa?"

"Of course, when will you arrive?"

"Hartsfield, tomorrow morning at a 9:45 from Miami, Gate A-17. Will thata be a problem?"

"Not at all, will you have luggage?"

"Only a small carry-on."

"Great, I'll meet you as you come up the escalator into the main terminal. I'll be there at the top with your name on a sign."

"If youa don't mind, puta 'Malifer' on the sign. You'll recognize me. I use a cane."

Tim hung up the phone, took a deep breath, "Bobbie, where's Gil?"

"He's not in, but Cecil said he would be back in five minutes."

Tim called Gil's phone, "Gil, Ricco Marionetti just called me! We have to pick him up at the airport tomorrow morning!"

"Tim, call Dad! He called me early to catch a plane to Louisville. Things are popping! I have to look at two more properties."

"You're not in town?"

"My plane leaves in ten minutes. Call Dad right now!"

"Shit."

"Tim, I'm glad you called. We need to talk, hold on — I'm on with Roy." In a few seconds, Zack was back. "Thanks, things are back on line. Ricco

Marionetti will call you."

"You're late. He just did."

"What'd he say?"

"You didn't tell me 'he'sa froma the olda country'."

"He's not but many of his investors are. So he saves the accent."

"Well, he'll be here tomorrow."

"He has talked to his clients. Mord says all but one is for the deal. The problem is the client against it lives in Fenton. Can you believe that?"

"Who?"

"It doesn't matter, but that's the glitch. It's one of those things. Bad luck always happens in your own back yard."

"You don't know who the guy is?"

"Mord says they must have the deal. They need it bad. So Ricco wants to see Cypress Tree for himself."

"I talked to Gil. He's on a flight to Kentucky. Should you be here?" Tim asked.

"Mr. Roy said no. Ricco will think we're too anxious. They might be playing to get us to panic."

"So the pressure's on me."

"I told Mord the bank had raised their offer. Only thing, Mr. Roy liked a couple of sweeteners Ricco threw in last Wednesday."

"You have a backup?"

"Tim, we have nothing."

"Maybe it's good you won't be here. You're too negative."

"Pick him up, show him around, take him to lunch but get him back on the plane with a smile on his face."

"Wham, bam!" Tim said.

"Wham, bam! Out of Dodge. For gods' sakes don't let him start to think. We want him to see it, say 'it's a deal', and leave. The paperwork's back underway."

"Anything else?"

Zack paused, "Good luck."

"Well thanks for not putting me under any pressure."

"Tim, you'll do fine."

He hung up. The cool rush of adrenalin ran up his spine.

Tim looked up Chet Quinn's phone number at the newspaper in Louisville. He had not talked to him in months.

"Chet, Tim Lichten. How are things?"

"Son of a gun! I told my wife it was about time that you changed jobs. Why is it I only hear from you when you change jobs?"

"I'm not this time. I need information on a company."

"So you might be looking?"

"No, honest, I will tell you more when I can. You know how it is."

"What's the name?"

"Marionetti Enterprises of the Cayman Islands. That's spelled: M-a-r-i-o-n-e-t-t-i. The owner's a Ricco Marionetti. There is also a Mord Doyle of Tampa. They're into banking and real estate. That's all I know."

"Give me an hour."

In about two hours Chet called back, "Tim, your Ricco Ladro Marionetti lives in Palm Beach. He has an office above a small art gallery on Worth Avenue. Marionetti Enterprises is registered in the Cayman's, but the address is an attorney's office. As far as we can tell the company has no real assets in the Caymans. Ricco is also on the board of Bank of Moddey Dhoo Ltd., on the Isle of Man."

"Between Ireland and England?"

"Right. His father's name was Genovese Giuseppe d'Marionettini. They shortened it when they came from the old country. Ricco was top of his class at Wharton. Degrees in Law and Accounting. His uncle is Sal Palmisano of Tampa."

"Wait a minute, is that the Tampa Sal Palmisano?"

"That's him."

Tim turned pale.

Chet continued, "Sal had a brother, Nanto, who moved to Kansas City. Another brother Giuseppe, controlled gambling from Memphis to Atlanta."

"So Ricco is related to Sal?" Tim asked.

"But there's no record of Ricco dealing with Sal or his brothers."

"I still don't like the connection."

"There's more. Several relatives were deported. My source at the FBI says they lost track of a couple of others. Your Ricco controls some family finances, which seem to be on the up and up. The Feds still watch him, but I couldn't find out why."

"An entrepreneurial family."

"I also had her look up Mord Doyle. His real name is Mordimer Doyle. He is a part-time contractor in Tampa. No police reports in last ten years except one drunk driving charge. Got his CPA but went to prison for murder. He was pardoned a few years ago."

"Is that it?"

"Well, one more thing."

"Lay it on me."

"You caught me at the right time. At the end of the week, I'm taking a position in New Orleans."

"With the Picayune? I thought they were laying off people."

"No, working with the Corps of Engineers, to improve their image. They have been hammered in the budget."

"You, the last investigative reporter alive?"

"I do what I do."

"We all do."

"Believe me, the money's better than writing facts."

"You are going back to where we went to school. Damn, wish it was me."

"Come down for Mardi Gras."

"When you go to the Camellia Grill, have the cheesecake. Tell Owen I said 'hello'."

"Who's he?"

"He is a waiter there. He'll remember you from college."

"I'll do it."

"Chet, thanks a million."

WEDNESDAY MORNING

Tim spotted his target with a cane as he limped off the escalator. He was 5' 2", in his late sixties but with pitch black hair and gold-framed glasses. He wore a tailored dark pinstriped suit, starched shirt with a maroon tie. His shoes looked handmade.

When he saw Tim's sign, he nodded and came straight toward him.

"Mr. Lichten? Thank you fora meeting me. I have a plane at 4:15. Willa that be gooda or shall I make a later flight? Ifa we get done early, I can leave at 2:10."

"That will be too early, Mr. Marionetti."

Tim slipped into his routine of inquiry. He would ask a question, listen for answers, ask another. Ricco Marionetti deftly slid past answers to ask his own questions and Tim responded.

In the car, Ricco opened a slim alligator briefcase. Tim saw only a Wall Street Journal, a phone and hotel stationary with notes. Ricco took out the notes.

Ricco's questions focused on the mall's hidden defects that Tim might know. Roof problems? Is there asbestos? What prospects did Tim have for tenants?

Tim focused on how he had organized a visit to all area desirable tenants. He told how they were able to get three state leases and two federal agencies in the office tower. He tried to throw in humor when he could.

Tim turned the car left onto Green Ave and drove past tree covered mansions by the college.

"We're now two miles from the mall, but Malifer has never targeted these students." Tim turned to double back and skip the blighted area. He wanted to drive Chestnut Boulevard to downtown.

"We were able to get in the Enterprise Zone drawn down this Boulevard."

"Mordie told me." His head turned to see a large home. "And both sides of the street are not in it, only di mezzo?"

"That's right."

"Did the signatura costa lot?"

"No."

At the mall, Tim drove the outside perimeter of the parking lot. He parked in front of the main entrance so Mr. Marionetti could take a few photographs.

A long black Bentley drove up next to him. The passenger window opened.

"Ricco, I have something for Griselda."

The dark-haired man handed Ricco a package with a few words.

When they drove off, "Thata was Angelo and hisa wife, Salma. I told them I wasa coming to look at the mall. He brought me a present for my wife."

"I didn't know you had family here."

"He's been here a few years. He a didn't wanta us to buya the mall."

"Why not?"

"He doesn't want other investors to think he pushed for Cypress Tree." He looked at Tim, "He'sa my problem. I think we can do it."

They parked closer to the mall's main entrance and walked inside.

"Is the mall always thisa clean?"

"What do you mean?" Tim asked.

"No spider webs." He pointed up to a store sign, "Looks gooda."

Tim smiled, "Always."

In the office, Cecil lauded the ivory dragon on his cane. Then Cecil pulled out his grandfather's cane.

Ricco ran his fingers over the carved fox face as if he had been handed a rare lost violin. "Thisa carved in the Black Forest, at least four hundred years ago."

Cecil's eyes widened. "I knew it was old, but didn't know it was that old."

"Mid sixteen hundreds I woulda guess."

Cecil said, "If you like this you should see the metal craftwork on the old war axe I have at home."

"My next trip I will make time to see it. I love old world craft."

At 3:00 they left Cecil and Tim made the dash with Ricco to the airport.

When he pulled into the drop-off Tim asked, "Will you need anything else?"

"No, I don't thinka so. Don't worry about Angelo. He didn't want the family to blame him, if it goes bad.

Ricco Marionetti opened the door to get out, and turned to ask, "Tim, if we buy, we may wanta you to stay with us for a while. Do you have an interest?""

Tim said, "It depends."

"We'll talk after closing."

"I'll be waiting."

When they shook hands, Ricco Marionetti put his left hand on top of

Tim's. It was the first time Tim noticed he had no left thumb.

"Mordie will be in touch."

With Ricco dispatched, Tim called Zack. "He's on the way home – wham bam – its over. It went well."

"Do you think he'll sign?"

"Absolutely," Tim said.

"Well, I guess we wait. I'll tell Mr. Roy." Zack still on the phone, started to talk to someone else. "Tell them to play through – I'm on the phone." His voice came close to the phone again. "I'll tell Gil, he is here with me."

"Is he near the phone? Can I speak to him?"

"Sure, Gil, Tim wants to talk with you. He says Ricco was positive."

"Hello, Tim, so it went well?"

"Couldn't be better. I thought you were in Kentucky."

"I am. Dad also flew in. We are checking out some real estate now."

"Gil, you know I planned to take off this Thursday and Friday."

"What about it?"

"I wanted to make sure it was still okay."

"Tim, tell you what, take Monday and Tuesday also. You deserve it. You'll have your phone won't you?"

"Sure."

"Good, see you next Wednesday."

"Thanks."

The Hunting Dog

41

The Recess

Tim woke as Aimee snuggled closer to him, "Good morning."

"Are the kids awake?"

"It's going to be fun to smell the ocean."

"Yeah."

"You tossed all night," Aimee said.

Tim rolled over, "What if they offer me a job?"

"If they give you more money, why not?"

"I don't know them."

"You didn't know Malifer."

Tim looked at the ceiling. "I need to think about it."

"You'll have time at the beach."

"I wish I could see the whole picture."

"We live but once."

"I know, but it's how that worries me."

"The kids are excited. If you have anything in mind, you better hurry. They'll be awake in a minute."

"That sounds like a hint."

"You wouldn't know a hint if it hit your head."

"Did you tell the hotel we want to stay two more days?"

"Yes, they said fine. The place looks neat."

"Where is it again?"

"Amelia Island."

Junior knocked on the door, "Mom, when will we leave?"

"As soon as we are all dressed." She heard steps run upstairs and a bathroom door slam.

Tim opened the bedroom to shout, "We will see alligators!" He closed the door to turn around, but a thousand pins stabbed his side. "Ouch, damn," He slumped on the bed. "My shingles are back."

"Let me see." Aimee looked at the row of red spots on his lower back, "Looks like it. I thought you only got them once."

"Damn, it hurts."

"I think we still have medicine." Aimee shuffled through her collection of outdated prescriptions.

"I'll be glad when the sale closes."

"What's the worry? You'll have a job."

Junior shouted, "Mom, I've put the 'nocklers in the car."

"It's bi-noculars. Make your bed." She heard feet run again.

Aimee turned the shower on, so Tim raised his voice. "I want to get away."

SATURDAY AFTERNOON

"Tim, this is 'Chicago' Mike, can you talk?"

"Hey, Mike guess where I am? Getting on a boat in the Okefenokee Swamp on an alligator hunt!"

"Sounds like you are desperate for tenants!"

"Free time with the family."

"Should I call later?" Mike said.

"No, not at all. The boat doesn't leave for ten minutes."

"Papa wants to look for a building in Georgia that could make a good factory. You know of anything? About 10,000 sq. feet in an area we can get rehab funds."

"There are several in Fenton. The mayor has an interest in a couple I know."

"Good, he could help us get federal funds."

"He controls the Enterprise Zone."

"What's that?"

"An area where you get put to the head of the list."

"Great, find out what you can. When will you be back in town?"

"Wednesday, I'll get you details, but is this a real deal or a game?"

"All life's a game, Tim."

"That's why I am afraid."

"Get me some info. We will talk next week."

"I'll see what I can do."

WEDNESDAY MORNING

Tim was at the office so early that he used his key to get in. He was on his second cup of coffee before Bobbie arrived.

"Boy, you are bright-eyed and bushy tailed this morning," she said. "Did you have a good trip?"

"It was great! What happened while I was gone?"

"Well the sale has Cecil in a tizzy."

"Sale? I thought we were refinancing," Tim said.

"Cecil let it out, but don't tell him I told you. He thinks he's in for a killing."

"Why's that?" Tim asked.

"He thinks this new company will beg him to stay with them. Maybe even give him a big contract."

"He had better be careful."

"Cecil thinks his knowledge is gold."

Tim shook his head, "A little knowledge is dangerous. He had better watch his back, or he could get cut out."

"You can't tell him that," she said. Tim nodded in agreement. Bobbie asked, "Why are you here so early?"

"I woke up ready to chop wood, so I came in early. Once here, I realize I have to wait for people to arrive." He held up several slips of calls to return. "Do you know what Paul Daniel at the home office needs?"

"He is the attorney handling the contract. Cecil talked to him several times a day."

"Is the paperwork done?"

She shrugged. "How do I know?"

Pete Gravel came in to pick up the trash from each wastebasket. "Mif Bobbie, Mr. Cecil didn't 'tred the paper as he normally do."

"Take it. It's trash that will be burned anyway."

"Good morning Pete," Tim said.

Pete smiled, to show a missing tooth. "Did'ja have a good 'stime?"

"It was heaven, Pete, pure heaven."

"Been suits here in'pectin' for Mr. Mord."

"Maybe they will give us some money, so we can paint the place."

"Maybe, I can get a new truth," Pete smiled.

"Tooth?"

"Yef fir," Pete smiled again and pointed to the missing front tooth. "I need to go to the dennift. I broke a truth."

"I think we all did," Tim said.

Tim called the home office's legal department. "Lucy this is Tim Lichten in Fenton. Paul Daniel called me."

"He's on the other line. Do you want to wait or have him call you back?"

"Do you know what he wants?"

"Something about the sale. That's all we've been doing."

"So when's closing?"

"Next Wednesday, if we can get the paperwork done."

"I hear it'll be unique."

"I've never seen such a convoluted contract. Marionetti's attorney is writing most of it."

"Isn't that backward?" Tim said.

"They insisted."

"You know the old rule," Tim said.

"What?"

"The man with the gold holds a club."

"That's true," said Lucy.

"Did you hear? We sold it twice."

She laughed. "Zack told us you drove the new owner around like a drunken cabbie to stay away from every bad area near the mall."

"There were a few turns in the road."

"Zack had us in tears with laughter."

Tim closed his door, "Lucy, can I ask a favor?"

"You want me to list you as an owner?" she joked.

Tim moved his mouthpiece closer, "When everything is done, I'd like to see a copy of the sales contract and closing documents."

She thought a second, "I could send you a copy of what we record at the courthouse."

"No, I want the real dope, the inside story, the skinny. I want your notes from the closing."

"I won't be in there when the chickens are in the bread pan dividing up the dough. Besides you know I can't do that."

"I know you shouldn't."

"But I won't be in the room."

"Look, the property will be sold. You will go in after to throw away the trash. Just send me the scraps on the table and the floor."

"Well," she paused.

"You know it's going to be a unique sale."

"Maybe. Paul might send Cecil something. They talked last week."

"And ?

"Well . . . " she paused.

"If he does?"

"Tim, I don't know. They have a relationship." She lowered her voice. "If you did get something, you'd never tell where it came from would you?"

"Never."

"Promise?"

"I promise, never ever."

The line was quiet.

"You there?" Tim asked.

"Put it this way. If anything goes to Cecil, and I am the one who sends it, maybe I could copy . . ."

"Yes, you could."

"I'll try. I cannot promise anything."

"Lucy, you're the greatest. Do you have my home address?"

"Yes, but understand, if something comes, you don't know from where."

"I understand."

"You will not tell," she said.

"Never ever."

The Hunting Dog

42

Confession

The closing was postponed for a week, but at 7:18 P.M on the following Wednesday, Mr. Roy put his pen down. "Gil, call Rami. Tell him there will be eight for dinner."

Mr. Roy Parino stood up, took off his sunglasses, extended his hand to Ricco Ladro Marionetti, Mord Doyle and their lone attorney.

"Ricco, I think this was a good example of a win-win. You have lifted an elephant off my back. I hope we could give you what you needed."

Ricco took Roy's hand with both of his, "Roy, you have been tough but fair. I thank you moltissimo."

After dinner at Rami's, Gil went to his hotel to call Susan. He told her the deed was done. They agreed that they should invite the Cypress Tree office for dinner. She immediately called Bobbie and Aimee to let them know of the plans for Saturday night.

Tim and Aimee arrived at Gil's house about sunset when long shadows lay on the golf course behind his house. A few players rushed in silence to finish their games.

Gil was in a turquoise silk Hawaiian shirt, white linen draw string shorts and sandals. His pony tail had an antique silver ring. A gold Gerald Genta watch dressed his tanned arm.

Tim brought a bottle of 25-year-old Dalmore Scotch. "It's the nectar of the gods."

"I thought that was mead," Cecil said.

"Those were Homer's gods. This is for our gods. Besides Homer never tasted Dalmore."

"A toast to Ricco Marionetti," Gil said. "He gave me a present at the closing." He got up and walked into the back and came out with a large Andy Warhol print of Marlyn Monroe. "It was something from his family collection." He set it against the wall for all to admire. "He gave Mr. Roy and Dad a work of art also."

"A toast to Ricco and his wealthy investors," Cecil said, "But I have to use water. I learned long time ago I cannot handle anything stronger than a soft drink."

Tim and Gil sat on the patio drinking scotch as Cecil put on the chef's apron to help set the table.

The clear sky was now a deep dark blue. The horizon had a touch of red. It reminded Tim of one of the Folon prints in the Kansas City office.

Their laughs pierced the dark as night crept into the bushes, past the patio torches.

Gil went to the door, "Susan, let's move this party to the patio. The weather's terrific."

Susan nodded acceptance, "We'll need to take the dining room table." Aimee and Bobbie helped her remove the table settings. Gil, Cecil and Tim carried the long table outside. Once reset, Susan added three lit candles.

Cecil poured himself another Seven-Up, "I guess I can now announce I made a deal to stay with Mord. They wanted me to sign a contract for five years, but all I agreed to was six months."

Gil smiled and offered a toast. "To Cecil!"

The air sizzled steak. Susan put Andrea Bocelli on the stereo.

"It's perfect to sit here and see the crystal and silver sparkle," Aimee said.

Gil uncorked a bottle of wine.

Tim picked up the cork and smelled. It was stamped Coche-Dury.

"It's a French Burgundy that will go well with the steaks," Gil said.

The steaks were prime and thick and juicy and melted in their mouths. The torches and candles danced on Susan's pearls.

"Carol Parino gave me her cheesecake recipe. Anyone interested?" Susan asked.

Tim said, "Aimee, let's get it before we leave." She gave him a glare.

Gil said with a smile, "We have ice cream if you're on a diet."

After dessert, the women collected dishes and the men brought the table back inside.

Gil and Tim returned under the stars for after dinner drinks. "Tim, we want you to stay at Cypress Tree for a few months during the changeover. We will see what happens."

"Who will be my boss?" Tim asked.

"Your check will be from Malifer. You will work for them for 120 days. They are hiring Cecil. We told them you would help with leasing until they hire someone."

They had discussed the changeover, but this was the 'official' notice.

Gil continued. "Let's walk. I'm moving to Kansas City." They both headed to the golf course that backed up to his property line.

"So, what was the final price?" Tim asked.

"It appraised at twenty-eight million plus our option rights on the Hotel. We owed over thirty million so there was little profit."

"Sounds like you paid for them to take it off your hands," Tim said.

"It was complicated," Gil said.

Tim lifted his drink in a toast, "To the simple life."

Gil toasted, "Nothing is simple. We all follow Medusa."

"It's as if the whole world drives drunk." Tim shook his head, "There's no map anymore, but men don't use maps."

"They use accountants," smiled Gil.

"I guess an era has ended," Tim said.

"It never ends," Gil said.

"Well, I've learned a lot - I mean dealing with Mord, meeting Mario."

"And you don't know the half of it."

They put their empty glasses on top of a post that marked his property line. Gil pointed toward a bench on the other side of the fairway. It glowed in the starlight.

"Things took place. You wouldn't believe."

Tim looked up at the stars. "There's no moon."

"Watch your step."

"It's amazing how, even in the dark your eyes get used to it," Tim said.

"Our deal was so dark I wish I could forget it." Gil sat, stretched his legs out and looked up, "It's as if I'm in a mine field."

A firefly blinked in the trees.

"Tim, what's a lie?"

"The opposite of a truth. No, the absence of a truth."

"How do you know, if you don't know the truth?"

Tim sat on the bench, "My dad always said lies complicate. Truth keeps life simple."

They looked at the house. The others were in the den. Cecil was singing, but they couldn't make out the words. Gil looked up at the stars, "The vastness of it all. Have you ever thought about it? I mean, how does it all play together?"

"No, not much."

"I used to come out here to think."

"People don't think anymore," Tim said.

"I know I don't."

"How often do you come out here?"

"It's been a long time. And this golf course was the main reason I wanted the house. So I could think." Gil searched the sky, "Have you ever seen stars in the Rockies? They'll take your breath away. Someday that's where I want to live."

"Tonight is clear."

"That's because you haven't seen stars in the Rockies," Gil said.

"Like Plato's cave."

"Exactly."

"People's words create haze," Tim said.

Gil stood up and paced back and forth, "Tim you don't know how lucky you are."

"Why?"

"What if I told you . . . " Gil didn't finish the sentence.

A frog started to croak behind them.

"Gil, smell this air. It's so pure and clean. Not a whiff of a cigarette."

"Tim, I wish this sale was behind me."

"I thought it was."

Gil walked in a circle around Tim, "A lie never dies." He came back and sat, "Motivation, if you know what someone craves, you can make any deal."

"How much did Marionetti give?"

"The partners did well."

"I thought you said they lost over two million?"

"That was the appraisal. Dad and I were only minor partners, but we can't spend it, not yet, anyway."

"Why not."

"The way it was done."

Gil sat, leaned and put his elbows on his knees. His hands covered his mouth and pressed hard against his lips. He whispered, then mumbled. His eyes watered, and tears glistened on his cheeks. His lips twitched and soon sentences flowed. "We didn't mean for it to be that way. It started small. We didn't mean for things to grow, but they did. Mr. Roy wanted profit. We all did. Dad wanted to get rid of Cecil, but Mr. Roy said he was forced to keep him."

Tim listened to the frogs praying to the night and waited. When Gil's lips started to quiver again, Tim whispered, "Why?"

"I don't know. Cecil knew something. Who knows what? Mr. Roy wouldn't cut Cecil off. Dad thought he was a problem. Mr. Roy moved me here to help him. Soon we were behind the eight ball."

Gil stood up and started to walk around the bench, "We refinanced. We fudged the books, when we couldn't take on more debt, the recession hit. Stores left. The doctors were caught by the Feds so their offices closed. Our cards began to fall. Mr. Roy, Dad and I all pledged personal assets, but the blood wouldn't stop."

Gil sat quiet for a long time. Even the fireflies were now dark.

Tim thought he saw a rabbit move on the fairway but didn't say anything. He listened to Gil's breathing in and out, in and out, each time faster than before. Gil then leaned over and whispered fast without pausing. Tim listened like a confessor.

"Cecil was to charge tenants a little more to increase cash flow. We squeezed to slow the bloodletting. Who would complain? Who would know? We padded. God, I'm sorry."

Gil sat and put his palms together as his mother taught him when he was three. "When someone rented 1,000 square feet, we billed for 1,100 and then 1,200. We had to do it. We weren't stealing. We were borrowing to keep our doors open. If we didn't we all would be on the street."

"I understand," Tim heard himself say.

"If someone caught our 'mistake' we would have corrected it. We were not crooks." Gil took two deep breaths, "But no one noticed. Not one. They presumed we billed them correct. They knew us. They played golf with us. We were friends. They knew we were not bad. Besides all tenants fudged their sales reports to us, they all do."

"Our damn New York bankers wanted their money. They didn't want the property. We tried to give it to them. Damn cash was all they wanted."

Gil went behind a bush and took a piss while reciting whispered words. Tim couldn't understand the fragments but let him talk. "Old tenants dried up. Others died . . . we made sweetheart short-term deals . . . stop gap grew to be long term . . . little rent better than no rent . . . the merry-go-round swirled into a black rabbit hole sucking cash."

Gil came back and took a deep breath and was silent again. Tim started to ask a question but all he could say was, "Wow."

"Tim, one day I woke up and couldn't justify it anymore. But I couldn't do anything about it. I was in too deep. We were all in too deep. We had to sell. Dad tried, but no one wanted it. Finally, Mr. Roy called Ricco Marionetti to look at it."

"Did he know him?"

"From way back. Ricco sent Mord to take a look. Mord saw we were in a vice." Gil made a fist, "And Ricco squeezed us in a corner, until we took his deal."

"You couldn't say no?"

"Nor could Ricco. We were both in a vice."

"How?" Tim asked.

Gil paused and licked his lips, "We both had things to hide."

Gil started to walk out on the fairway so Tim followed him. "Maybe it started when Cecil got a friend at the electric company to remove meters.

That gave us free electricity. It was free money because we charged tenants for it. We thought it was a way out."

"No one saw it as stealing?" Tim asked.

"We weren't thieves. We just wanted to stay above water."

" . . . in the dark." Tim muttered.

"Cecil required a trash hauler that all stores had to use. They billed stores direct and paid Cecil a percentage collected, a finders fee."

"Cecil suggested we start a construction business with two contractors he knew, so Cecil and I partnered with them, and they got all the small jobs at the mall when an outside contractor was needed. It became a nice bonus."

"I wasn't aware of that."

"It was before you started. But things got tight. We couldn't pay ourselves."

"Kansas City didn't mind? Or did they know?"

"Mr. Roy, Dad and a few others at the home office formed BCM Construction Co. They own the airplane we lease."

"BCM does all the big jobs we borrow construction money for."

"So Malifer . . . "

"Don't go there." Gil waved both hands.

Tim said, "Merchants didn't complain their construction was too expensive?"

"What could they do?" Gil shrugged, "What could I do? I put the checks in the bank and moved on."

"You didn't smell something?" Tim asked.

"I held my nose. Damn Tim, you're not stupid. You should have seen it."

"I guess I didn't want to. If cash flow was so bad, how did we get money?"

"As tenants left it became harder and harder. We started to give away free rent to get the cash flow. We got Cecil's bank to increase our line of credit. The more we borrowed, the more lenders wanted to see new leases, so Paul in the home office made some up. Like the banks did on home mortgages. They never checked. They only wanted to see paper. So we printed some." Gil talked so fast he couldn't stop, "We changed lease clauses, so we could collect more fees. Soon we charged more. Damn the paperwork. No one checked. The lenders worked in offices. No one visited the mall to look . . . Even our real tenants, didn't check to see if charges were legit. Hell, most of them were cheating too."

"A den of thieves," Tim whispered.

"We had to increase cash flow." Gil waved his hands. "Family vacations merged with business trips. Our condominiums in Aspen were legally offices. Our lives and our business were one. Hell, my party at Callaway Gardens was well over a hundred thousand dollar expense that we charged to merchants."

"The cursed hunger for gold," Tim said.

"Tim, Mr. Roy is a good man. I had no idea his relationship with Marionetti was so old and deep."

Gil bit his lip and started to cry, "Mord Doyle killed a guy when he was young. When he was released from prison, he went to see Dad in Kansas City for a job."

"Mord said he knew Mr. Roy years ago," Tim said.

"I think their fathers did business in Atlantic City. Mr. Roy's wife is the daughter of one of Marionetti's clients."

"I thought she was from Kansas City railroad money."

"Her Godfather is Angelo Saulora, who lives in Fenton. He was at my engagement party. The short man with dark glasses and a young South American wife? He's the man who told Ricco not to purchase Cypress Tree."

"Ricco Marionetti's cousin," Tim said.

"How do you know?"

"Ricco told me."

"Damn."

"I think their money is . . ." Tim stopped. Gil's eyes pleaded for him not to finish.

"Tim, Marionetti gives money distance and respect." Gil looked around as if looking for someone. "Dad is named in memory of a close friend of my grandfather, Genovese Issac d'Marionetti, who went to grade school with their family back in the old country. Our family name was Palmisano, but granddad cut it to 'Palm' when he moved to Kansas City."

Gil's face was now in panic. "Tim, I've got a wolf by the ears, and I can't let go. You can't tell anyone, you just can't." He waited, and Tim nodded. "Tim, my father was involved with the Enron scandal and went to prison for a year. While in prison he met Mord."

"He said they lived in the same complex."

"Anyway, when Dad got out he went to work for his dad's real estate company in Kansas City and there met Mr. Roy, and the rest is history." Gil took a deep breath.

"Gil, what can I do?" Tim asked.

"Go, run, get as far away and forget what you know."

"I cannot run from the truth."

"For God's sake, go while your hands are clean. Go, and forget everything."

Gil turned and stood face to face with him and whispered. "Tim, you know nothing. You can prove nothing, get the hell out. The rest of us must wallow in this until we die. Take your freedom and go."

Gil took out a handkerchief, wiped the sweat and tears from his face.

"Gil, you've done your best. That's all you can do."

The silence was broken by a frog.

"Tim, what time is it?"

His Rolex dial glowed, "Looks like 11:32."

"I think it's time."

Without a word, both stood and started toward the light of the house. Tim put his hand on Gil's shoulder.

"Watch your step. Keep your eye on the lights and aim straight. Step like you are planting corn."

The Hunting Dog

43

Breakfast at Red's Truck Stop

Aimee and Tim left Gil's party but drove without a word. When they approached the flashing red neon sign for Red's Truck Stop, Tim said, "Let's stop for a bite."

"Here?"

"If you don't mind. Louie brought me here once."

"What's wrong?"

"I need breakfast," Tim said.

"OK, but it's after midnight."

Heads of smelly overweight truckers turned to look at Aimee as they walked in.

A waitress came over. Aimee ordered decaf. Tim didn't look at a menu, "Two eggs over easy, sausage patty, grits, biscuits with black coffee."

Aimee asked, "You didn't have enough to eat?"

"When I worry I get hungry. Gil and I had a long talk tonight. He said that I should run while I can."

"From what?"

"The whole mess. I told you how I felt about Ricco. Well, Gil confirmed it."

"So stay with Malifer, they've treated us fine."

"After tonight I don't know."

"You want another job?"

"It might be wise."

"Why? They've treated us well. We own our house free and clear."

"Trust me, I think it needs to be done."

"He didn't fire you did he?"

"No."

"How will you find something that pays as much?"

"I don't know. Mike wants to put something together."

"I'm not moving back to Chicago."

"He wants to do something in Georgia."

"What?"

"I don't know. He always has a get-rich plan. He is supposed to be down here in a few weeks."

"What do you want?"

"I wish I knew."

The waitress placed breakfast in front of him. Tim cut up the eggs and sausage to stir them into the hot grits. "Louie, taught me this. Right now, this is bliss."

"Tim, remember, no matter how hard it gets, you're not alone."

"I know."

"But think before you jump."

"Maybe I can find a sales job on the road."

44

Meeting with Mike

Tim walked into the lobby of the Peachtree Hotel, and there was 'Chicago' Mike on the escalator right on time. He now had a short beard.

They shook hands, hugged and headed to the bar.

"You've changed," Tim said.

Mike laughed, "Yeah, the old days are gone. I haven't been in a bowling alley in years. It's now scotch and golf. Do you play?"

"I visit a driving range once in a while."

Mike ordered 25-year-old Chivas, Tim his normal Beefeaters and tonic. Soon they started to bring back some of the Saturdays they had together.

"Do you ever see the old gang in Chicago?" Tim asked.

"The only one I talk to is you. You know how often that's been."

Tim saw Mike look at his Rolex, "I need to thank you for that. Aimee loves hers. They never stop."

Mike said, "Beats a Timex."

Tim smiled.

"Tim, Papa died. We've been thinking about options. I might expand to Georgia and let the brothers have Chicago. Georgia will have some advantages. I'm here to look for a small factory location."

"So business has thrived?"

"Plus, I've learned a lot."

Tim asked, "What exactly was papa's business?"

"International sale of used equipment. He was able to sell to old factories behind the iron curtain. When China started up, we sold scrap iron to them also. Something old to us is new to them. We also import new German equipment, so we get it both ways."

"Will it be a big office?"

"Maybe, depends on what I find. I might even move here." Mike's eyes followed a girl who walked by. He lowered his voice, "I'm thinking of doing another bid with the feds." He smiled at Tim.

"Not again?"

"Bigger than ever."

Tim shook his head. "Mike, you've got the biggest brass ones I know. You're not serious?"

Mike said, "With the revamp of the government, they will be selling all kinds of surplus stuff. We could sell it abroad. But now they control everything by computers."

"You don't know anything about computers."

Mike held up his index finger to make a point, "I do know how to make money on a bid." He leaned in, "I know how to move money before they see where it went."

"Like a magic act with computers?"

"Sort of."

Tim sat silent so Mike changed the subject, "So how's life treating you?"

"The mall has been sold so I'm in a transition phase. I'm on loan to the new owner for a few weeks. After that, options are open. I could stay with Malifer, or make a complete switch. I've had a good interview to sell on the road."

"We had a lot of fun with those Christmas kiosks. Plus we made great helicopter 'candy' together."

Tim touched his Rolex.

Mike said, "We wanted to help you and Aimee with her hospital bills and all. This time you can help me."

"How?"

"You remember the bid list? Well today it's even larger. With the cutting the size of government they have farmed out a lot."

"Yeah, to make things more efficient. Fat chance."

Mike smiled, "Well private companies run by former politicos are now in control."

"We've become a mercenary government," Tim said.

"That makes the process more complicated but better for us."

"Why?"

"Tim, they don't know what they are doing. No one does. They are farming it all out, and startup funds are bigger than ever. They want an efficient computerized government."

"Big brother."

Mike punched the air towards Tim. "We will make some real money this time."

"How long will it take?"

"I don't know, maybe a year or two." Tim shut his eyes and shook his head. Mike continued, "This time I want to go for big bucks, really big bucks. Things must be set up right. It can't be a paper company or a post office box. This time we'll need a real address, have an actual factory. I'll need solid local connections. So I need you."

"Mike, Aimee wants me to take this job on the road for a while."

"All I need is advice. Point me in the right direction."

Tim held up his glass and asked for a refill, "Well, go to the state and tell them you might want to expand to Georgia. You'll be wined and dined for a while if you wear that suit. They'll show you around, introduce you. What will you tell them?"

"I'll be honest. My father-in-law died. The family wants to expand to a city with direct flights to South America and Africa."

"If you want South America, the mall's owner has connection down there. I could make a call for you."

"Let's focus on Georgia," Mike said.

"Do it low-key. Don't march in asking for money. Just be educating yourself. Always ask about competing areas. Make them sell you. The more jobs you have available, the more they will offer you."

"Let them smell the cheese."

"Banks will want to get involved. Luke Douglas will be glad to take you to Chamber and Rotary meetings."

"I like the way you think."

"Don't sell them. Get them to sell you."

Tim continued, "The mayor in Fenton owns some buildings and can help get rehab money to get your factory up and running."

"How well do you know him?"

"Mike, I'll point you to the right people, but I can't get into it."

"Why not?"

"It's personal. I just can't. I'll help you any way I can, but I can't be involved, not now, not here."

Tim looked over Mike's left shoulder and watched a long haired tanned girl in a sleek white dress walk toward him. He smiled, and she smiled back as she squeezed the hand of the man she was with. When she passed, Tim said, "I can't do it again."

Mike looked straight at him, "Even if we clear ten million each?"

Tim turned pale. A chill ran down his back, "Shit."

"If we do it right maybe twenty or thirty million."

"Damn!"

Mike leaned in, "And it will be legal. We will walk away clear, with no one able to touch us, or make us pay taxes."

"Mike, you're dreaming."

"Am I? Think about the billions and billions spent in Iraq. Name me one man who went to jail taking money from the Government."

"Bernie Madoff."

"Wrong, he had a Ponzi scheme that took from rich people."

"Mike, I wish you luck. I don't have the guts."

Mike looked at Tim's Rolex, "What did you do with the 'peanuts' in the package?"

Tim was silent. He did not want to tell him it was still in the bank vault, "I paid off Aimee's bill, and bought some stocks."

"Think about what you could do if you won the lottery."

Tim sipped his gin. "How did you convert to cash? I was stunned the FedEx had cash and diamonds."

"It's easy when you are in the import-export business." Mike smiled, "Cash is not the problem. Keeping it is."

"Mike, millions will be a much larger problem."

"Papa's man specializes in transfers. He knows all kinds of ways."

Tim said, "Can you trust him?"

"I think so."

"Mike, you can't think, you must know." Tim leaned back in his chair, "So what is your plan?"

Mike opened his brief case and handed some papers to Tim. "This is part of the latest bid list."

Tim went down the sheet. "There are hundreds of items."

"It's crazy. We could buy old supplies they have in storage, such as bookshelves, and sell them to a different agency." Mike smiled, "Papa would say: they're all crooks."

"You have to employ people. If you don't have a plan to put a lot of people to work you won't get a dime to start anything."

"You're giving me something to think about," Tim said.

"It will take time to set things up, but it's the basic thing we did."

"What's that?"

"Skimming the cream, the essence of all business," Mike said.

"You don't think they have safeguards against this sort of thing?"

"That's why it's important you point me the right way. You'll earn your share and have clean hands."

Mike pulled out a yellow pad and handed it to Tim. "Write down all the people I need to meet. I'm a business man from Chicago. We might expand to Georgia. Who do I need to see?"

Tim started to write.

45

Ashes

SIX MONTHS LATER

Mord Doyle awoke in a motel somewhere in South Georgia with the squeak of a cart's wheel. His eyes jumped open when someone tapped on the door. He rolled over and rubbed his face. He had to get back on the road, but for now he would lay quiet. He closed his eyes.

It had been 2:30 when he gave cash for the room through a night security window, picked up a key, towels, and TV remote control.

"Housekeeping." A key slipped in the door lock. "Housekeeping!" The door chain stopped the door from opening.

Mord shouted, "Later. I'm still in bed!"

"Excuse me." The door closed.

A spring in the mattress poked his right shoulder.

A call from Cecil on Wednesday had concerned Mord enough that he made a quick trip from Tampa. He now knew Cecil would not be a problem. Tonight he would go fishing with his brother.

"What town is this?" he asked himself as he looked at the bedside clock, found the TV remote, clicked it on, only to close his eyes.

The constant TV chatter aroused his brain. On the wall above a fiberboard table was a faded framed print tilted a quarter inch to the left. The bare gray asbestos tile floor had collected balls of dust. There was a scent of Pine-Sol.

"No coffee pot, damn."

He sat on the side of the bed. In the mirror, he did not recognize the man with matted gray hair and pointy eyebrows. There was a dark stain on his silk shirt.

"Damn, Cecil, you ruined it." He pitched the shirt in the plastic wastebasket, checked his shoes and slacks. They were clean.

"I have to hit the road," He pulled a toothbrush and some Lava soap from his bag.

"Damn, the tub has mold. No one gives a shit anymore."

After a shower, shave, and fresh clothes he started to gather his things and saw the shirt in the trash. He took the trash bag with the shirt, rolled it into a ball and stuffed it under his truck seat. He checked again in the room to make sure he didn't miss anything.

He slipped on his sunglasses, jumped into his green pickup. He turned in the first place for gas, then went inside for supplies.

"Gas, half pound hamburger, crackers, six-pack of Bud, Vidalia onion, a carton of Camels, is that all, sir?"

"Add a bag of ice."

"One bag of ice. Cash or credit?"

Mord pulled out a hundred-dollar bill.

"Got anything smaller?"

"Don't forget the gas."

"Thank you, sir. Your change, praise Jesus."

"You bet."

At his truck, Mord Doyle removed a red ice chest, put in the fresh ice, beer and hamburger. Then ran back in for two glazed donuts and coffee for the road. He showed what he had taken and threw down ten dollars, "Keep the change."

"Have a good trip."

When he opened the truck door, a large envelope addressed to Cecil Malcour sat in silence on the passenger seat. Mord turned it over. "Cecil, you're a damn amateur."

A little after two, Mord left the interstate to drive four miles to a state park.

"Can I have a park map?"

The park ranger gave him one, "Two dollars parking fee."

"Do you have grills?"

"Yes Sir, make sure the fire's out before you leave."

Mord drove the park before he found a lone shaded table away from anyone else. If he had stopped on the Interstate, noisome kids would run around.

He parked at a table near a tall oak, looked for twigs to start a fire, found a half bag of charcoal someone left. Soon on a sheet of foil, he laid the fatty hamburger, sliced potato, carrots and onion. He sealed the foil, buried it deep in smoking coals.

He picked up the package Cecil gave him, sat at the concrete table, rolled up his sleeves, opened a beer and began to read. There were copies of computer printouts, legal documents and various handwritten notes. He placed each finished page under a stone on the table.

The trees stood still. Cicadas chanted to their gods. When all the pages were under the rock, he removed the stew. Set it on the concrete table and opened another beer. Steam rose when he opened the foil.

Afterwards, he pulled the papers from under the rock, looked at them one last time as he fed them to the coals. Tongues of flames lashed, twisted and hissed as they consumed forbidden truth.

When the fire died, Mord took a stick, raked the ashes for unburned paper. He sprayed on lighter fluid. Flames jumped and gasped but soon were still.

He remembered the stained shirt. Added it with lighter fluid on the coals. Flames again swirled to release a sweet burnt odor.

Finally, he brought the ice-chest to the grill to pour ice on the dead ashes.

He didn't turn his mobile on but at the welcome station, found a pay phone and called his answering machine in Tampa. There were no messages. He passed by the grill one last time to make sure he had not forgotten anything. The site was clean.

His mother always said a man had to run his business like her kitchen. Clean things up or the job was not finished. Mord got the documents from Cecil. Things were now clean.

He was now going to fish. He looked at his watch. He would make the boat before the high tide.

Mord started to whistle as he did in prison. It was a way to pass the time, to not think about history. He whistled a mix of bird calls, insect chirps, cat sounds and loud screeches. His favorite was that of an alley cat. It sounded great in a bar full of drunks.

He popped open another beer.

46

TV News

Tim pulled into his driveway at 6:12. When he opened the door, the aroma of pot roast hugged him.

"You're early!" Aimee said.

"After three months, I've started to get the hang of selling pasta. Thank God for audio books." He rolled his travel bag into the bedroom.

"Did you have a good week?"

"Oh yeah, Tim the 'joke telling' bird-dog pasta man! We had an excellent week. They all like to see me. I have extra tickets to Atlanta's games. I have stories. Like my dad always said, "Get their attention with a funny story. Listen to theirs. Become a friend. Then show them the diamonds." Tim grinned and said, "In my case, it's great semolina pasta."

Aimee gave him a kiss, "Junior's spending the night with Jimmy. They're having a camp out for about five boys."

"His dad's going to have his hands full."

She handed him a gin and tonic, "They're at their cabin on the lake."

"I wish them luck," Tim said.

"Ray wanted to camp out with Dexter in their back yard."

"So we will be free until 2 A. M. — when I'll go get him." He stirred his drink with his finger.

"That was last year, he's eight . . ."

"Whoa . . . how much gin did you put in this?"

"I gave you two shots. Anyway, Ray promised he'd stay."

"Do I smell peach cobbler?" Tim opened the freezer, "Hope we have ice-cream."

"I told him we'd leave the back door unlocked."

Tim walked onto the back patio to look, "There is a tent pitched, but I don't see the kids."

"Pam took them to Mellow Mushroom for Pizza."

Tim went to his home office. In the stack of trade magazines was a thick, oversize fiberglass envelope from Kansas City. Tim raised his voice, "When did this come?"

"What's that?"

"The big FedEx envelope. This is hell to open."

"Two days ago."

Inside was no cover letter, only an inch stack of documents wrapped with two rubber bands.

Tim remembered he had asked for details of the sale from Paul's paralegal, but that was months ago. He forgot all about it. Funny how when your mind moves on. How things loose importance. Tim set the envelope down to go to other mail.

Aimee asked from the kitchen, "Do you think he wears a wig?"

"Who?"

"The new anchor on Channel 3. I think he wears a toupee."

"Maybe."

Tim started to scan the Chronicle for new restaurants in the works, but the package from Kansas City beckoned like midnight ice cream. His right hand set on the fiberglass envelope. His fingers slithered inside to twang a rubber band. Tim soon held the bundle, and his eyes were checking the dates.

"Tim, did you hear that?"

His ears perked. "After this message, we will have a story about a local executive found murdered in his home."

"Who was it?"

"They showed a picture of Cecil." Tim set the papers down and walked to the den. The roast was on the table. He uncorked wine as the reporter came back.

"Today the gruesome body of Cecil Ricatto Malcour was found in the Malcour family mansion on Bluff View Lane. Someone killed him with an antique battle-ax blow to the back of his skull. His elderly mother found the body at 10:30 this morning when she came downstairs for breakfast. Mrs. Malcour told police she had heard nothing out of the ordinary."

"Cecil Malcour was a resident of Fenton. He was the grandson of Isaac Naher Malcour, founder of Fenton National Bank. Mayor Canaglia named Cecil Malcour one of five outstanding business leaders last year. The Exchange Club gave him their Top Executive Award seven years ago."

"In recent years Cecil Malcour had been the General Manager of Cypress Tree Mall. Six months ago, a private investor group purchased Cypress Tree Mall from Malifer Properties of Kansas City."

"Police are looking for a dark pickup, seen on Bluff View about 9:30 last night."

"Can you believe that?" Tim's mind flooded with thoughts of Cecil and the secrets he knew. But why would anyone want him dead?

Death steals a face and fades it into the fog of the past. But the murder of someone you know will brand their face on your mind.

Tim shivered.

They sat at the table, but the roast had no flavor. The wine was bitter. Tim tried to speak, but his voice had no air.

Aimee asked, "Do you have Mord's number in Tampa? Maybe you should let him know."

Tim found his number and called. A machine answered. "I'll be fishing until Monday night. Please leave a message with your number. I'll get back to you . . . beeeeep."

"Mord, this is Tim Lichten in Fenton. It is Friday night. I've called to make you aware that Cecil Malcour was found murdered today. It was on the news tonight."

Tim felt obligated to call Gil Palm in Kansas City.

"Tim, who do they think did it?"

"I have no idea. They didn't mention any suspects. Do you have an idea?"

"I don't even want to guess. He screwed everyone. Maybe it was one of his weird friends." There was silence for a few seconds, "Tim, you know nothing, — nothing."

"Gil, I can't imagine who did it."

"No, Tim, Cecil's death is not what's important. Remember, what is: you — know — nothing." He made a long silent underline. "Understand?" He paused again. "Not — one — thing."

Tim understood, "I — know — nothing."

There was another long pause.

"Nothing." Gil repeated.

When Tim heard a dial tone he slumped in his chair.

"I know nothing," he muttered, "I . . . know . . . nothing."

Tim remembered Gil's eyes on the night golf course, Cecil's thin smile as he left Star's with his cane, Mord's cigarettes. What did Tim not know? What was he to forget?

Aimee put a bowl of peach cobbler in front of him, "Well? What did he say?"

"He's shocked."

"Who does he think did it?"

"No idea."

They watched Jeopardy in silence. Tim couldn't answer one question. His mind was mush.

The phone rang. "Did you hear about Cecil?" It was the jeweler, Falconi.

"We're stunned." Tim said.

"I wish you were still working here. Do you have a number for their Miami Office?"

"I called their people."

Falconi changed his tone, "Cecil called me yesterday. He wanted to show me an envelope he received from Kansas City."

"What was in it?" Tim looked at the package on his desk.

"I don't know. He never came."

The hair on Tim's neck shivered. Words blurred. All Tim could see was the smile Cecil had when he came from the mayor's office with the signed papers. "Mr. Falconi, my head's a mess. I'll call you when I contact them."

He hung up, tried to talk to Aimee but could not. She gave him another drink.

"Is it strong?" Tim asked.

"It's the last one you'll need tonight."

"Good."

47

The Next Morning

Tim woke at 2:18 a.m. gasping for air. At 3:10, he jumped and twitched in his sleep. He started to snore at 3:46. Aimee moved to the couch. When she did he laid awake and begged for sleep. Each time it approached, he would hear, "You know nothing, not one thing."

At six-thirty, NPR's silk voice announcer started to talk. A few seconds later the automatic coffee maker started. When he smelled coffee, he went in the kitchen.

Aimee was at the table with the paper.

"You jumped all night," Aimee said.

"Sorry."

"I finally moved to the den."

Tim said, "I had this weird dream. I was in a cave. I couldn't turn around. The walls were so close I couldn't breathe."

"Well you're awake now, and you've survived." Aimee passed him the front section. Cecil's picture was on the bottom of the first page.

Tim read aloud "Mrs. Malcour, his mother, found his body when she came down for breakfast. She saw a pickup drive up sometime after 8:00 P.M. She thought it left about an hour later."

"I already read it," Aimee said.

"Sorry, I wanted to make sure you didn't miss anything. An antique 13th century battle-axe was still in his skull when police arrived."

Aimee asked, "Wonder where that came from?"

"He collected everything." He continued, "The police found his sister, Roberta Malcour unconscious but alive in her bed. Both are now under a doctor's care."

"That sounds funny," Aimee said.

"What do you mean?"

"Unconscious? I'll bet they didn't tell everything."

Tim passed the paper back to Aimee. "The article doesn't tell much more than the TV."

Aimee started to read the section aloud. They both examined each word in hope to hear something new. They didn't.

Tim picked up his cup and went out on the patio. Next door the boys were asleep in the tent. He listened for birds but there were none. He sat on the damp bench and shut his eyes. He still wanted to sleep.

Back inside he refilled his cup and walked to his home office where the large envelope waited. He opened it to find Xerox copies of the closing agreement, the deed transfer, ledgers, several scraps of yellow legal paper with hand-written notes.

One page was filled with arrows, squares, dollar figures and names of properties in Austin, Nova Scotia, Cayman Islands and The Isle of Man. Some were hen scratches that Tim couldn't read. Mord's demonstration with beer bottles, napkins and cigarette butts, made the jots a Rosetta Stone.

Tim probed single words, followed the sketched arrows, all as if they were some witch's recipe. Soon he felt he knew too much.

He still could hear Gil's voice, "Tim, you know nothing -- understand -- not one thing."

He went through every slip of paper until only two items were left. One was a hand written list in block letters:

ROY
- Rembrandt's 'A Lady and Gentleman in Black'[delivered]
- Manet's 'Chez Tortoni' – [delivered]
- 10,000 oz gold bullion in a safe-deposit box, Bank of Moddey Dhoo, Peel in Isle of Man, depos- it box #244 – key received
- Jan Vermeer's 'The Concert' [To be picked up at Bank of Moddey Dhoo in Peel, Isle of Man]
- Folon Sculpture, Printemps 40x15x12cm – deliv- ered
- Folon Sculpture, 79éme pensée 30x10x10cm – delivered

ZACK
- 2,000 ounces of gold – Banc de Louis box #34
- Stock Certificates with 100,000 preferred shares of Nokia deposited in safe deposit box #34 Banc de Louis, key received.
- 45ft sailboat docked in Cancun, key and title re- ceived
- 100,000 shares of Chile Telephone Co. – re- ceived

GIL
- 25,000 shares of Chile Telephone Co. –received
- Warhol print M.M.[delivered]
- Gold Gerald Genta watch –– signed [delivered]

He read the list over twice. Marionetti may have had problems with certain assets. Now they were problems of others.

A brownish-yellow paper dropped out. It was an actual page #277, from a book. Someone had marked in yellow, which glowed as if neon.

The Catcher in the Rye

I don't know what I think about it. I'm sorry I told so many people about it. About all I know is, I sort of miss everybody I told about. Even old Stradiater and Ackley, for instance. I think I even miss that goddam Maurice. It's funny. Don't ever tell anybody anything. If you do, you start missing everybody.

-277-

Tim could never forget. It would be hell, but even hell does not let the truth die.

Tim picked up the phone, but his mind went blank. He couldn't remember whom he wanted to call, so he hung up and pulled out his car keys.

At first, he drove in a daze. He started toward downtown Atlanta but turned to get out of traffic. He went into a neighborhood, turned around to go down a country road. He headed toward Stone Mountain but circled back to go toward Callaway Gardens.

He pulled over to the side of the road. He didn't know where to go. He drove past Lamar's Hardware but didn't stop. He pulled into the downtown parking garage and drove to the top floor. There he sat for several minutes. He thought about talking to Jacob Dabe but didn't.

The memory of Cecil's smirk stalked him. It's not who you know, but what you know.

When Tim found himself outside Cypress Tree. He didn't remember driving there. When he heard the echo of his steps in the hollow hall, he started to focus on the spider webs in the corners of store signs. He turned the corner. There was Archie with his checkered "Bear Bryant" hat. He sat on the bench by the fountain. A man in hospital whites was reading to him.

As Tim got close, Archie held up his hand to stop the reader, "Is that you Tim?"

Tim smiled but didn't answer until he was in front of him, "You're still good Archie, darn good."

"I didn't think I'd see you again." He slapped his hand on his leg. "They told me, you found another job."

"I did, but I had to come back to see you."

"Well, thank you."

"So how you been?" Tim asked.

"I sold my house and moved into Glen Acres, so I guess I'm officially old."

"Good for you."

"Those McDonald stocks came in handy."

"Archie, you look good."

"I get Lester here to bring me to the fountain a couple times a week. Sure beats sitting in a rocker."

"There's something about this water," Tim said.

"This is the last week for the fountain. The new owners are taking it out."

"That's stupid."

"Tim, they don't understand. They're afraid of it."

"The world needs more fountains," Tim said.

"They want to put in carts to sell more stuff."

"It's all about money," Tim said.

Lester stood and with his hand, offered Tim his seat. Tim said, "Archie, if you don't mind, I'm going to sit with you to let Lester take a break."

Lester stood up. "Thank you sir, I'll walk down the hall."

"Archie, your new home has helped. You look ten years younger."

"They help me with my medications. If I get off them, I go to yah-yah land."

"Well, you look to be back on earth."

"I hope to stay."

"Did you hear about Cecil?"

"Lester read me the article."

"Who did it?"

"Tim, who is not important. Why is."

"Why?"

"Always ask why."

"Ok, why?"

Archie shrugged, "Maybe blackmail. Cecil learned the craft from his father."

"I never heard his father was a blackmailer."

"It was a Malcour craft passed down for ages. Did you ever notice the cane in his office?"

"He was proud of it," Tim said.

"Cecil stroked it when he felt weak. He had a ritual with it. He would put it in his hand, caress it, play with it. It was as if it had some power."

"Do you think he was blackmailing who killed him?"

"He had something on everyone, even Mr. Roy."

"Like what?"

"God only knows."

"Knowledge is power." Tim said.

"But it killed Cecil."

"I guess Bobbie's upset."

"She had to be admitted." Archie leaned toward him, "You know she was born a boy?"

"What do you mean?"

"When she was three. There was a hatchet accident with Cecil. So they gave her an operation and raised her as a girl."

"Damn."

Archie held his index finger to his mouth, "No one is to know."

"How do you know?"

"My late brother was the surgeon."

"Son of a bitch."

Tim looked at Archie's eyes. He was now blind. Tim couldn't think of what to say, so he sat back to hear the burble of the fountain.

"This fountain is a clear space in the woods," Tim said.

Archie nodded, "Where one can grow corn."

"Now they want to kill it for profit."

"Tim, do you know why profit's a cancer?" He tilted his head to hear Tim's answer, but he said nothing so Archie continued, "Business wants profit, and unstoppable growth is the creed of any cancer."

"So profit becomes a cancer?" Tim asked.

"Which mutates from a good business dream to a social evil. It changes ethics, chokes men, and kills creative souls."

"Every dream has a monster," Tim said.

"Tim, look what happens to public institutions when they taste profit."

"Like hospitals?" Tim asked.

"Hospitals, colleges, churches — even city governments." Archie paused, "When the focus is profit, the value of life dies."

"Archie, making a profit is the essence of America."

Archie rubbed his forehead, "Evil is like mold that has been active for eons. It moves slow, but is alive. We have the plague of electricity. Then with faster speed came telegraphs, telephones, televisions, now computers. I'm telling you Tim, man's spirit can't cope with the speed."

"I agree, there is a lot of stress."

"Man's very soul is in conflict."

"You think it's a war at his core?"

Archie nodded, "Mankind will do anything to stop this rush for speed and the weight it puts on his spirit. He has fled to the new world, to the west, to the suburbs. When electricity came he ran to lakes and mountains. But man can't escape."

"Archie, you're talking about progress," Tim said.

"Rust is progress? A society running like a rabbit on steroids is progress? Mankind is on a rocket into the sun. It's not progress to do something just because it can be done."

"I don't think . . ."

"Tim, no one thinks. That's the problem."

"We're human. We think."

"Stress burns man's soul. Stress causes heart attacks, cancer, even Alzheimer's. That's what it does, you know. Stress fries the brains of people. It causes neurons to clump." Archie held up his hand then closed it into a tight fist that made his fingers turn red.

"I don't think?" Tim asked.

"No one thinks! Companies don't want their employees to think. They tell employees the boss will do the thinking, but the boss doesn't think either. He only reacts to cold financial numbers. He stomps creative thought."

Tim didn't respond this time but let his eyes roam the mall. Dust balls ran across the floor. Falconi's store was closed and dark. Lester was at the hotel's entrance on his way back.

Archie said, "That's why I appreciate this fountain."

"With its electric pump! Archie, you always make me think."

Archie smiled, "How about that, even the fountain lives a lie without knowing it."

"Cecil was killed with an ax," Tim said.

"I'm sure it was the one they played with as kids."

"Wow."

"Tim, I quit Malifer because they monkeyed with the books. They bent rules. I wanted to quit, but I was trapped. Evil forces you into a corner where you have no choice."

"Money warps ethics." Tim said.

"You know, I was in the cancer as part owner of Cypress Tree."

"I know."

"Tim, we've all made love to a beast."

They both listened to the water gurgle.

Tim said, "We should have listened to the Indians and the land, and the breeze, and the brooks."

"People take drugs for the symptoms. They must learn to cure the ill," Archie said.

"How?"

"Don't be afraid." Archie squinted his eyes. "Don't let them control you by fear."

"OK."

Archie's finger started to shake as he pointed in the air, "Everyone must kill the big cause of the cancer."

"Profit?" Tim asked.

"Indifference."

48

New Orleans Return

Lightning flashed above the door of the Corps of Engineers. Chet Quinn dashed through the downpour to Tim's car. The heavy clouds gave the rain a purple cast.

"Tim, what brings you to New Orleans?"

"Cheesecake."

"Camellia Grill here we come!"

"How do you like living in New Orleans?"

"It's not the same city where we went to college. Katrina has changed everything."

"Chicago had a fire, San Francisco an earthquake. New Orleans will recover."

"But you wouldn't believe what changed."

"Maybe we have changed."

At St. Charles, Tim handed Chet a stack of typing paper bound by rubber bands. "Would you read this for me?"

"What is it?"

"A novel I've worked on since I left Malifer."

"About what?"

"Business, life, hell I don't know."

"Do you want me to edit it?"

"No, I want your opinion, your ideas. Tell me if you think I can get it published. Mark it up all you want, but you don't have to edit."

"Sure."

"You don't mind?"

"No, no, I'm glad to, it'll be a good change of pace from the government bullshit."

"Do you think you can help me find a publisher?" asked Tim.

"One step at a time. First, I read."

"I understand. Can you recommend an agent?"

"First I read."

It was still raining when they parked, so Chet took the rubber bands off to look at the first page, "You know you're not going to make money."

"That's not why I wrote it."

"Good." He skimmed the beginning. "So why did you write it?"

"I had to."

"Do you show anything?"

"I think so, I hope the truth. Tell me what you think. I need feedback."

"No problem."

The rain stopped, and sun glittered on the oak leaves. They walked toward the white columns outside the front door. Thick air steamed off pavement like incense. Soon they were seated at the Formica altar.

Owen gave them a smile. "Good to see you again, Mr. Tim. Is Mr. Chet going' write about your search?"

"No that's my job but he might help," Tim said.

Owen set a place mat with silverware for them. "What would you like today?"

"Owen, I want to thank you."

Owen looked puzzled.

"You gave me the answer."

"I did?"

"The last time I was here."

Owen rubbed his chin. "You had your regular. You said 'don't forget the cheesecake, I remember that." Owen twirled his yellow pencil in silence and looked at Chet.

"My usual with cheesecake."

Tim chimed with, "My usual."

"You think I don't remember?"

"Owen, we know you remember," Tim said.

Owen smiled as he checked off their order. When they confirmed he was correct he chanted in a loud voice to the chef. "One BLT with fries, one strawberry freeze, one cheesecake, one burger extra pickle, no onion but onion rings on the side, one chocolate freeze, one cheesecake with coffee." He looked at them making sure they agreed.

The chef echoed the order as he rang his steel spatula on the hot griddle.

Owen looked at Tim. "Last time, I gave it to you?" Tim nodded. Owen furrowed his forehead and walked off.

Tim turned to Chet. "It's amazing how he remembers."

"He's a treasure. Maybe I should write an article on him."

"You still write? I thought you worked for the government."

"I freelance some." Chet said.

"I came in here after fifteen years and would you believe he remembered me?"

"When we moved back, he remembered not only what Tracy and I ordered but also what we were wearing on our last visit."

Owen came back with their two freezes. "I told you?" He opened and offered straws to them.

"Owen, you gave me the answer." Tim took the straw. Owen left still puzzled. Chet smiled at the game.

Owen brought their orders but put both hands firm on the counter. At first, he didn't say anything. He looked at each one of them, turned to eye the cheesecake still in the display. "No one gets cheesecake until you explain."

"Owen, think about what you gave me," Tim said.

Owen removed his hands. "Let me think some more."

When they finished, Owen returned with coffee. "Mr. Tim, always takes coffee after his meal." He put his hands firm on the counter and looked at them. His head nodded towards the cheesecake behind him.

Tim eyed Chet, "Owen you drive a hard bargain." Tim touched Owen's hand. "Owen, it's inside."

Owen smiled, reached for the cheesecake.

Tim grinned and leaned toward Owen, "You treated me with respect. You touched my heart. I'll never forget it. None of us, given respect, can ever forget."

They clasped each other's hands.

"Thank you, Tim."

"Thank you, Owen."

Tim bit his lip. Owen's eyes watered.

"Owen, it's simple, but it's everything."

"Don't let that truth die, though weak it may lie," said Owen.

"Owen, you should write a book."

"I do with each straw I open."

Owen walked off twirling his pencil. The chef barked back another order. Bacon sizzled. Dishes clanged. Coffee perked. The cash register rang. Life was jazz. Somehow Tim started to understand its voice.

Chet and Tim were on the way back to the car when Chet said. "Tim, that exchange with Owen started me to think."

"Be careful, you might find truth."

Chet smiled, "Like a spark in gunpowder?"

"Insight with a bang," Tim said.

"Damn, I forgot to give you something." Chet pulled an article from his coat pocket. "This was on 'Huffington Post' this morning. I made a copy for you but forgot all about it." Chet handed the article to him.

"What's it about?"

"They arrested the sister of the mall manager that was murdered. You know, where you worked."

Tim looked over the article. "It's crazy. They arrested his sister. They say after she killed him she tried to commit suicide. She's been in a psycho ward but was let out yesterday. Now the prosecutor says he will press charges against her."

"She'll plead insanity," Chet said.

"I worked with her. She never laughed, didn't even smile. Something made her snap."

Chet said, "I saw it all the time; individuals, groups, whole societies going insane. I thought I would escape it now that I write for the Corps. Except I feel like Jack Nicholson in that movie."

"One Flew Over the Cuckoo's Nest?"

"That's it."

"Bobbie's different somehow." Tim said. "Anyone would go insane if something basic snaps your world view." Tim popped the paper like Archie would.

"Like a bomb?"

"Bigger, a paradigm shift. It's happening around the world."

"But people learn to live with it," said Chet.

"Not when you get your manhood whacked."

"Ouch!" Chet grabbed his crotch. "What brought up that? Now that would hurt!"

Tim said, "Sure made Bobbie mad as hell."

49

Visit to Bobbie

A year passed before Tim was able to get his novel published by a small publisher. Once it was, he set up book signings at night when he was on the road. On one trip, he would find a bookstore to let him do a reading. Give them some posters and books to display. Then drop by the weekly newspaper with his photograph and a press release, a big smile and a free copy of his book. On the next trip through he would have a reading. The most he ever sold at any signing was six books. He started another novel.

Tim never visited Cypress Tree again except the day of Archie's funeral. Where the fountain was, stood one lone cart that sold memberships to the Channing Family Spa Life Center.

Tim tucked the memories of Archie by the fountain in the caves of his mind.

He tried to focus on his new job selling on the road. One week he would drive west to Montgomery, Jackson, and Birmingham. The next he would go north into Tennessee. However, when he went east and passed Plant Scherer, the ghost of Bobbie haunted him. When he passed the sign: Do not pick up hitchhikers, he always slowed and looked for her.

One early Friday afternoon, on the way back to Fenton, he drove past the two large magnolia trees at the prison entrance. He parked in the visitors' lot and walked to the brick gatehouse. Inside was a guard behind bullet-proof glass.

"What do I have to do to visit Bobbie Malcour?"

"You an attorney?"

"No, Ma'am. Only a friend."

"You on her visitor's list? You must be on her list." She started to search her computer screen. "What's your name?"

"Tim Lichten, I've never visited."

"I don't have a Bobbie Malcour. Could you be talking about a Roberta Malcour?"

"Roberta, that's her."

"What's your name?"

"Lichten, Tim Lichten. What do I do to be put on the list?"

She pointed to the screen, "Here you are. You're on it, but it doesn't say anything about you coming."

"I was in the area," Tim said.

"I'll have to get permission for you without an appointment." She reached for the phone but didn't pick it up. "You can't come back tomorrow? It will be visitors day."

"No, I can't. I wrote a novel about something she knows. I want to give her a copy and say hello."

"I'll need to see your I.D?" Tim passed her his driver's license.

"You can't touch her. If you want to give her money, give it inside to the funds manager. Cash is contraband. Leave the book with me, I will see the warden gets it, but you must fill a book gift form inside to be approved." She looked at a stain on Tim's tie as she picked up the phone to talk to someone about his visit. She checked Tim's driver's license, eyed his book, then hung up the phone. "OK, they say you can visit."

"Thanks."

"Don't thank me. You're the first person to visit her since I've been here. You know she's special, don't you?"

"How's that?"

"She's the Spider girl."

"Spider girl?"

"I'll let her tell you about it. You locked your car?"

"Yes."

"No pets or people in it?"

"No."

"I have to keep your I.D. and car keys. You'll get them back when you leave. Talk to the warden's secretary inside about the book."

Tim handed her his car keys.

She pointed to a door, "Now go through the metal detector to the sally port."

"The what?"

"Sally port, the gate. I'll buzz you through," she pointed again. "I will buzz and the gate will open, step in the cage. I'll buzz you out the other side. Go direct to the main door. You won't get lost."

Tim walked up to the gate. It buzzed and rolled to the side. He stepped to a sidewalk between two tall chain-link fences with razor wire on top. Before he reached the other end, the gate behind him slammed shut. He froze. He was trapped. He grabbed the far gate, but it wouldn't open. He pushed in panic and looked back at the small brick building. The guard waved and smiled as the gate buzzed open.

Straight ahead on the other side of a small manicured courtyard was another door.

"I'd like to see Roberta Malcour, and fill out a form, so she gets a book."

The receptionist gave him a form. She picked up the phone and called someone. "She's on her way. You will only be able to visit for thirty minutes."

"I appreciate it," Tim said.

When a guard arrived the lady said, "Follow Betty." She pointed to the guard. Tim followed her into a long room with seats along the wall.

The floor glistened better than any hospital. Even the corners sparkled. The air had a heavy green high-pitched smell, unlike any he knew. Tim's hands were cold.

When Bobbie came in she wore an institutional jumpsuit. She had gained a few pounds. Her eyes were clear, her smile broad.

Tim stood, "You look good, Bobbie. How are you?" They hugged and sat down.

"I'm all right." She sat across from him, "But Bobbie doesn't live in here. I'm Roberta in here."

"They told me I could not touch you."

"Well they allow us to say hello and good-by."

"I was lucky to be able to see you. It's not visitor's day."

"You surprised me Tim, but then life sends kind wonders."

"Thanks for putting me on your list," he said.

"When I first came, they told me to list anyone I would want to visit if they came. I tried to remember everyone."

"Roberta, you look great."

"I recognize your tie."

Tim looked at it, "It's an old one."

"It's the one you bought to celebrate leasing to some state office."

"I guess I did."

"I haven't seen anyone from the outside since Mother died."

"How do they treat you here?"

She nodded, "You learn to make adjustments. God knows I've done that."

"We all have."

She tilted her head, "So why did you come?"

"Things have changed since I saw you."

Roberta's eyes smiled, "Life is a journey."

"I now sell pasta wholesale on the road. Every time I pass this way I think of you."

"Oh jeez, why?"

"I don't know. I just do. I brought you a copy of a novel I wrote. Will they let you read it?"

"They'll get it to me, once the Warden approves. What's it about?"

"You'll recognize the story. It's about Cypress Tree's purchase by Marionetti."

Her eyes widened, "It's about Cecil?"

"You'll recognize him, but I changed some things. It takes place in Texas. The mall became a small oil town. I added a series of murders by one of the roustabouts."

"It doesn't sound like what happened."

"I guess that's why I came. You'll recognize a lot. I changed the facts but not the truth."

"Is it about Bobbie?"

"You'll recognize her. I hope you don't mind."

"Oh, I'm sure I won't."

"How do you know?"

"Bobbie's no longer, remember? Besides, I'll be the only one in here in a novel."

"People won't know."

"They'll know."

"How?"

"I'll tell them." She looked straight at him. "You're giving me worth, you know."

"Well, I didn't want you to hear it from someone else."

"Tim, in here, I found something."

"What?"

"They let me read. With books, I have found a freedom."

"So you are locked up but free?" Tim grinned.

Roberta nodded, "Yes, but at first it was lonely. I had no visitors or mail. I started to read anything. Reading taught me to think. I like to write poems. The writing puts those thoughts down in words. Somehow I feel," she gestured with her hands trying to find a word. "I feel something."

"What?"

"I feel warm, like I am talking to my soul. More so when I write poetry."

"That's a good thing," Tim said.

She started to relax, "Bobbie killed Cecil. She admitted it. When she was ten, she electrocuted Daddy. He was stone drunk. Everyone said it was suicide. When she was fourteen, she poisoned Judy at camp. She got even with Joan for walking out on Cecil when it was only his second day on the job. There were several more. She even strangled Mom's dog, Fritz with her own hands."

"Bobbie was sick."

"Tim, I need to be in here until I can get all of Bobbie out of me."

"Maybe they'll figure out how to do that."

"Books help, writing helps."

"Roberta, if you want to write your version of what happened, I'll help."

"Poems help a lot." Roberta smiled.

"I am glad you write."

"It's sort of a meditation."

"Good."

"Tim, this is my world now. Many in here have bigger problems than Bobbie. When you get to know them, I mean when you can get close enough to touch them, you find they're people, simple people with feelings who need hope."

"But you're in here to learn to help yourself."

"The truth is, to do that I must help others. They have become my family."

Tim leaned in, trying not to miss a word.

"I have learned, in here." She pointed to her heart. "Life is all about family, only about family."

"Just some of us are locked up," Tim said.

"You know what I like best in here?" she paused, "The structure. I know what will happen tomorrow. It's secure. It gives me a freedom."

"Freedom?"

"And the time to think."

Tim nodded, "People don't think anymore. They follow."

"My life today is better than the one Bobbie had on the outside."

"Good," Tim said, "you are in the world but not part of it."

"Out there Bobbie had to have a big car and control. Status is funny. In here it's measured by small things."

"So by bringing you a book, I've raised your status?"

"Until now I was only Spider Girl."

"What's that all about?"

"Did you notice how clean everything is?"

Tim nodded, "Even the grass looks like it was hand clipped."

"Well my job is to go around with a long pole with a rag on top to take down all the spider webs. I'm Spider Girl!"

"That's status?"

"The best you can have! Easy job, I go everywhere. I get to hear and see a lot." She sat up straight, "I am the walking newspaper!"

Tim added, "Roberta's Rag?"

She laughed, "Yea! And we had a real-live author visit." Her eyes sparked, "What more can a news editor want?"

"Roberta you're making my day."

"You'll sign the book won't you? That'll add at least another star," she laughed.

"I think this is the first time I ever saw you laugh."

"Bobbie's dead, not me."

"Roberta, you lift my spirit."

"Tim, you can't imagine how this visit helps."

"I'm glad."

"Tim, if you never forget people, you'll live forever."

"Wow!"

She paused to let her words sink in, "They will change you. You will change them. The world will never be the same."

Tim was quiet as it sank in. "Roberta, I wrote a novel, but now I wish I'd left in all the facts."

"Sometimes facts don't tell the truth. Truth talks to hearts. It takes fiction to show it."

"I think you might be right."

"I know I am," she said.

"Roberta, can I ask you a question?"

Roberta nodded, "Sure."

"What happened that night?"

"The night Bobbie got mad at Cecil?"

"Yes?"

"Mord Doyle came to see Cecil. Mama was drunk in her room watching TV. Bobbie sat on the second-floor landing. As kids, Cecil and Bobbie would sit up there and listen to Mama and Daddy downstairs."

"That night Mord Doyle brought some Maker's Mark for Cecil. They both began to drink. The more Cecil drank, the more he talked. He gave Mord a large envelope."

"Do you know what was in it?"

"No, but Mr. Doyle was glad to get it. Daddy always said to listen when people drink. You will learn things you can use. Mr. Doyle kept pouring Cecil another drink."

Tim said, "Mord liked to get people to drink."

"He told Cecil he was going to show Ricco the papers." Roberta looked at the clock on the wall, "Mr. Doyle said he wanted Cecil to get Bobbie out of the office."

"I guess that made Bobbie mad," Tim said.

"No, not at all. Bobbie didn't need the job. She only worked to help Cecil when Joan quit. No, Cecil started to talk about Bobbie's accident. Cecil swore on a Bible with candles in front of Mama and Daddy that he would never tell anyone, ever, about the accident. Cecil told Mord Doyle everything. And Bobbie heard him."

The guard eyed Tim again, as she tapped her watch. Tim nodded acceptance but motioned with his hand, they were almost finished.

Roberta took a breath, "Bobbie stayed upstairs until Mord left. The voice inside her told her to tiptoe downstairs, to take the Saxon ax off the wall, sneak up behind Cecil and whack him in the back of the head. He should have never broken his promise to Mama and Daddy." She bit her bottom lip, "You cannot break your word to your parents, never ever."

She got up, hugged him and turned to go to the door, but turned back and said, "Tim, you will never know how far a kindness will go." When the guard unlocked the door she said, "Remember Tim, we are both survivors, and all survivors are heroes." She started to leave again but turned back one last time, "Tim, don't ever forget what you did. If you don't remember, you cannot know who you are."

Outside, Tim walked to his car. There were heavy clouds with a moist breeze. He rolled the window down to smell the coming rain. He closed his eyes and let his hand feel for sprinkles.

He sat and remembered the last words Roberta said. "Tim, my whole life I have wondered why the world was so against me. Somehow your visit gives me hope. I need to be in here. I can help people living in this place."

His hand was wet, so he rolled up the window and listened to the rain dance on the roof. Thunder roared as a cloudburst hit. He waited for it to pass and thought about what she said.

He watched the rain bounce on the hood. The radio started to play Willie Nelson singing "Blue Eyes Crying in the Rain." When it slowed he started to drive. The car's odometer would pass 200,000 miles before he got home.

Right before he got on the Interstate, there was a place to pull off. He wanted to call Aimee.

A gypsy pelican sat on a fence post on the right. It sat there and watched Tim. Then a deer came out of the trees and walked through a gourd patch to the water. A warbler with a malformed bill that looked swollen like an engorged tick was on it, landed on the car's hood.

Tim called Aimee, "I'll be home in about an hour. How's it going?"

"Great! A man came and bought the old freezer we had in the garage. He gave me fifty dollars, so I bought a pot roast."

"Let's have it tonight."

"It's cooking now."

"I'll buy some wine," Tim said.

"That new store has opened. There was an ad in today's paper."

"What store?"

"Anthony's Vino-Vino. It's a huge liquor store out of Florida. Its right where you get off for Fenton."

"I'll look for it."

"And Beth called from Chicago a few minutes ago. She and Mike will be in Atlanta Wednesday. They want to take us out to Ruth's Chris Steak House."

"That sounds great!"

"Mike wants to move to Atlanta."

"And leave Chicago?"

"Maybe you can work for him."

"We'll talk about it."

"We need to talk more."

"I agree."

"Yesterday I was waiting to get Junior from practice when he walked in. 'Hey, buddy, how'd you get here?' I asked. He looked at me, 'Oh, we started a carpool. You have tomorrow.' He was completely oblivious how that would impact me. I told him I couldn't do it as you were coming home. He waved his hands in the air and told me I should talk to Tucker's mom."

Tim said, "We all need to talk more."

"You might make more money with Mike."

"Right now I want some corn and roast."

"It will be ready when you get here. Is it raining there?" she asked.

"With the sun shining."

"Buy some wine."

Tim looked at his Rolex, and started his car. Trees sparkled. He turned the radio on and it was playing Charlie Daniels' *"The Devil Comes Back To Georgia."*

"Damn, he never gives up."

Grand Opening

10,000 different wines -- 400 different beers

Georgia's Largest Party Store

Exit NOW – Exit NOW – Exit NOW

Anthony's Vino Vino

Tim pulled in their parking lot. He realized life moves on but never forgets. Rain comes to wash sins away, but the heart of a hunting dog never dies.

Ω

.

Acknowledgments

The author wishes to thank all those who helped with this project. This includes the Chattanooga Writers' Guild through their small critique groups and monthly meetings.

Also the Southern Lit Alliance that sponsors a fantastic bi-annual gathering of Southern Authors in Chattanooga where the author has been able to meet and talk to many of the icons of Southern Literature. Allen Weir, Roy Blount, Jr. [who can make a simple Sunday meal a verbal feast you remember forever], Allan Gurganus [who taught how detail shows], Richard Bausch [who teaches more with a joke than anyone I know], Betty Adcock, Beth Henley, George Garrett, Ellen Douglas [she confessed to me all authors borrow everything], Wendell Berry [who brings respect in everything], Clyde Edgerton [who also plays mando] and Tony Earley [who always brings a conversation back to the topic].

The encouragement the Meacham Writers Workshop brings to new writers has been most helpful.

Chattanooga State College's Writers at Work promises to be an excellent motivation to local writers.

I also would like to thank those who took the time to give editorial suggestions. Calvin Hayes, Duane Baker, Scarlet Richards, John Reihle, Donald Betzen, Raj Diwan, George Kemp, Anne Ford-Melton, Julian Goodrich, Ray Zimmerman, Jim Moore, Francine Fuqua, David and Lori Powell, Charles Lefory, Gary Sedlacek, Linda Peters and Mary Kelly Reviews. Special thanks goes out to Joyce Walters, who gave a critical eye as only a former teacher could.

Questions for Book Clubs

Have a bookclub? The author is available for online SKYPE questions and answers for those that request it. Make contact through: southernlitagent@aol.com

1. Is The Hunting Dog a mystery, a social commentary or a literary novel?
2. Does "The Hunting Dog" live up to title?
3. Which characters did you like the most? Why?
4. Is Tim a good man?
5. Is Tim's search resolved?
6. Where does Tim first become aware of evil that exists?
7. Is Tim simply nostalgic about the past or is he seeking solutions?
8. What makes Tim run?
9. Do forces outside Tim control his life? In what way?
10. What influences Tim's actions and why?
11. Are there any evil characters in the story? Who and why?
12. How is Archie a victim or simply wrong?
13. What symbols did you see and what did they represent?
14. Why was a mall the backdrop for the book?
15. What do you see happening in the next two books of the series?
16. What scenes stood out in your memory?
17. Some think this is a "journey" story. If you agree with this, why? If you do not agree, why not?
18. What are the major themes?
19. What symbols were used?
20. Was the ending a surprise? Was that good or bad?